Praise for Sue Henry's Jessie Arnold mysteries

"Suspenseful, intelligent, and filled with the spectacular beauty of the northern wilds." —*The Dallas Morning News*

"Twice as vivid as Michener's natural Alaska, at about a thousandth the length." —*The Washington Post Book World*

"The twists and turns keep you turning the pages . . . a thoroughly good read." —*The Denver Post*

"Henry revels in the wilderness of Alaskan scenery and keeps the tension mounting. . . . A fine adventure." —*The Cleveland Plain Dealer*

"This fast-paced page-turner will make the miles fly during any trip." —*Boston Herald*

"Henry has once again succeeded in crafting an engrossing mystery that . . . keeps the reader well-occupied." —*Anchorage Daily News*

"[Henry's] descriptions of Alaska's wilderness make you want to take the next flight out, buy heavy sweaters, or at least curl up with an afghan, a cup of steaming hot chocolate, and the book." —*The Phoenix Gazette*

"Real thrills set against the wild beauty of Alaska." —*Minneapolis Star Tribune*

continued . . .

MURDER AT FIVE FINGER LIGHT

A JESSIE ARNOLD MYSTERY

SUE HENRY

AN ONYX BOOK

ONYX
Published by New American Library, a division of
Penguin Group (USA) Inc., 375 Hudson Street,
New York, New York 10014, USA
Penguin Group (Canada), 90 Eglinton Avenue East, Suite 700, Toronto,
Ontario M4P 2Y3, Canada (a division of Pearson Penguin Canada Inc.)
Penguin Books Ltd., 80 Strand, London WC2R 0RL, England
Penguin Ireland, 25 St. Stephen's Green, Dublin 2,
Ireland (a division of Penguin Books Ltd.)
Penguin Group (Australia), 250 Camberwell Road, Camberwell, Victoria 3124,
Australia (a division of Pearson Australia Group Pty. Ltd.)
Penguin Books India Pvt. Ltd., 11 Community Centre, Panchsheel Park,
New Delhi - 110 017, India
Penguin Group (NZ), cnr Airborne and Rosedale Roads, Albany,
Auckland 1310, New Zealand (a division of Pearson New Zealand Ltd.)
Penguin Books (South Africa) (Pty.) Ltd., 24 Sturdee Avenue,
Rosebank, Johannesburg 2196, South Africa

Penguin Books Ltd., Registered Offices:
80 Strand, London WC2R 0RL, England

Published by Onyx, an imprint of New American Library,
a division of Penguin Group (USA) Inc. Previously published in a
hardcover edition by New American Library.

First Onyx Printing, March 2006
10 9 8 7 6 5 4 3 2 1

ACKNOWLEDGMENTS

WITH SINCERE THANKS TO:

Jennifer Klein and Ed McIntosh, owners of Five Finger Lighthouse, who extended a warm welcome for a week's visit to their small island in Southeast Alaska, acquainted me with its history and eccentricities, and openhandedly shared everything from information to a very good cabernet. (To support the Juneau Lighthouse Association contact Jennifer Klein and Ed McIntosh at P.O. Box 22163, Juneau, Alaska 99802.)

Good friends Barbara Hedges and Vickie Jensen, who went along as research assistants and work crew—though none of us did much more than add a lick or two of paint and polish brass in the tower.

The city of Petersburg—particularly the Tides Inn, Harbor Bar, and Northern Lights Restaurant—for generous hospitality.

Tina Green and Nancy Zaic at Sing Lee Alley Books with its great assortment of helpful and tempting materials.

Ginny Arthurs, Dispatcher and Jail Guard for the Petersburg City Police, Fire Department, and EMTs, for information concerning the dispatch of law enforcement to Frederick Sound.

Rod Judy of Pacific Wing Air Charter, who ferried us from Petersburg to Five Finger Light in his floatplane and pointed out some of the many whales in Frederick Sound.

Steve O'Brocta of Temsco Helicopters, who, at short notice, flew us back when the weather turned too rough for floats.

Bruce Wing, Fishery Research Biologist at the Auke Bay Laboratory of the National Marine Fisheries Service, for identifying and providing information on the isopods we found on Five Finger Island.

My talented son, Eric, who does the maps and photography for my books.

For Jennifer Klein and Ed McIntosh—

The real owners of Five Finger Lighthouse,
who are restoring and keeping alive
an important piece of Alaskan history.

Anythin' for a quiet life, as the man said wen he took the sitivation at the lighthouse.

Charles Dickens, *Pickwick Papers,* 1836–37

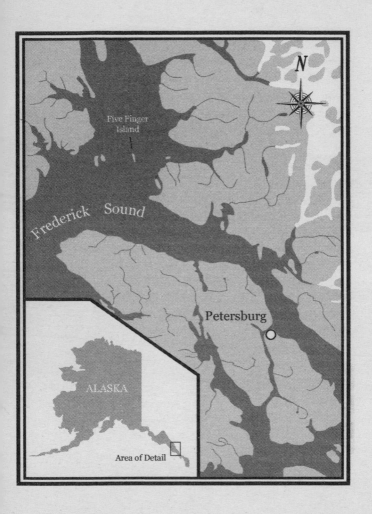

Five Finger Island

1. Lighthouse
2. Tower
3. North Porch
4. Platform
5. Manhole
6. Cove
7. Helipad
8. Boathouse
9. Carpenter Shop
10. Stairs to Trail
11. South Cove

TRAIL TO SOUTH END OF ISLAND

N

INTRODUCTION

There is little warm and welcoming about a lighthouse. Like medieval castles, lighthouses are solidly built not to attract, but to survive and repel; to withstand the assault of armies of waves, weather, and misguided ships. Most stand in solitary isolation where sea meets land, casting sweeping Cyclopean beams of warning into the dark. Their existence is all about hazard and the prevention of disaster.

But there is something captivating about a lighthouse—something mysterious and legendary that relates to remoteness and solitude, singular purpose, unique structure, reclusive keepers, and, sometimes, haunted reputation—that enthralls and compels consideration.

Many North American lighthouses are accessible to visitors by road, or waterway. But those that stand guard over the thousand-mile maze of Pacific Coast islands and channels of the Canadian and Alaskan Inside Passage are not easily available. Most rise where there are no roads, in splendid seclusion, often secreted by veils of mist that make them invisible to travelers of daylight waters. These are not the more familiar, tall, cylindrical structures designed to cast a light many miles out to sea. Surrounded by the islands that form the channels of the passage north, most have no need to be seen from such great distances. They are often built on high ground, so they are lower and, for the most part, square and solid in appearance.

Many of their names are resonant reminders of wilderness and grandeur, the early history of these wild coastal shores with their many perils, and the disasters of explorers and gold seekers that prompted the placement of light stations: Prospect Point, Discovery Island, Trial Island, and Gallows Point in British Columbia; Cape Sarichef, Eldred Rock, Guard Island, Cape Decision, Scotch Cap, and Cape Saint Elias in Alaska.

With two assignments, Five Finger Lighthouse was placed in Alaskan waters, where Stephens Passage opens into Frederick Sound, to guide ships on their way to and from the gold fields through that part of the tangle of passages, and to warn mariners away from the jagged rocks of five low, narrow islands that resemble a nefarious reaching hand that is all but invisible in dark or rough weather and could rip the bottom from any vessel unfortunate enough to founder upon them. On one of these, a tiny, three-acre island, six to seven hundred feet long, north to south, and around a hundred and fifty feet wide, depending on the tides, the deco-style lighthouse (a replacement for the original wooden structure that burned in December 1933) rises from its rocky base near and facing the north point.

This historically significant light holds distinction as the first of Alaska's lighthouses to be lit, in March of 1902, and the last to be automated, in 1984.

CHAPTER ONE

SHORTLY AFTER MIDNIGHT IN THE DARKEST HOURS OF AN early morning in mid-September, the grumble of a marine engine slowly and cautiously approaching a tiny, three-acre island was little more than a mutter within the pulse of the incoming tide that splashed and gurgled ceaselessly against the sharp stones, the dying result of a windy rainstorm that had swept through the area the previous evening.

In the northern reaches of Frederick Sound, midway in the Alaskan length of the Inside Passage, the island was the largest of five narrow ridges of jagged rock that had come to be known as the Five Fingers, for seamen contended that they resembled a grasping hand. Four of these barely broke the surface, but the fifth and largest was unique for rising some fifty feet at its highest point above the salt waters of the sound, and for the lighthouse that had been placed there and operated for just over one hundred years specifically as a warning for mariners to navigate farther to the west and avoid the risk of foundering upon the lurking, treacherous fingers that were well and dangerously concealed at high tides, in darkness or rough weather.

The growling powerboat approached gingerly and without running lights, the operator well aware that, without an available dock or landing, caution must be taken to avoid being caught by the surf and bashing the hull against the ragged natural stone ramp rising up from the sea to the level of a wide concrete platform below the lighthouse. Between this rough ramp and a support wall below the platform lay a narrow but deep cove that provided partial protection from the insistent waves. With its two heavy Mercury outboard engines off the transom, the operator carefully maneuvered the twenty-six-foot Kingfisher into this semiprotected space, close enough so that a second figure could hop off and help to rig a pair of opposing lines that would hold the craft off both the rocks and the wall, but close enough for unloading their small but valuable amount of cargo.

High over their heads in the cupola of the tower the automatic solar-powered light revolved steadily, sweeping the line of its powerful beam across the underside of a low-hanging layer of cloud that threatened more rain and reflected just enough light to make the area visible to eyes already accustomed to the dark. It would probably rain again, but the accompanying wind had died and the waters of the sound calmed their thrashing to mild whitecaps and lacy foam.

Tied off safely with two lines, the operator cut the engines and stepped out onto the aft deck, opened a hatch, and removed two carefully waterproofed packages about eighteen inches square.

"You're sure there's no one here?"

"Yeah, sure. They won't show till around noon next Sunday."

"It better be like you say. I'm not up for any surprises on this one."

"It's fine. We've got plenty of time to stash this stuff and head for Petersburg. They'll never know we were here. It's like I told you—perfect cover."

"It better be. Here, take this. I'll bring the other one."

"Bring a flashlight. We'll need it."

"No inside lights?"

"Not unless we start a generator and we don't want to do that, do we?"

Each warily carrying one of the packages, the two figures, one shorter and huskier than the other, but both mere shadows in the dark, carefully climbed the uneven, slippery stones of the ramp to the platform and crossed to a pair of double doors that led into the lower floor beneath the lighthouse that towered over them.

"Got the key?"

Balancing the package on one arm to free a hand to dig into a jacket pocket, the answer came with a nod. "Yeah—same one I used last time I was here."

"Hey—be careful you don't drop that. Just open the damn door. Let's get this done and be gone."

Swinging the doors wide, the pair vanished into the blackness of the basement, returning empty-handed in a few minutes to lock the door behind them.

In less than ten minutes they were gone and the island was once again left to the enduring isolation of its automated duty.

Far across the wide waters of Frederick Sound the pilot of a fishing boat took comfort in recognizing the familiar beam and in knowing that he was finally nearing his home-port, little more than an hour south. Briefly he wondered about the people from Juneau who now owned Five Finger Light and the whale-watching station that, rumor had it, they intended to locate there.

Shrugging, he took another swig of rapidly cooling coffee and focused on achieving the most direct route across the sound to Petersburg.

CHAPTER TWO

EARLY ON A MONDAY MORNING IN MID-SEPTEMBER, without opening her eyes, Jessie Arnold rolled over in her big brass bed, pulled the quilt down far enough to uncover her face, and took a deep inquisitive breath. The scent of freshly brewed coffee that had wafted enticingly up from downstairs filled her nose, mixed with that of bacon frying and a hint of toast.

Yawning, she tossed back the quilt, sat up, and swung her feet over the edge of the bed, feeling for her slippers. Not finding them, she peered over the edge of the mattress and spotted them a foot or two away, where she had kicked them off the night before. Scuffing them on, she slipped a robe over the pajama bottoms and green T-shirt in which she had slept, and left the bedroom, headed soft-footed for the stairs.

Halfway down she was able to see Alex Jensen busily cooking breakfast in the kitchen of her new log cabin. He was humming softly to himself as he removed the bacon from the pan to a paper towel before draining the grease and turning to stir a bowl of eggs for scrambling, unaware of her presence until she spoke.

"You're up early, trooper. Can't wait to get back to catching bad guys?"

He turned with a smile. "Hey there, sleepy. You want eggs?"

"If you're cooking—you bet."

Jensen added two eggs to the bowl, stirred, and emptied it into the pan. As the eggs sizzled invitingly, Jessie made a quick dash into his work area to pour a mug of coffee and snitch a crispy strip of bacon from the pile on the towel. Knowing that the kitchen could be a hazard zone as, long-armed, Alex tended to unexpectedly reach out for things without looking as he cooked and was currently waving a fork, she retreated to the safety of the table to watch and enjoy the fact that someone other than herself was playing chef.

Both hands around her steaming mug, she wrinkled her nose at the aroma and savored not only the brew, but also having Alex back in her kitchen, as well as her bed. The months he had been gone from Alaska now seemed dull and ephemeral, as if his return had brightened her world and let her see everything with new eyes after a stretch of bad weather.

It *was* a sunny morning, and a glance out the window brought a smile of appreciation to her face at the glorious September gold of the birches that surrounded her cabin and dog yard. As she watched, a breath of breeze brought a few more leaves fluttering down to litter the ground beneath and she knew that, once again, there would soon be only bare limbs against the sky.

Turning back, she found Alex, careless of the eggs sizzling in the pan, leaning against the kitchen counter with a smile of his own at her admiration of the fall's generosity.

"Your favorite season," he said. "It'll be your birthday in another month."

"It will," she agreed. "But I won't remind you that you still owe me an earring to replace the one I lost somewhere in the brush on Niqa Island."

"So I do. I'll have to consider that."

Refilling his own coffee mug, Alex brought two full plates to the table and, settling in a chair beside her, moved the butter and jam so they both could reach them.

"M-m-m," Jessie said, when she had made a significant inroad on the food on her plate. "It's nice to have someone else in the kitchen for a change. May I expect you to continue to spoil me rotten?"

"We'll see how you appreciate it," he answered with the hint of a leer, wiping strawberry jam from one side of his luxurious handlebar mustache with a paper napkin. "What's up for you today?"

"Well . . ." Jessie frowned and hesitated, considering. "I'm not sure. It's a pain not to be able to run the mutts, but there's always cleanup that wants doing in the dog yard. You?"

"Hm-m." Jensen pursed his lips and wrinkled his brow, miming deliberation.

"What? You've got something in mind—yes?"

Mischievously, he forced her to wait as he slowly chewed and swallowed another mouthful of eggs and toast before he answered with a grin.

"We-ell, if you haven't anything pressing on your dance card for the next few days, maybe you'd consider driving to Dawson with me to visit Del and Clair Delafosse."

RCMP Inspector Charles "Del" Delafosse and his wife Clair were friends met when he and Alex had worked a case together in Dawson City several years before. They had also helped Jessie, when she was involved in delivering a ransom demanded for the release of an abducted musher during the Yukon Quest sled dog race.

At Alex's suggestion of a visit, the impatience on Jessie's face was replaced with pleased surprise. "Really? That's a great idea. Why're you going to Dawson?"

"Del called yesterday afternoon. The Canadian government's put money behind its decision to create a joint plan to improve border security. So Commander Swift is sending me to help get the cooperation started with a planning meeting between the Alaska State Troopers and a new RCMP Border Enforcement Team that Del's been assigned to as well."

"There're only two, aren't there? The main customs station on the Alaska Highway at Beaver Creek and the one on the Top of the World Highway, though that road's closed in the winter. Oh, I forgot. You have to cross the border coming north from both Skagway and Haines, don't you? That's four."

"A couple of guys are coming up from Vancouver to coordinate with us on those two that cross into British Columbia, then back into the Yukon. But you're forgetting the entire Southeast. There's a lot of water traffic along the Inside Passage—cruise ships, private power- and sailboats, fishing boats, oil tankers, commercial container ships—probably more people crossing the borders in both directions than ever use the highways. And there is one other that's off the Cassiar, between Stewart B.C. and Hyder, though it's probably got the lowest use.

"We want to have everything organized and in place before the tourist season rolls around next spring and all those motor homes and boats start pouring back and forth across the borders. Then we'll be looking hard for drug dealers, gun smugglers, and border runners."

"So you guys'll really be working?"

"Yup. But you can visit with Clair, and we'll all get together in the evenings except for a day or two when Del and I have to go down to Whitehorse."

"Won't be much that's really active for Clair, considering she's just a couple of months from presenting Del with twins," Jessie reminded him.

"Yeah, well. It'll be cool over there this time of year anyway, but we shouldn't have real snow for another week or two. You can always stay inside and knit booties," he teased.

"Bloody likely! There are a lot of things I *can* do but knitting's close to the top of the I-can't or I-won't list. You know Clair. She's no knitter either. Now that they're adding to the people living in that small cabin of hers, she'd probably rather build on an additional room."

Alex got up to retrieve the coffeepot from the kitchen and lifted a questioning eyebrow at her before replenishing her cup along with his own.

"When are we leaving?" Jessie asked as she shoved her empty plate aside with a sigh of satisfaction and leaned forward to put both elbows on the table, coffee steam once again warming her nose.

"Well, I've got a few things to clear up at the office and the paperwork to finish on a robbery case, but I thought we might get an early start Thursday morning. Would that suit you?"

"Perfectly," she agreed. "That'll give me time to do laundry and get Billy set up to take care of the few dogs I have left in the yard. I'd like to get a present for the new twins too. Can Tank go with us?"

"Sure. Bring the dog." Alex collected the plates, ferried them to the kitchen, and turned back. "You okay to clean up here? I'd better hit the road."

"Ah-h," she sighed theatrically. "Should have guessed I'd be relegated to bottle washer. I'll call Billy and then take care of the kitchen. Tonight you can sort out what clothes you want washed and I'll do that tomorrow."

Billy Steward, the young man who worked with Jessie in caring for her dogs and kennel, often joined her on training runs with a second team. Though the injury to her knee had removed *her* racing possibilities, Jessie felt Billy was ready to run one or two of the shorter sled dog races during the approaching winter, and she had kept enough dogs at home for his use, along with one that would soon have pups and two past racing age. Steady and dependable, Billy had more than earned his privileges, the practice would be good for him, and a couple of races would give him experience and entrée to the racing community.

Alex soon disappeared down the drive to Knik Road and Jessie, who had kissed him and waved goodbye from the front porch, turned thoughtfully back to her chores inside. It seemed a little strange to have someone else living in her house, even Alex—or, perhaps, especially Alex. Seven months earlier, when he had left Alaska, having taken a job in his home state of Idaho, she had assumed their relationship was over. His sudden return less than a month ago in time to rescue her from a nasty imprisonment in a remote and abandoned cabin in the wilderness had renewed their bond, and she was content to have him back in her new cabin and her life. At times it was almost as if he had never left at all, though at others she knew there were questions still to be answered and adjustments to be made. For now they were both inclined to give it time without examination. Things for them had always had a way of working themselves out, with patience.

The idea of a trip to Dawson, across the border in Canada's Yukon Territory, was appealing and raised her spirits. The injury to her knee, the result of a fall down the steep side of a mountain that summer, had been severe enough that the doctor had given her little choice in the matter. "If you're wise," he had solemnly advised her, with a penetrating look over the rims of his glasses, "you'll give it a rest this year, Jessie. If you compromise now, you'll be able to race next year without it bothering you unduly. I can't promise that if you don't. So no training runs or heavy kennel work, okay?" The tendon she had torn enough to require surgery was healing well, and she was no longer wearing a brace, but there would be no sled-riding behind her dogs. Billy Steward would make training runs with the few dogs left in her kennel, keeping them and him fit for the racing she would encourage him to do.

Before attacking the laundry and kitchen cleanup, Jessie made the call to explain why she intended to be away from home for the next week or so, and Billy agreed to show up shortly to feed and water the stay-at-home dogs and house-sit for her while she was gone. "I'll be taking most of them out on runs anyway, so I might as well stay there."

True to his word, when she had finished the dishes and, finding she had enough for a load to wash already, was adding detergent into the machine, Billy could be heard whistling as he clattered food pans in the dog yard.

She was about to go out and help with the morning routine of caring for the dogs when the telephone rang.

"Arnold Kennels," she answered.

"Jessie? Jessie Arnold?" a vaguely familiar voice asked in her ear.

"This is Jessie."

"This is Laurie Trevino. Do you remember me?"

The name, like the voice, rang bells from somewhere in her past, but a distinct memory eluded Jessie.

"The *Spirit of '98* and the Ton of Gold Run from Skag-

way to Seattle in July of 1997? Remember, Alice La Belle—
the 'bird in a gilded cage'?"

Recognition chimed a harmonious chord in Jessie's mind
as she recalled a friendly face to go with the name and voice
from the Klondike Gold Rush Centennial celebration several years earlier. This caller had played a dance-hall girl in
a melodrama enacted on board during their voyage down the
Inside Passage.

"Laurie! How *are* you? Still singing the oldies?"

There was a chuckle from the other end of the line before
Laurie answered.

"Off and on, but I've taken on some other, very different
things. We now own a lighthouse."

"A lighthouse? Who's 'we'? Where? Tell me everything."

"Well, Jim Beal and I. You remember Jim, right? He
dressed as a riverboat gambler on the *Spirit*. Anyway, the
Coast Guard asked for proposals from anyone interested in
leasing one of several Alaskan lighthouses. We applied and
were given a thirty-year lease on Five Finger Lighthouse in
Frederick Sound north of Petersburg. Then they decided to
simply turn it over to us, so we own it. Now all we have to do
is restore it. And, boy, does it need restoring! Nobody's lived
here since 1984, so you can imagine."

"So you're moving into a lighthouse?" Jessie asked.
"That's a long commute from your interest in the theaters
in Juneau and Douglas, isn't it? Do you have to keep it
working?"

"All the Alaskan lights are automated now, so they run on
solar energy and don't need live-in keepers. We're not moving down—just going back and forth on weekend restoration
parties, or for a week or so at a time, which is why I'm calling you. It's already September and we want to get the main
building painted and a new roof on a storage shed before we

close it up for the winter. The weather is supposed to be good for a change, so we're organizing an end-of-season work party for next week, as large as we can put together in a hurry. I thought you might like to come down and help. We can't pay your plane fare, but we can promise to feed you well—and that trooper of yours, if he can come."

Jessie hated to refuse, but this would clash with the trip Alex had mentioned. The idea of a week in a lighthouse was very appealing—she had long had a yen to visit one or more of the historic lighthouses in Southeast Alaska. Why did it have to come at the same time as the trip to Dawson?

"I'd love to come," she told Laurie, then explained the conflict between the two trips and why Alex would not be able to get away.

"Damn," Laurie swore. "I'd hoped he could come too. There was something I wanted to talk to him about. Ah well, another time, I guess."

Jessie considered the concern she recognized in Laurie's voice.

"Problem? I could have him call you when he comes home tonight."

There was a thoughtful silence before Laurie continued. "Oh, no. It's nothing *that* important. Just . . . Hey, listen, if I remember right there's a way you *could* come from Dawson, even if he can't. I think you could fly to Juneau on Air North from Dawson early next week. From there it's an easy hop to Petersburg on Alaska Airlines. Some of us from Juneau and Skagway are going down in our boat on Sunday. We're waiting to hear from a couple of others who are hoping to come on their own during the week. But the thing is that Jim's going on down to Petersburg on Tuesday to pick up one guy and some roofing material for the shed. You could come back with him from there. What do you think?"

Jessie hesitated, considering, tempted by the idea.

"I'd have to check and talk to Alex about it," she told Laurie. "Give me your number and I'll call you back when we've had a chance to think it over and check the flights to see what's possible. I'd really like to come if I can work it out, but I know Alex won't be able to make it."

There was a laugh from the other end of the line. "Hey, we'll take whatever help we can get. I'll expect to hear from you."

With a click in the receiver Laurie was gone.

Jessie stood for a long moment staring at the receiver, then dropped it back into its cradle and headed out to help Billy in the dog yard, wondering briefly what Laurie had wanted to talk over with Alex. There had been something about her tone that raised mental flags of concern and now she wished she had questioned her about it.

But her mind soon turned to making the trip herself. Would it work out? She hoped so. It was at least worth checking on flights and Alex's reaction to this unexpected opportunity. When she and Billy finished the chores she would get online and see if she could find the connecting flights Laurie had mentioned.

Slipping on a warm fleece vest over her long-sleeved shirt, she headed for the dog yard, glad to be back in fall clothing again, even if this year they wouldn't be the insulating kind she wore in the deep of winter on the back of a sled behind a dog team.

CHAPTER THREE

"I KNEW THE COAST GUARD WAS GOING TO TURN THE lighthouses over to private groups for renovation and received a flood of applications and proposals. So Laurie and Jim got lucky," Alex said that evening, when Jessie told him about the invitation to visit Five Finger Lighthouse. "Doesn't surprise me a bit that the two of them would take on something so dramatic, and a work party is a great idea—should be a lot of fun. I think you should go."

"She asked us both," Jessie reminded him.

He frowned and shook his head. "Sure would like to, but Del's already scheduled that meeting for Monday and Tuesday next week and the guys are practically on their way from B.C. Since I'm our only representative this time, I've got to be there. But you don't. So—go."

"But what about our visit with Del and Clair? You've already told them we'd both come."

"Do what Laurie suggested. Come to Dawson with me on Thursday, visit for a couple of days, then catch that Air North flight out of Dawson on Sunday afternoon. I can take care of business and start home from Dawson on Wednesday or Thursday at the latest. I'll be back to pick you up when you fly in to Anchorage on the weekend."

"So I can have my cake and eat it too—so to speak."

"I guess you could look at it that way. Just keep in mind that I'm not baking cakes till your birthday and that's a month away. Even then, my baking usually turns out more interesting than epicurean, if you recall."

"I seem to remember a lopsided tendency," Jessie agreed with a grin. "Okay. I'll check on the flights and call her back. But I wish you could come with me."

"Me too, but maybe we could go down together next spring. It sounds like restoring a lighthouse will be a long-term project. Take the camera this time and bring back lots of pictures?"

Jessie agreed and headed off to check online for possible flights, forgetting to mention that Laurie had wanted to speak to Alex. She would remember later—too much later, unfortunately.

The following Sunday, after two enjoyable days of visiting in Dawson, Jessie flew Air North to Whitehorse, as Laurie had suggested, then on to Juneau. After staying overnight with a friend, she was at the airport a little early to catch the afternoon Alaska Airlines flight to Petersburg, less than an hour away in the maze of islands that define the waterways of Southeast Alaska's Inside Passage.

Checking in and relinquishing her duffel bag, she headed for the departure gates upstairs, where she found a long slow parade of passengers inching their way toward security. Making a detour into the nearby gift shop, she took a few minutes to browse the magazines, hoping the line would shorten. As she thumbed through the latest *Mushing* magazine a harried woman with an awkward carry-on bag and two children in tow shouldered past her, headed for the cash register, holding a paperback in one hand, pulling a child along with the other. The four- or five-year-old boy struggled to twist away from his mother's firm grip on the shoulder of his jacket, failed, then spitefully punched his younger sister, who instantly howled a protest. Jessie suspected reading was more wishful thinking than a realistic expectation for the woman, and hoped, if they were on her flight, that she wouldn't be seated anywhere near them.

Traveling with sled dogs is easier, she thought, putting the magazine back in its place and picking up an Alaskan husky from a rack of stuffed animals. Checking dogs through baggage in their portable carriers meant you could relax without having to contend with a whining, squirming presence in the seat next to you.

A glance told her that the number of people waiting to go through security had dropped by half, so Jessie put down the stuffed dog and left the gift shop to join the line. Moving up a step or two at a time behind a man who shoved his briefcase ahead with one foot while scanning the front page of the local *Juneau Empire,* she watched a little girl in a bright pink sweater come out of a nearby restroom. Her pale blond curls bounced as she scampered across the room and threw her arms around the legs of a tall man carrying a suitcase. He smiled and took her hand as they went down the escalator together. A father coming home from a business trip, Jessie guessed with a grin, mentally comparing this child with the two she could see ahead of her in line.

As the girl and her father sank out of sight, a slender young woman with shoulder-length dark hair half-opened the same restroom door and stood looking out. In a navy blue skirt and blazer over a white-and-yellow striped top, she was half hidden behind it as she glanced around outside with a concerned frown. Apparently not seeing anyone she recognized, she turned quickly to vanish inside and the door closed itself behind her.

The mother of the child in the pink sweater, Jessie guessed again, then amended that assumption. Maybe not. There had been a hint of caution in the woman's scrutiny of the area, as if she was checking for someone she didn't care to see. *Must be a man,* Jessie thought, *if she's hiding out in the one place he wouldn't venture. Or maybe she's just afraid she'll miss whoever she's looking for.*

The line lurched forward again and the woman with the two children arrived at its head to dump her carry-on bag onto the conveyer belt that fed the maw of the X-ray machine. Swinging toward her son, she grabbed for the small daypack he was wearing, but he ducked out of reach shaking his head.

"Mine," he told her defiantly.

"Stop it, Michael. You give me that—right now."

With the help of a security guard, she cornered him and stripped off the child-sized daypack while he yelled resentfully. Tossing it onto the moving belt, she marched him by the scruff of the neck through the security gate and collected their carry-on items and her daughter, who had obediently followed them through. Jessie could still hear her scolding as they turned left and went off down a hallway toward a distant waiting area.

She took another step forward and heaved an audible sigh of relief. Wherever they were going it was not Petersburg, for she could see that gate from where she stood.

The briefcase man turned to give her a rueful grin. "I know just how you feel. Unfortunately, I'm afraid . . ."

"You have my extreme sympathy," she told him with a grin.

"Wanna switch?"

"Not for any amount of bribery. I'd for sure wind up sitting next to Michael."

He stepped up to deposit the briefcase and newspaper in one of the plastic bins provided, adding his jacket and shoes before it all slid away into the machine to be scrutinized by an eagle-eyed woman operator while he was occupied in emptying his pockets of car keys and change.

"Good trip," he wished Jessie, and walked on through the gate with a resigned shrug and shake of his head.

With a few minutes left before boarding, she found a seat in the waiting area and sat down to casually assess the people who *were* about to join her on the way to Petersburg, or beyond it to stops in Wrangell and Ketchikan, before the plane reached its destination in Seattle. As usual for Southeast Alaska, and the state capital of Juneau in particular, they were a mixed assortment of mostly permanent and temporary residents, but few tourists, for that season had slowed to a trickle with cool weather and the beginning of the school year.

From pictures seen in the news, she recognized a senior legislator from Fairbanks who stared at the floor and leaned close to listen with seeming attention to the appeals of either a constituent or a lobbyist who was emphasizing points with a forefinger jabbed repeatedly into the palm of his other hand.

A group of five commercial fishermen—easily identified by the worn coveralls or jeans, and sweatshirts or flannel shirts they wore—were sprawled loose-boned in seats facing each other for somewhat spiritless conversation across the aisle. At least one slumped half asleep, his cap pulled over his eyes.

An older woman in sensible shoes and a tan raincoat passed up a seat near them with a sniff and scowl of disapproval for their appearance and colorful language. She moved on to the opposite end of the row, where she plumped herself down beside Jessie, clutching her handbag to her ample bosom. "Disgusting," she muttered. "Simply disgusting."

Visiting from Outside and not used to the typical behavior of some Alaskans, Jessie guessed, and suppressed her smile as she turned her attention to the rain that was falling steadily outside the wide western windows. Across Gastineau Channel bands of mist below sodden clouds obscured most of the forest that velveted the mountain slopes of Douglas Island. As she was hoping it wouldn't continue to rain all week on the lighthouse island and feeling glad to have brought waterproof gear, the loudspeaker blared to life announcing first-class boarding. She stood up and moved closer to the gate, knowing her section of seats in the rear of the plane would be next, leaving the woman to cradle her handbag until her turn came.

On board the plane and settled in her window seat, Jessie turned attention to the crush of passengers shuffling single file in her direction, bottlenecking traffic as they reached to cram their bags into overhead bins or bent to tuck them, like her daypack, under the seats ahead of them. One of the fishermen dropped heavily into the center seat next to her, nodding a hello after tossing his worn insulated jacket to the floor and stuffing it under the seat with a booted foot. "Petersburg?" he asked Jessie.

"Yes," Jessie told him with a smile. "You?"

"Yup—back to another damp and miserable search for the elusive shrimp. But it's already getting—ah—friggin' cold out there."

"You from Juneau?"

"Ketchikan," he told her, massaging his temples with hands that were nicked and scarred.

An image of taut lines and sharp knives on cold flesh reminded her that fishing was in many ways a dangerous business.

"Just hopped across to the big city for a weekend of R and R," he continued. "Damn, I've got a head. Spent too much time and money in the Triangle Bar last night."

Slouching in his seat, he pulled the long bill of his cap down over his face and she recognized that he had been the one half asleep in the waiting area. "Wake me when we get there, will ya?"

"Sure."

As near as she could tell, he was instantly asleep.

Slowly, as the last of the passengers located and took their seats, the aisle cleared. A flight attendant moved along it tucking in a dangling strap or handle here and there before snapping closed the overhead bin covers. The seat beyond the now gently snoring fisherman had remained empty and Jessie, feeling lucky, was considering the possibility of waking him enough to ask him to move over and give them both more room when a final passenger stepped aboard at the next to last minute and came hurrying to practically fall into it. Hugging a small black suitcase against her, she leaned cautiously out just far enough to look back up the aisle as if she expected someone to follow.

"Please put your bag under the seat in front of you," instructed the flight attendant. "And fasten your seat belt for takeoff."

"Oh—right." Startled, the young woman bent to slide the bag into the space suggested, then wriggled to find and fasten the belt while still keeping an eye on the forward door. As soon as it was closed and no further passengers had appeared, she heaved a sigh that sounded like relief, settled back, stretched long jeans-covered legs to put her Reeboks on the bag, and, retrieving a paperback from a denim jacket pocket, began to read.

There was something familiar about her. As the plane began to back away from the terminal and Jessie searched her memory for a clue, the woman turned to look out the window. Turning back, she started to read, then stopped and flipped the book over on one knee to keep her place. Reaching up, she pulled off what turned out to be a wig, then used both hands to run her fingers through the revealed waves of short auburn hair and shook her head as a person might in the relief of removing a hat. The motion caused her jacket to fall open to expose a yellow-and-white shirt beneath it.

It was enough for Jessie to remember the woman who had stood in the doorway of the terminal restroom, though her present appearance was so different she couldn't be sure of that identification. Without the wig, it was obvious that the woman's red hair was her own. In the more casual denim she looked younger, perhaps in her early thirties, but it was the same woman. Thoughtfully, Jessie turned to stare unseeing at the tarmac outside the window, considering the odd transformation. Curious—definitely curious.

As soon as they were airborne she gave up wondering, reclined her seatback and settled herself for the short flight.

Whatever the young woman's reasons for changing her looks, it was, Jessie decided, none of her business after all— was it?

CHAPTER FOUR

RAIN DRIZZLED FROM OVERCAST SO LOW THAT THE MISTY tree-covered slopes of the distant islands and mainland defining the dark Alaskan waters of the Inside Passage were barely discernible from the deck of the Alaska State Ferry that plowed steadily north of Ketchikan through Clarence Strait.

On an outside observation deck, beneath an overhang that provided scarcely more than a suggestion of shelter, the husky figure of average height that leaned, hands in pockets, against a cabin wall was only slightly protected from the damp. Now and again a drop of moisture fell from above to darken one broad shoulder of the gray canvas jacket he wore over a maroon sweatshirt and well-worn jeans.

With little visible of the spectacular scenery that often introduced visitors to the Far North, the few collar-clutching passengers who scuttled past Joe Cooper's vantage point, bent on finding warmth and refuge inside, cast him looks that questioned the judgment of anyone who would elect to endure the damp chill of the deck in such weather. His gaze never shifted to meet their questioning stares. But when they were not looking in his direction he assessed each with a single investigative glance and returned his attention to the wake that churned a long line of roiling water and foam behind the ferry until mist dropped a curtain to hide it. A careful appraisal, however, would have revealed that, although seemingly at ease, there was a hint of tension about him—a stillness and patience as purposeful as a coiled spring.

A boy of eight or nine in a hooded yellow slicker came trotting along, probably sent out by a mother frustrated by his confinement-induced surplus of energy. Abruptly he interrupted his solitary circuit of the deck to stare curiously up at the man. Cocking his head to one side, he grinned, exposing the space left by two missing front teeth. "Arnchu cold, mithter?"

Under the bill of his cap, the man moved only his eyes to stare down at his pint-sized interrogator. Then, without change of expression, he twitched one shoulder in what the boy correctly interpreted as a shrug.

"It'th purty cold out here, ya know?"

Making no further response, Cooper continued to consider the path of the wake.

"Okay. Thee ya later maybe."

Cheerfully accepting disregard as unspoken dismissal, the boy trotted off, leaving the man to his solitary perusal of the nautical miles quickly falling behind.

It had been a week since Cooper bought his ticket for the trip north and waited until the last possible minute to board the Alaska State Ferry *Malaspina* in Bellingham, Washington. From a spot near the boarding area he had carefully observed the passengers making their way onto the vessel, hoping to recognize the one in particular he had followed north from Seattle, believing she was either heading for the ferry or attempting to disappear into British Columbia. Having identified the car she had abandoned in the parking lot, he had taken up his surveillance post. From past experience he knew she was clever in creating disguises for herself, so when he had not been able to pick her out of the crowd of people boarding—though knowing she could have planted the rental car as a ruse—he had felt certain enough that she had somehow managed to escape his vigilance that he had followed the last of the passengers onto the boat, a commitment that left him no options if she had not.

He had carried little: a single duffel containing a sleeping bag wrapped around a change of clothing, a few personal items and papers, several photographs, and a consuming, resentful anger that the preceding months had honed and focused, along with a cast-iron determination that the woman should not slip away to escape him again. Assuming usual security in boarding the ferry, he had reluctantly locked his handgun in a concealed compartment of the truck he had left in long-term parking, planning to retrieve both upon return. A gun was an easy enough thing to obtain, probably more so in the Far North where, he understood, most people owned them, and where the woman was seemingly headed.

There had been cabins available when Cooper bought his ticket. But preferring to remain where he might catch sight of his quarry, he had not acquired one. Instead, each night he had spread his sleeping bag on the floor of a forward observation lounge, or in one of its recliners, when one was available. Being in the common areas meant it was possible for her to notice and identify him, but he thought it worth the risk, as it was clear that she was aware that he had located and was following her again or she would not have taken flight. As soon as the ferry left Bellingham they were both committed and confined on the vessel until it reached another port. So far, however, there had been no sign of her and he was growing restive.

During the thirty-seven hours of running between Bellingham and Ketchikan, first of the Alaskan ports, he had spent a considerable amount of his time in the cafeteria watching people come and go, reasoning that she would probably not risk the dining room, but had either brought her own supplies or would venture in to pick up food to take away. The woman had to eat sometime, didn't she? But not once so far had she appeared. The best answer to the puzzle of her disappearance was that she had taken a cabin and meant to stay invisible for the duration of the voyage. But how long, he had wondered, would that be? Where was she headed? Though he had asked, even offered the suggestion of a bribe, the purser had been unwilling to part with any helpful information on either the destination or the cabin assignment of any passenger—would not even confirm that she was aboard.

In carefully analyzing the situation, Cooper had calculated that she would not disembark in the small towns of Wrangell or Petersburg along the route. They were communities where, except for the influx of summer fishermen and tourists, residents knew each other and in September a stranger, especially a woman, would stand out. It was possible that she might remain aboard until the *Malaspina* reached the northern end of its run in Haines or Skagway, both of which connected with highways that led into Canada. But these were also small, ingrown communities, and besides, the woman had left her transportation in Bellingham. After consideration of schedules and maps, he had decided that she was most likely to leave the ferry in either Ketchikan or Juneau, where she could more easily blend into a larger population, hoping to vanish into a city-sized port.

Upon docking in Ketchikan, he had traded anonymity for

the assurance of close scrutiny and had stood leaning against the rail near the gangway as disembarking passengers passed him one by one. From there he had also been able to see cars, trucks, and one motorcycle leave the vehicle deck. A couple of senior citizens had also left from the vehicle deck: An old man with a cane had walked slowly beside his wheelchair-bound wife, who was pushed down the ramp and into the terminal by a steward.

For the three hours the vessel remained at the terminal he maintained his observation post, strolling away only when the lines had been cast off and the ferry drew slowly away from the dock to resume its journey, certain that the subject of his search had made no appearance. Though he expected to watch again in Wrangell and Petersburg, he was now convinced that the larger capital city of Juneau must be her intended destination.

Giving up wake-watching, Cooper abruptly pushed away from the cabin wall intending to stroll forward along the deck to the door that was closest to the cafeteria, another of his endless cups of coffee in mind. As he turned, a disturbance in the rain-dimpled channel caught his attention and he paused to watch as, perhaps half a mile away between the ferry and the distant shoreline, the distinctive "humped" dorsal fin that gives the humpback whale its name came into view above the surface as the giant mammal rose to breathe. As he watched, the huge animal blew a mist of spume into the air, though the spatter of the rain, thrum of the ferry's engines, and splash of the water they were cutting through obscured the distant sound. In what seemed slow motion because of its size, the whale rolled forward until the giant flukes lifted clear of the water, then disappeared into the depths of the channel once more.

Cooper waited a few minutes to see if it would reappear. When it did not, he was about to resume his walk toward the cafeteria when against the far shore the vague shape of a boat appeared like a shadow, half hidden in the mist. Motoring slowly south close to land, as the fog thinned it gradually grew more distinct until he could see that it was not a fishing boat, as he had first assumed, but a recreational powerboat of some kind, large enough for extended travel with living space similar to a seagoing motor home. Some family of tourists on their trip of a lifetime, he figured, watching it with mild interest. In a moment or two the cloud that hugged the shoreline thickened and the ghostly vessel vanished, leaving Cooper to feel that the sighting had been a trick of his imagination. Shrugging, he swung toward the cafeteria and the continuation of his search.

If the woman he sought managed to leave the ferry undetected and found a place to stay somewhere in the north, he felt he could eventually run her to ground. Though Alaska was a huge state, the bulk of it was wilderness through which ran only a few roads and a limited rail network. Access to many of its towns and villages was restricted to air travel. To Cooper, this meant that its population was contained in a searchable number of communities, even if they were scattered and isolated.

He needed to find her soon—was running out of patience and the wherewithal to continue or extend the hunt. Following her as she attempted to elude him had seriously depleted his resources. But, one way or another, she could not be allowed to escape this time. He felt that he was closing in and savored the idea that when he found her, pleasant or not, he would collect the debts she owed—to him and to others.

CHAPTER FIVE

AS THE PLANE CAME DOWN, JESSIE COULD SEE THAT THE rain falling in Petersburg was lighter than what she had left behind in Juneau. The airport they taxied up to was several miles south of the town, and the terminal part of a line of buildings and hangars that included private charter companies that flew all kinds of support for locals and flight-seeing for tourists during the season. Through a window she caught sight of a sign for Pacific Wing Air Charters and two mechanics in coveralls working on a Temsco helicopter beyond it.

Most rural and many urban Alaskans take flying in large or small planes as much for granted as city dwellers do catching a subway or bus. But maintenance on any kind of aircraft is regarded very seriously, especially by those who fly in the southeastern parts of the state and who know that making unscheduled landings—in country that is little but heavily wooded slopes, or abrupt rocky shores that descend steeply and immediately into the saltwater depths of the Inside Passage—are to be avoided at all cost. Strict and conscientious care *is* that cost.

The fisherman in the seat beside her had not even moved when the wheels hit the runway with a bump. When they had stopped at the terminal, Jessie nudged his shoulder and he sat up, rubbed his red eyes, and yawned before reaching down to retrieve his jacket. The young woman on the aisle was already on her feet and, evidently as anxious to get off quickly as she had been to get on, paid no attention to her seatmates. By the time the departing passengers around them had begun to collect their carry-on baggage and move forward, she had crowded ahead of several people and was already headed toward the exit with her black bag.

Space was limited inside the small terminal and the conversation of many people loud, as arriving passengers greeted friends and relatives while they waited for their checked luggage to appear, joining the throng of others who had formed a haphazard sort of security line to board the continuing flight to Seattle. Hating crowds and not in any particular hurry, Jessie avoided both and found a semiclear space on the opposite side of the room to wait till the worst of the crush had either claimed their bags and vanished through the front door, or had been allowed to board the plane. When the room had almost emptied she retrieved her duffel and approached the ticket counter to inquire about transportation to downtown Petersburg. A friendly agent gave her the number for a local taxi and pointed out a pay phone near the door.

Fifteen minutes later, she was waiting on a bench under an overhang outside when a brown, semi-antique Chevy four-door sedan with one gray fender pulled up in front of her, with a rattle and screech of brakes, and a girl of around twenty, wearing jeans and a bright yellow sweatshirt, bounced out and came around to offer her hand with an eager grin of welcome.

"Hey. You must be Jessie Arnold, right? Are you really the Iditarod musher? Oh, hell—I know you are. I've seen you on television and in the paper enough times to recognize you easy. I'm Connie, the local cab jockey—when my brother Dave isn't doing this job. Welcome to Petersburg. Hop in."

Snatching up the duffel, she trotted to the rear of the Chevy where the trunk, lacking a mechanism to secure it, was held shut with a purple bungee cord, and tossed the bag in with a thump that made Jessie glad she was carrying her camera equipment in her daypack. Opening the rear passenger door, she waved Jessie into the backseat with a flourish, slammed it behind her, and, still talking, hurried around to fling herself behind the wheel.

"Okay," she said, revving the engine to life and shifting into a gear that screeched in protest. "Where do you want to go? Downtown—yes? Or are you staying with some friends while you're here?"

"The Tides Inn," Jessie informed her, managing to get a word in edgewise while catching her balance with a grab at the back of the front seat as Connie let off the clutch with a jerk and made a quick U-turn. Clearly, her driving was as enthusiastic as her nonstop conversation.

"Cool," she approved, tossing the words back over her shoulder. "Tides Inn is a good place—great people and close to downtown. But then everything is close to downtown. Petersburg is so small you can practically see it all in an hour. Be prepared for Scandinavians though. The place is overrun with Norwegians and most of them like to dress up as Vikings and have parades as often as possible. I'm a Swede myself, but they're generous and let me live here anyway."

As Connie continued with a wealth of details on the attractions of Petersburg, a fishing and logging community that had come into being in the 1890s, Jessie turned her attention to what they were passing. While fall had definitely come to her home in the Mat-Su Valley, gilding the birch leaves and scattering them in a ground-covering carpet, she was pleased to see that here the leaves on the trees were still green and there were beds of late flowers blooming in the yards of the houses that sped by the windows of the car. It would be a while longer before winter made an appearance in Southeast Alaska, which was more prone to rain than to snow.

"How far is it into town?" she interrupted Connie's continuing monologue to ask.

"Oh, not far at all—couple of miles. We'll be dropping into it in just a few minutes. Nothing's far from anything else here—even the airport. That's why the cab doesn't have a meter. We just know how far everything is from everything else. It's impossible to get lost because—"

"That *is* a grocery store, isn't it?" Jessie asked, seeing that they were passing what appeared to be a large modern supermarket, prominently labeled HAMMER & WIKAN.

"Oh yeah. That's our new one. You want something there? We can stop if you want. I got some stuff I could pick up anyway, so I won't charge you any more."

She was already swinging a right turn into the parking lot as Jessie, amused, agreed. As they turned, she glanced out the window at the road they were leaving. Not far along it, a figure was walking toward town with a small black suitcase in one hand—the young woman from the plane, without a doubt, for her auburn hair was a dead giveaway. Though the rain had all but stopped, she walked with her shoulders hunched, had turned up the collar of her jacket, and had her free hand thrust into a pocket of her jeans.

She must live here, Jessie thought—but forgot to wonder

as they pulled up in front of the grocery and parked with a lurch.

"Take your time," Connie said as the automatic doors swept open in front of them at the entry. "I'm in no hurry."

Wheeling a cart through the aisles, it wasn't long until Jessie, remembering that Laurie had promised to feed the working crew, had collected the few things she wanted to take to the island. Still, she thought snacks were a good idea, as were two cases of soft drinks, fruit, cheese, salad greens, and a couple of tomatoes. She added a box of her favorite peppermint tea, milk and sugar for it, and picked up a few candy bars at the check stand, where a friendly woman was waiting to tally up the bill. When Jessie asked if her purchases could be packed in a box or two, explaining that she was going out to Five Finger Lighthouse, the clerk improved on the idea.

"We can put all this in the cooler and deliver it to the dock tomorrow if you'll let us know when and where. No charge. It's a service we provide—mostly during the summer for boat people, tourists, and fishermen."

Handing her a credit card, Jessie gratefully agreed, glad to be relieved of carrying the groceries to the hotel—to say nothing of getting them, along with her personal gear, to the dock to meet Jim Beal and his boat the next day. Knowing she might like some later in the evening, she put the box of tea, a couple of candy bars, and a box of cookies into a plastic bag to take with her, then helped carry Connie's purchases to the taxi.

Back on the road, they were shortly headed downhill into Petersburg and soon pulled up at the front door of the Tides Inn on the corner of First and Dolphin Streets, a block from the main street, Nordic Drive. Connie had the duffel on the

sidewalk before her passenger could make it out and close
the door of the Chevy.

"Thanks," she said as Jessie handed her a large tip along
with the fare she quoted. Trading the cash for a battered
business card from the same pocket of her jeans, she handed
it over. "If you need wheels while you're here, just call me at
this number."

"I might need a lift to the dock tomorrow if it's very far.
But I don't know where the boat will come in yet."

"Probably the public dock, but maybe not if, as you said,
he's picking up construction materials. Anyway, the hotel
has a complimentary van that could take you—could actually have picked you up at the airport for that matter—but
call if you need me. Or Dave, who will probably decide to
drive if he knows you're the passenger." She grinned imp-
ishly. "Maybe I just won't mention that then, will I?"

"Thanks, Connie," Jessie said, laughing. "And for the
grocery stop."

"You bet. Anytime. If I don't see you, have a good trip. A
week at Five Finger Light! Wow. You'll get to see a lot of
whales."

She was gone, a hand raised to wave out the window, before Jessie could respond.

Hefting the duffel, Jessie walked into the hotel, where she
was met by the smell of coffee that filled the air from a pot
on a low table across the room. The coffee was, she could
see, accompanied by paper cups and packets of sugar and
creamer. As she filed away this visual information as a
source for a morning brew, a short dark-haired woman came
out of a rear office to stand behind the counter with a welcoming smile.

"Have some if you like. It's fresh. Can I help you?"

"Yes, please. You have a reservation for Jessie Arnold?"

The woman's smile grew broader and she held out an eager hand to shake Jessie's with some excitement.

"Oh *yes,* we certainly *do*. The whole staff's been looking forward to having *you* here, Jessie. We've seen you in the Iditarod reports—and the year you ran the Yukon Quest—though we could only get part of it. You've got some real fans in Petersburg, including all of us here at Tides Inn."

All of them—*really?* Jessie wondered.

It always made her slightly uneasy when someone was so obviously impressed by her. This was one of those times that left her a little embarrassed and not quite sure how to respond. *That's nice* wouldn't quite do it, but what would?

"Thanks," she said finally, with her usual smile. "Glad you like the races."

Though she could understand Alaskans' pride and fascination with what had become the state sport, to be singled out had always seemed inappropriate in some odd way. The taxi driver's recognition had been filled with a particular brand of humor and it was doubtful that Connie was as impressed with much of anything as was this woman, whose fervor bordered on a sort of unrealistic, starstruck awe that seemed to have more to do with who Jessie was than with what she did—race sled dogs. She'd rather people were rac-*ing,* instead of rac-*er,* fans. The feeling, however, was not one she could, or should, communicate to anyone but other mushers—who had experienced the same thing and sympathized. So she smiled and signed the register, relieved that she wasn't asked for an autograph.

Given a key, carrying her duffel and daypack, she went, as directed, back out the front door and around the side of the building to where the Dolphin Street sidewalk sloped steeply downhill. A passage halfway down it led to the left like an alley between the multilevel hotel and its annex next door. Turning in there Jessie soon found the room she had been assigned.

It was dark and a bit crowded with two queen-sized beds, but pleasant enough, though a little cool. Turning up the thermostat, she left the duffel, washed her hands and face clean of the feel of travel, and thought for a minute about calling Alex to let him know she had safely completed the airplane part of this adventure. Checking her watch, she decided that he and Delafosse might still be finishing up their meetings and would soon settle in the bar of their hotel for a beer before dinner, probably with the visiting officers from Vancouver. She would wait till later to make the call, when he might be back in his room. For now, she would go out, get a look at downtown, and find a place to have her own dinner in the process.

It was raining again, so she put on the waterproof slicker she had brought along and, shouldering her daypack, closed the door, checked to be sure it was locked, and headed down the hill into Petersburg.

CHAPTER SIX

AT JUST AFTER SIX O'CLOCK IT WAS ALREADY EVENING, FOR the sun had disappeared behind the mountains to the west. The rain had, at least temporarily, slowed to what was almost a mist but, though the general temperature was noticeably warmer than at home in the Matanuska Valley, the breeze off the waters of the harbor was chilly. Jessie zipped her green insulated slicker and tucked her hands into its pockets, rather than bother to retrieve her gloves from the daypack.

At the bottom of the hill, she rounded the corner onto Nordic Drive, where the tantalizing scent of pizza wandered in suddenly from somewhere to tickle her nose, but was immediately whisked away by the wind. Walking west past several closed businesses, a little way down the block she came to the Harbor Bar with an adjoining liquor store, both open and casting warm inviting lights onto the sidewalk from their windows. As she paused to look into the bar the door swung open, letting out the sound of canned music, the cheerful buzz of conversation, and two young men, one wearing a bright blue hooded sweatshirt with VIKING printed in white across the front and smaller print below. He turned left and went on along the street with his friend, leaving Jessie to wonder about the small print, but she smiled at the appropriateness of the larger word. Petersburg people were clearly as proud of their Scandinavian heritage as Connie had indicated.

Peering through the glass, she could see a large room that was well lighted for a tavern, with a long bar against the left-hand wall. It was lined with tall stools, a few of them empty. More than half of the chairs clustered around an assortment of tables in the remaining space were occupied by a casually dressed, cheerful crowd of people sharing relaxed conversation along with their drinks. A carryout box on one table held a crust or two that were left from a pizza. A poolroom occupied the rear of the space and a dartboard hung on the back wall, both in use.

The atmosphere was persuasive, so when the door opened for an arriving customer, she followed him in and claimed one of the tall stools near the front window, slipping off her slicker and depositing it with her daypack on another stool beside her, leaving two spaces between herself and the nearest occupant.

"Hi there." The bartender, a tall young woman wearing a plaid shirt tucked into her jeans, a metal bottle opener slipped into a hip pocket, greeted her with a smile. "What can I get you?"

"A Killian's Red," Jessie told her, naming her favorite lager.

It appeared in rapid order along with a glass that she pushed back as she laid a bill down to pay for her drink, which she sipped straight from the longneck bottle.

The first taste was always best, Jessie decided appreciatively, setting the brew down with a satisfied sigh. Though it had taken three air hops to arrive here, her plane travel was over for the rest of the week and it felt good to know that on this evening she had no commitments, could relax and make decisions on dinner for one. Glancing inquiringly around she saw no source for the pizza she had observed on the table across the room and had a question ready when the bartender returned to lay her change on the bar and remove the unnecessary glass.

"From a place down the street," the bartender told her. "You can get one to go and bring it back if you want—lots of people do. We don't serve food, so we don't mind."

Though pizza was not without appeal, the idea didn't satisfy Jessie—not in seafood country.

"Where would I go to find a place with crab or shrimp on the menu?"

"The Northern Lights will be open," the woman told her, glancing down the bar to where a pair of mugs had been set back to indicate their drinkers were ready for refills. "Oops. Hold that thought. I'll be right back."

Jessie watched as she filled the mugs and came striding back with a grin. "Sorry. It's usually slower on Monday, but we've got a thirsty crowd tonight for some reason."

"You said the Northern Lights?" Jessie prompted.

"Right. Where are you staying? I'll walk you through it from there."

"The Tides Inn. But I'll go from here."

"Okay. If you go across the street and walk west for two full blocks you'll come to a garden on the corner with the statue of a bear with a fish in its mouth. Take a right, then curve to the left on Sing Lee Alley. Keep going, and where it turns into a bridge that goes over the slough, you'll see the Sons of Norway Hall. From there you can see the Northern Lights Restaurant—on pilings at the other end of the bridge."

"Great. Thanks," Jessie told her. "I think I'll try that."

"They have a good menu—all sorts of—"

"Hey, Carol. This'd be a great place to open a tavern," someone interrupted with a call.

The bartender shook her head and grinned. "If I had a nickel . . . You'll like the Northern Lights," she called back as she hurried off to fill the order for the impatient someone at the other end of the long bar.

Jessie leaned forward on her elbows and, taking another swallow of the Killian's, returned to her thoughts of spending time on her own. The Harbor Bar was warm, dry, and comfortably full of agreeable background music, the crack of balls hitting each other on the pool table, and easygoing conversation—all in all, an undemanding and relaxing place to be for the moment. Purposely, she had chosen a seat away from others, feeling a need for time by herself and knowing the week at the lighthouse would be crowded with other people.

As she considered it and sipped the lager, someone gave a hoot of laughter at a table behind her.

"You made that up, Hal."

"Did not—I swear it really happened."

"Yeah, sure it did."

For a second or two, Jessie wished she were in a pub at home and could walk over and join the friendly conversation, but quickly returned to appreciating time on her own.

She was used to being alone and independently making her own decisions as by necessity a majority of her time as a sled dog racer was spent in training teams for competition, which involved hours, even days, in the wilds of Alaska with only her dogs for company. It was a solitary occupation that was not for everyone, but suited Jessie for she was introspective at heart. Sometimes she wondered if she liked it so much because the sport was matched to her personality, or vice versa.

Growing up in a family of extroverts, she had not been a shy child, but had learned early in life to be on her own, when the loss of a younger sister had focused the attention of her parents on an endless, anguished search for the seven-year-old who disappeared on her way home from school one afternoon and was never found. As a result, Jessie knew she had felt unreasonably responsible and had come to be most comfortable when depending on no one but herself—being in control of what went on around her and what she did. If it hadn't been for the loss of Lily things might have been different and . . .

I'm not going there, she decided firmly, realizing such thoughts were taking her into territory that, unresolved, was deeply painful.

Casting about for something else onto which to turn her attention, Alex Jensen immediately came to mind, along with a vague sense of discomfort about their relationship. His return had somehow made her feel uneasy in her own living space and she wanted to know why—but not at the moment. *Not going there right now either,* she told herself sternly, and swinging partway around on the bar stool once again noticed the pool table in the back of the room. It was a game she enjoyed. Should she go and lay a quarter on the edge of the table—play a round or two? No. She didn't want the rituals of meeting new people—what she wanted was dinner, and soon. She would finish the half-emptied Killian's and go, she decided. Petersburg was known for its shrimp, so she might as well take advantage of it.

Turning the other way, she took a look out the window

and saw that it was full dark, but the rain seemed to have ceased for the time being.

Raining now or not, the short, heavyset man who came through the door as she watched had clearly walked through some before it stopped, for he shook water from the worn yellow slicker he removed and tossed over the back of a stool between himself and Jessie before he climbed onto another and settled comfortably, with a nod of greeting in her direction.

Time to go, she thought, *before he tries to start a conversation.*

But he turned to the bartender instead.

"Ferry's in," he told her as she set a Budweiser in front of him—clearly his usual, for he had not given her an order.

"It's a couple of hours early," she responded.

"Yeah. Heard they skipped Wrangell this run—some repairs being made to the dock, so they couldn't put in."

"You can usually set your watch by the *Malaspina.*"

"Yup. They'll be putting in after dark from now on. I coulda used a couple more months of summer."

"Couldn't we all?"

At the sound of the door opening again behind her, Jessie paused, bottle halfway to her mouth, and glanced over her shoulder to see who was next. Expecting another stranger, she was surprised to once again see a familiar face—the young woman from the afternoon's plane. The redhead hesitated momentarily and gave the room a searching look before, with long, jeans-clad strides, heading directly for the back where she disappeared into the restroom. As she passed she focused her attention on the long bar and her eyes widened, startled, when she recognized Jessie.

Three—no—four times I've seen her now. Is she follow-

ing *me?* For a moment Jessie wondered, but had to smile at her paranoia. *Everything,* she told herself—draining the lager before collecting herself to go find Sing Lee Alley, the Northern Lights, and dinner, in that order—*is* not *about you.*

CHAPTER SEVEN

THE SKY WAS DARK, NOT A STAR TO BE SEEN, WHEN JESSIE left the warm, cheerful Harbor Bar. Before following directions to the Northern Lights she stepped next door into the liquor store to ask how late they would be open, intending to pick up a bottle of Jameson and some Killian's to take with her to the island the next day. Learning she would have time after dinner to take care of this errand, she went along the street past a number of storefronts, some decorated with colorful rosemaled patterns that she recognized as typically Scandinavian. Baskets of still-blooming flowers hung from the streetlamps that cast pools of light on the sidewalk, and she noticed that in several places circles of intricate brass designs had been set into the pavement. One was a fishing trawler, the water depicted under it filled with salmon. Two others were done in the familiar patterns of local Haida or Tlingit people. She was pleased to find that a raven, her favorite Alaskan bird, was one of these. The other portrayed an eagle.

All the gift shops and art galleries were closed for the night, but their windows were full of interesting things that she mentally filed away to examine in the morning, knowing her transportation to Five Finger Lighthouse would not arrive until the middle of the day. At the end of two blocks she crossed the street and found the small garden mentioned by the bartender, with its statue of a bear and its fish.

Following directions, she almost immediately found herself in Sing Lee Alley. It curved to the left and was so narrow that she thought it might have been one of the original Petersburg streets that began its life as a wagon road. Away from the lamps that lined the main street the lane was dark and full of the shadows cast by old houses and buildings that clung so close that their doors opened directly onto the street. As she strolled along she could hear the slow drip of rainwater falling from eaves into puddles, and her footfalls created echoes that came back to her in the confined space almost as if two people were walking.

Noticing a raven cleverly painted over a doorway as if it were perched on the frame, Jessie stepped closer and saw two others painted near it, their wings spread in flight. As she smiled in appreciation of the unknown artist's sense of humor, she was startled to hear the echoes of footsteps continue for a step or two after she stopped. Swinging sharply around, she peered into the dark in the direction from which she had come, but the narrow lane was empty of anyone but herself and some inky shadows. Almost she retraced her steps to take a look, but deciding that her imagination was taking over, continued toward the restaurant she knew must be close ahead. Purposely, she made her footsteps loud, listening carefully, but did not hear the double echo again. Must have been a trick of that particular building or doorway, she decided—unfamiliar town, street, and sounds. But as she went on, she increased her speed slightly.

Just past a large white house with a sign reading SING LEE ALLEY BOOKS—another goal for tomorrow morning—the

pavement turned to timbers and she identified the barn-
shaped Sons of Norway Hall, built on pilings like the bridge
beyond it. Along the bridge were lampposts with a Norwe-
gian flag, bright red with a white-framed blue cross, hanging from each, and on the other side the Northern Lights
Restaurant proclaimed itself with fairy lights below its sign.
Jessie abandoned all thought of imaginary echoes behind
her and hurried across into the warmth of a pleasant dining
room that wafted a delectable aroma of food into her
nose—dinner at last.

The front section of the restaurant was a pickup area for
orders to take out. As she hesitated, a waitress hurried forward with a greeting and led her to one of the tables in the
back, where she could look out the window onto a marina
and a long causeway on tall, thin pilings that led out to a
large commercial-looking building. Jessie shed her slicker,
deposited it and her daypack on the bench of the booth, and
settled in satisfaction to open the menu she was handed, in
which she was pleased to find an appealing assortment of
options including, as anticipated, plenty of seafood. After a
short equivocation, she chose a dinner salad, shrimp Al-
fredo, and another Killian's to keep it company.

While she waited, she glanced around the room, which
was attractively appointed with hanging lamps and plants. A
wide decorative wallpaper strip with an amusing collection
of roly-poly chefs topped a wainscot along one wall and she
could hear real cooks, roly-poly or not, making a busy clat-
ter in the kitchen. Glad she had forgone the pizza in favor of
the Northern Lights, she thanked the waitress who delivered
her drink, then turned to appraise the marina below, which
was crowded with the power- and sailboats of private owners, local and transient.

The tide was out and the access ramp formed an acute angle with the dock that was designed to float up and down on its pilings. Though there was a soft hint of light in one or two of the boats and the area seemed mostly deserted at this late hour, movement on a large powerboat caught her attention. As she watched, two men, one with a duffel bag over one shoulder, left the boat and hiked along to the ramp, which they were forced to climb slowly and carefully considering its low-tide steepness. When they stopped at the top under an overhead light he set the duffel down and she could see that he was dressed in tan work pants and a faded green sweatshirt under a black slicker. From his graying hair, he looked older than his companion, perhaps in his fifties. Back turned, silhouetted against the pool of light, the other seemed to be dressed in waterproof coat and pants, but she couldn't see his face. They exchanged a few words and then separated. As they disappeared into different parts of a parking lot, she wondered where they had been in such bad weather, but supposed it was possible they had spent the day working on the craft and hadn't left the harbor at all.

"That was quick," she started to say, turning with a smile, aware of someone approaching her table. But the smile faded into surprise, when she found, not the waitress she anticipated, but the young woman she had noticed on the plane from Juneau that afternoon and again in the Harbor Bar.

"Hello," the woman said quietly, with a nervous, hollow sort of smile. "Would you mind if I joined you for dinner?"

When Jessie didn't say no, she slid quickly onto the bench on the other side of the table. Her hair, once again dark and shoulder-length, Jessie could now see *was* a wig that she must have put back on in the Harbor Bar. Her face was thin, eyes a greenish blue with lashes heavily darkened with too much mascara that gummed them together in clumps.

"Thanks," the young woman said, reaching across the table to offer a hand that Jessie automatically took, noticing that the nails were chewed raggedly short. "I'm Karen. Karen—ah—Emerson. And I appreciate the company."

"It's okay," Jessie told her, still confused. "We came in on the same plane. I'm Jessie Arnold."

There was no flash of recognition at the mention of her name, which told Jessie that Karen was either a stranger to Alaska or not a sled dog racing fan.

"You were in the bar a little while ago," Karen said.

Jessie remembered the sound of footsteps behind her in Sing Lee Alley and decided she had not been imagining them. "Did you follow me from there?"

"Yes," Karen admitted, "I did. Sorry. I wanted to see where you were going. You might live here and be headed home. But you don't, do you? You're just passing through, like me, right?"

It seemed unusual criteria for selecting a dinner companion to Jessie, but perhaps not. In a town as small and friendly as Petersburg, such a request for company from a local could have elicited an offer of residential hospitality. This woman seemed to be seeking contact of a less personal nature, the kind that could be assumed in the neutral territory of a restaurant. As Jessie watched, Karen glanced nervously over her shoulder toward a woman who had come in and gone directly to the pickup counter. *Why is impersonal company important?* she wondered. *Why me?*

"I am passing through," she answered the question, "sort of. I'm on my way to spend the next few days with friends on an island."

"Really?" Karen said brightly. "How fascinating. Tell me."

The question seemed defensively designed to focus the conversation on Jessie rather than herself and Jessie found that she felt somehow oddly reluctant to share her plans with this stranger. As she hesitated the waitress appeared suddenly with a second menu and glass of water. "Your dinner will be right up," she told Jessie. "Or would you want to wait while your friend orders?"

"Oh, please don't." Karen waved off the offered menu. "Whatever it is, it'll be cold if you wait. What kind of soup do you have?"

"It's minestrone or clam chowder tonight."

"I'll have a bowl of the minestrone, toast, and coffee, please."

She watched the waitress cross the room to the kitchen, then turned back to Jessie, renewing her simulated smile of interest. "Now, tell me all about your island. Is it close to Petersburg?"

What harm? Jessie decided, wondering why she should feel disinclined to share. There was something about this woman that seemed slightly off-key, as if she were pretending to be something she was not, but maybe she was naturally nervous in getting to know new people.

"Not really. It's a very small island at the north end of Frederick Sound and has an historic lighthouse. And it isn't mine. It belongs to friends of mine and I'm going to spend the rest of the week there with a volunteer renovation crew."

"Interesting. How do you get there, by boat?"

"Yes. A friend is picking me up tomorrow, when he comes to town for roofing materials."

She had been watching Karen carefully as she spoke, noting that the woman's attention still seemed a little scattered as she directed another glance or two toward the front door of the restaurant, as customers came and went through it. About half of the tables were full, but the place seemed to have a fairly steady flow of people, either sitting down for dinner or picking up take-out food. Though appearing to listen, Karen was evidently on the lookout for someone. Jessie wondered who—and why. But, if she was anticipating the arrival of someone else, why had the woman asked to sit with *her?*

"Are you expecting someone?" she asked.

"Oh—no," Karen said almost too quickly, turning back. "Of course not." But the bright interest faded from her face and was replaced by a guarded expression as she turned her head to look out the window at the public dock where a series of lamps on tall poles cast pools of light at regularly spaced intervals.

"Is something wrong, Karen?" Jessie asked.

"Not at all," Karen denied, turning back with a smile that faltered and did not reach her eyes. She hesitated, then seemed to give in. "Oh hell—yes. Very wrong."

"What?"

The waitress chose that moment to appear at their side with a tray, bearing the pasta, salad, and soup they had ordered. As she arranged their food on the table, Karen once again turned her head to stare out the window.

When the waitress had gone, Jessie leaned forward over her plate and gave up all pretense of politeness.

"Look, Karen. I don't know anything about you, but it's obvious that you followed and picked me as a sort of cover for some reason. If you've got trouble, don't I at least deserve to know what's going on? I won't be part of anything I don't understand. So you'd better tell me what it's all about."

Surprised at Jessie's straightforward demand, Karen faced her, eyes wide.

"I'm sorry," she said after a second or two of silence while Jessie waited. "I wanted to get to know you a little and see if you were someone I could trust."

"Trust about what?" Jessie countered. "If I don't get answers, I can always move to another table."

Karen took a deep breath, put elbows on the table on each side of her soup bowl, laced her fingers together so the gnawed nails were hidden and leaned over them.

"I'm in trouble," she said in a low conspiratorial voice.

"*That* much I got. And?"

"Okay. There's a guy following me that I'm trying to shake."

Jessie thought back to the woman's nervous observation of the door of the plane and the way she had relaxed after it was closed.

"That's why you were wearing the wig you have on now. You were afraid this 'guy' would get on the plane this afternoon, right?"

"Right."

"But he didn't."

"No. So I thought I was okay and took it off."

"Then how would he get here now?"

"The ferry came in awhile ago. I think he was on it."

"How do you know that?"

"When I heard it was coming in early, I went down to see and I'm almost sure I saw him getting off."

It didn't make sense to Jessie.

"That ferry," she said, "was headed north. I heard a man in the bar say it was supposed to stop in Wrangell on its way here, but couldn't—some kind of problem with the dock. So if this guy was on it he couldn't have come from Juneau."

"So he wasn't in Juneau, but I was afraid he might be. He's very smart and scares the hell out of me. He caught the ferry in Bellingham when I did four days ago." She frowned, remembering. "Look. I was living in Ketchikan and he was my . . . we had a relationship that didn't work out, okay? When I finally had enough of him hitting me, I moved out. But he refused to believe that I meant what I said and it was over. He's been following and making threats for a long time now. It was time to leave town again."

"Leave where?"

"Seattle."

"I thought you said Ketchikan."

"That was before. I left there eight months ago and went to Seattle."

"How long has he been threatening you?"

"Almost a year now."

"Why didn't you go to the police?"

"I did, in Ketchikan, just after I moved out, but it made him furious. I also got a restraining order that he ignored, but they couldn't do anything because I couldn't prove it. They talked to him and he gave them some alibi so they thought I was making it up. They *wouldn't help!*"

Karen pounded a fist on the table lightly in frustration, sighed, and more pieces of her story came pouring out.

"I'd finally had enough, so I moved—to Seattle. When he showed up there again a couple of weeks ago, I left, drove up and caught the ferry in Bellingham, but somehow he followed me and got on too. I took a cabin and stayed in it. When we got to Ketchikan I knew he'd be watching to see if I got off, so I said I had sprained my ankle and had them take me off from the car deck in a wheelchair, like an old lady. It worked, for once. I saw from inside the terminal that when the ferry left he was still on it—near the gangway, watching everyone getting off and looking for me. I caught the next plane to Juneau, then to here, thinking he wouldn't expect me to double back. When I saw him get off here, I knew that somehow he'd figured it out. Now he's looking for me here, so I'm in real trouble."

"We might try the police," Jessie suggested, realizing she had said "we."

"They'll just call Ketchikan and I know what those guys will say. Believe me, law enforcement will do no good at all."

Probably not, Jessie thought. The police could seldom provide the round-the-clock protection this kind of stalking demanded. A sinking feeling played havoc with her appetite as she sat staring speechless at Karen over the rapidly cooling seafood dinner she had anticipated enjoying. The relaxing evening she had expected to spend on her own had suddenly taken an unwelcome and confusing turn. She knew the fear of an abusive relationship from a past, but less intense and stressful, experience of her own. She also knew that because of it she was inclined toward sympathy and assistance. This was not the same, however, and she only knew a little about one side of a situation that made her hesitant to involve herself—but her reluctance was mixed with understanding and support.

"I've got to find someplace to hide tonight and figure out how to get out of here tomorrow somehow," Karen said, frowning, her eyes still full of anger, fear, and fatigue. "Do you have any ideas? Where are you staying?"

With a sinking sensation, Jessie, envisioning her hotel room with its two beds, knew that, chancy or not, she was about to suggest it as a solution for the night.

CHAPTER EIGHT

KAREN'S ACCEPTANCE OF THE SUGGESTION THAT THEY share the hotel room did nothing either to lessen or to justify Jessie's edgy feeling. But her effusive appreciation and evident relief seemed sincere.

"That's a generous thing for you to offer when you only just met me," she said slowly. "If you're really sure it's okay, I won't say no. Where else can I go? I don't dare have my name on a hotel register. Thank you."

When she insisted on picking up the check for both dinners, Jessie relaxed her wariness a little and turned instead to considering a less conspicuous way to return to the Tides Inn than the route down the main street that she had taken on her way to the Northern Lights. Leaving the restaurant, they once again crossed the bridge over the slough and went quickly along Sing Lee Alley. Then, instead of turning left on Nordic, they crossed it and climbed another block up the hill to First Street, which in three blocks brought them to the upper level of the hotel.

"Didn't you have a suitcase?" Jessie asked as they went down to enter the passageway that led directly to her room.

"I left it with the bartender at the Harbor Bar," Karen told her. "But I sure don't want to go back in there tonight to get it. Would you mind terribly doing me one more favor?"

Jessie agreed, remembering the errand she had planned earlier. "I wanted to stop next door for some booze to take to the island tomorrow anyway."

So leaving Karen safely ensconced in the hotel room, she went first to the liquor store, then to the bar next door.

"Oh, sure," the bartender said, when asked for Karen's bag. "It's right here, safe and sound." She handed it out from behind the bar with a smile. "Your friend said she'd be along to pick it up after you had dinner."

"She did?"

"Yes. She seemed surprised to find you had already gone when she came out of the ladies'. Asked if I knew where you were headed and could she leave the case temporarily so she could hurry to catch up. Guess she found you at the Northern Lights. How was dinner? Enjoy it?"

"Yes," Jessie told her, forcing a smile to accompany her thanks, "we did."

My friend? She questioned the term as she hiked back up the hill, laden with Karen's black bag, a bottle of Jameson and two six-packs of Killian's in plastic bags—glad she hadn't far to go. Karen would bear watching, it seemed, and she wondered if she shouldn't have continued to maintain, as she had decided on the plane, that this woman was none of her business. Still, if Karen had spent a year avoiding a man who seemed to qualify as a stalker, she must have gained some experience in what it took to stay out of his reach by seeming to fit in with other people, and being with Jessie might be part of it. Remembering her own encounter with physical abuse, Jessie couldn't actually blame her for doing whatever it took to escape.

Once again, she let the issue go, put down the bag to retrieve the room key from her pocket, opened the door, and
found Karen staring at the door like a deer in the headlights,
having jumped up from a seat on the bed farthest from the
door at the sound of the key in the lock. For just a second
Jessie, startled, didn't recognize her, for she had removed
the dark wig and was once again a redhead.

Gotta get used to that wig, she told herself, as Karen
quickly crossed the room to help with the load she was
carrying. But the transition from brunette to redhead was so
extreme it was astonishing.

"Thanks for retrieving this," Karen said, taking her bag
after setting the lager and whiskey on the floor in a corner by
Jessie's duffel. Then she hesitated and asked politely,
"Which bed is yours?"

"It doesn't matter to me. Take the one you were sitting on
if you like."

Dropping her daypack on the foot of the other bed, Jessie
slipped off her green slicker, kicked off her shoes, and
flopped back onto the bed with a tired sigh to stare at the ceiling, which, she noticed, had a long crack across it that looked
a little like part of an airplane propeller. It had been a long
and confusing day, to say the least. There had been more food
on her plate at the Northern Lights than she would normally
have eaten, but even after cooling during their conversation it
had tasted so good that she had eaten most of it and found she
was now more inclined toward a nap than the shower she had
planned to wash away the grimy feeling of travel.

Karen sat down again on the edge of her bed beside the
black bag she had opened to find a toothbrush and pajamas
that she held clutched in one hand while she paused to look
across at Jessie.

"I want you to know how much I appreciate this," she said. "I realized while you were gone that I felt safe for the first time in several days and that means a lot."

Jessie turned her head to look across at her unplanned guest. "I'm glad if you do," she told Karen. "I know what that's like—was in a bad relationship myself once, a long time ago. I should think you *are* safe here, so just relax and forget about it, okay?"

With a nod, Karen went to brush her teeth.

As she listened to the water running, Jessie thought about that old abusive relationship and how different it was with Alex, who was a much stronger and more self-assured person. She could not imagine him ever hitting her. When her cell phone rang in the daypack, she knew who it was, as if he had felt her thoughts. Sitting up, she retrieved the phone and answered the call on the third ring, shoving the bed pillows behind her to lean on.

"Hey there," said his voice in her ear. "How's the Southeast?"

"Hey yourself. Petersburg's its usual rainy self. How's Whitehorse?"

"About the same as always, but it isn't raining. We got everything done that we wanted to accomplish today. So the RCMP's going to give us a quick hop back to Dawson tonight, then Tank and I'll head for home tomorrow instead of Wednesday."

"That's good, if you aren't too tired."

"Nope. It's been pretty laid back."

She could hear music and voices in the background. "Where are you?"

"At the bar in the Gold Rush Inn—sampling the good beer these Canadians have been keeping on tap for us."

There was a self-satisfied grin in his voice and she could imagine him and Del relaxing in the bar she remembered from a prior visit as pleasant.

"I assume you made it to Petersburg okay," he said.

"Without a hitch," she assured him, glad to hear his voice and know that he cared that she arrived safely. But somewhere next to the gladness there was also a small, resentful feeling of having her independence intruded upon—as if he thought she needed to be checked up on. She shrugged it off as she told him about Connie the taxi driver and the grocery clerk's offer to deliver supplies to the dock the next day.

"Hey, that's pretty slick service. Do you know when Jim's going to pick you up?"

"Laurie said sometime around noon. But he's going to call me from the boat on the way in, so I'll know where to meet him. How's Tank?"

"Clair says they're having a fine time in Dawson. He likes her."

"He likes being the center of attention and she spoils him," she pointed out, missing her favorite sled dog.

"Well, I'll check him out when we get there. We'd wait and go tomorrow, but Del's anxious to get home and be sure Clair's okay. You know—new father syndrome."

There was a pause as he said something aside, then returned to the phone laughing. "He's threatening to leave me here if I make any more comments concerning his imminent fatherhood."

As Jessie joined his laughter, Karen came out of the bathroom in her pajamas.

"Do you think . . ." she started to say. "Oh, sorry. I thought you had the television on."

"That's okay. I'll be through in a minute," Jessie told her, watching as Karen dropped the toothbrush back in her bag and laid her clothes on a chair before moving the bag to the floor beside it.

"Somebody there with you?" Alex asked in her ear.

"A friend I met here," she told him. "We're sharing a room tonight."

"She part of the lighthouse crew?"

"Ah . . . well"—she hesitated—"ah . . . probably not."

Alex had never been slow on the uptake. "She's right there and you don't want to talk about it?"

"That's right."

"But it's okay and you'll tell me all about it when you get home, yes?"

"Sure."

"Everything really okay?"

"Yes, fine." Again, she felt a twinge of *I can take care of myself, thank you very much,* and was surprised when Alex chuckled, catching it.

"Independent as ever. We do better in person than on the phone, don't we? Why is that?"

"Oh, I think we both like seeing who we're talking to. There's a lot that gets said nonverbally."

"You're probably right. Well, my beer bottle seems to have a hole in it, so I'll let you go and find another one. Oops, no more beer—Del says our ride is here."

"Tell him hello and have a safe flight," she said. Then, feeling she was relenting in some odd way, "Glad you called, trooper. I'll call you from Five Finger Light tomorrow night to be sure *you* get home okay."

"Don't call too early. It's a long drive so I'll leave at the crack of doom and drive till I get there. I love you, Jess."

"I love you too. Take good care."

"You bet."

He hung up and she immediately missed him.

Can't have it both ways, she told herself, and dropped the phone back in the daypack.

"Trooper?" asked Karen. "Sorry, I couldn't help over-hearing."

"My friend's an Alaska State Trooper," Jessie told her.

"Oh. What do *you* do?"

"I run a kennel and race sled dogs."

Recognition dawned on Karen's face. "I thought your name sounded familiar. You're that Iditarod racer, aren't you?"

The conversation turned in that direction for the next few minutes, until Jessie escaped to take the shower she had planned earlier. When she came back, clean and refreshed, rubbing her short honey-colored curls semidry with a towel, Karen was already in bed watching the news on television with a frown.

"Death, disease, and disaster," she said, turning it off. "Can't they ever report anything positive?"

Jessie grinned and shook her head. "My feelings exactly. Well, for a week at least I don't have to know what's hap-pening anywhere but on a tiny island in the vastness of Fred-erick Sound. What are you going to do about the situation tomorrow, Karen?"

"I don't know. But I'll have to figure out something—just not right now."

"True."

"But maybe . . ." Karen began, but stopped suddenly at the sound of heavy footsteps that hesitated in the passage-way outside their door. Her eyes widened and she sat up straight in the bed, listening intently, one hand clutching wrinkles into the sheet.

"Come *on,* Craig," a male voice called. "Get a move on or I'm gonna leave without you."

"Keep your shirt on," they heard someone answer faintly, then the sound of a second set of footsteps came along the passage and the two continued together, sharing quieter conversation that faded into silence with distance.

Though she had noticed that the curtains of the room were closed when she came in from the Harbor Bar, Jessie watched with interest as Karen got up, crossed the room, and tugged at them till not a hint of space remained for anyone outside to peer through. Returning to the bed, she gave Jessie a self-conscious smile.

"I know. I'm more than a little paranoid," she said. "I'm also really tired. Goodnight, Jessie. And thanks again."

With that, she turned over to face the wall, clearly meaning to go to sleep.

"You're welcome," Jessie answered softly, reaching to turn out the light between the two beds.

But from the expression on Karen's face throughout the incident, Jessie doubted paranoia had much to do with it. What she had seen and recognized was the kind of fear that she didn't believe could be faked. Whatever the veracity of Karen's story, there was no doubt in her mind that the woman was sincerely terrified.

In Whitehorse, Alex Jensen put his cell phone away thoughtfully with a frown that lowered his eyebrows half an inch closer to his handlebar mustache as he drained the last swallow of his beer.

"Something wrong?" Inspector Delafosse asked from

where he sat next to Alex at the bar, raising a finger to let the pilot who was waiting for them at the door know he'd been seen.

"No, not *wrong*. We're just getting used to each other again, I guess. Mostly my fault for leaving Alaska in the first place."

"Mind my asking why you did leave?"

"Well . . ." Alex hesitated, casting memory back to the preceding February. "When my father died suddenly and I went back to Idaho to help my mother, Jessie was running the Yukon Quest."

"I remember that situation," Delafosse reminded him. "And I knew that they had offered you a job as sheriff and that you went back and took it."

As they both stood up and put on jackets, Alex agreed.

"That's almost right. I had already taken it—without talking it over with her—before I heard she was in trouble and came back. The timing was all wrong, but I'd already accepted it anyway."

Delafosse gave him an understanding nod. "Big mistake?"

"Oh yeah. Part of it was misplaced concern for my mother—I told myself I was doing it for her. Didn't take long for her to let me know that, as always, she was perfectly capable of taking care of herself and I should go back to Alaska, where I really wanted to be. But I think that I was really testing Jessie. I'd asked her to marry me and I guess I thought taking the job might influence her to say yes."

"Bad assumption."

"Got that right!"

The bartender collected the bill Alex dropped on the bar and extended thanks for the tip it included. The two men turned to meander their way through the tables to join the waiting officer.

"The real mistake was my determination to go ahead with the Idaho job when Jessie wouldn't say yes. I should have refused it and come back. There was a certain amount of trust lost between us because of my stubbornness and her resistance."

"I noticed there was something a bit tentative between you these days."

"That obvious, huh?"

"Only to someone who knew you then and now, I think. Clair mentioned it."

"Well, women talk to each other, don't they?"

Del shook his head. "Clair said Jessie wasn't talking, so she wasn't asking. She just noticed.

"Hey, Ted. Thanks for the airlift," he said, reaching a hand to the officer as they reached him.

"Not a problem. You ready?"

Following the two Canadian officers out into the night, Alex gave his relationship with Jessie final, silent consideration. *It'll either work out—or not. Probably just needs time. When she gets back, maybe we'll talk—if she's ready.*

He couldn't know that a lot would happen before they had such an opportunity for face-to-face conversation, meaningful or not.

CHAPTER NINE

IN THE DARK OF THE EVENING, THE HARBOR BAR WAS A bright oasis on the main street of Petersburg, leading Joe Cooper into it after a long walk from the ferry terminal at the edge of town.

Luck and misfortune had brought him there: his luck at catching a mere glimpse of auburn hair when the headlights of a car pulling into the parking lot illuminated shadows at the side of the terminal building; her misfortune in being in the wrong place at the wrong time, which allowed that sighting to happen. There was no doubt in his mind what he had seen from his vantage point at the rail of the ferry, where he had once again stood waiting to watch passengers disembark. Another might have questioned identification based on so little, but long surveillance and more than one such sighting had given Cooper an instinctive ability to recognize the woman he was following.

How she could be in Petersburg and not on the ferry was a question for which he had no concrete answer. She could not yet have left the ferry at this stop, so the only plausible explanation was that she had managed to elude his surveillance in Ketchikan, left the ship there, and had reached Petersburg some other way, probably by plane to be there so quickly.

It didn't matter. A satisfaction lay in knowing he had picked up her trail again—that she had not managed to escape him. So he had gone quickly to collect the duffel he had left tucked in a corner of the observation lounge and joined the few people waiting to leave the ferry. Waiting in line to go ashore had been frustrating, but finally the gate opened and the Petersburg passengers had moved forward, allowing him to all but sprint to the place where he had seen her standing. It had been empty, of course. She had disappeared into the night. If he had been able to see her from the rail in the glare of the ferry and terminal lights, the reverse was true and she had fled. But in a town this size some local resident would have seen her and it remained only for Cooper to find that person.

He did not expect to see her in the well-lit, cheerful atmosphere of the Harbor Bar, but in such a gathering spot, where he could wait and watch without notice, he might learn something that would lead him to her. The place was clearly a casual after-work hangout, for many of the seats were taken by fishermen and processing plant workers, by themselves, or with their wives and girlfriends. The hum of conversation and crack of pool balls hitting each other on the table filled his ears as he hesitated just inside the door to give the room a sweeping glance. Confident his quarry was, as expected, not among the current patrons, he dropped the duffel and his jacket under the window, where he could keep an eye on them, and crossed to an empty stool halfway along the bar.

"A shot of Jack Daniel's and a Bud," he told the female

bartender and, as she turned away, cast a look at the way she filled out the front of her red plaid shirt. *Nice hooters,* he told himself, allowing his appreciation to slide south when she bent over to pull the beer from a low cooler.

"Not bad, huh?" A low comment from the man behind the leer on the bar stool on Cooper's right. "And the legs go all the way up under those jeans."

"And how would you know, Perry?" A well-padded woman in coveralls on the left leaned forward to speak disdainfully around Cooper. "In your dreams maybe! You guys never quit, do you?"

"You'd just bitch about *that* if we did."

"You like to trade places?" Cooper asked her.

"Naw. You're better looking than he is—probably more interesting too. I'm Sylvia. You gotta name?"

But Cooper was already on his feet and switching her blended margarita with the beer and shot the bartender had just delivered.

"Okay—okay!" She gave him a resentful look. "Sorry to have *inconvenienced* you."

She slid over and Cooper took her abandoned stool, staring straight ahead to discourage further conversation.

In the mirror behind the bar, he watched Perry hook a sympathetic arm around her shoulders and snuggle her up to him. "Hey, who loves you, babe?"

Tossing a last indignant glance toward Cooper, she gave Perry an exhibition kiss that drew whistles and cheers from one of the tables in the room behind the pair.

"Hey, man. Don't count your loose change in public!" someone called.

Disinterested, Cooper tossed down the shot and chased it with a swallow of beer. Catching the bartender's attention, he pointed at the shot glass and she brought the bottle to pour him a refill.

"Seen a redhead you didn't recognize in here tonight?" he asked casually.

"Not one I didn't know." She nodded toward a table across the room, where a woman with carroty hair was part of a group. "But it's been busy, so I could have missed one or two."

"Buy yourself one," he told her, laying a bill on the bar.

"Thanks. I'll drink it later."

When a stool nearer the front of room became available, Cooper moved closer to the window and his duffel, where for the next hour he nursed another beer, patiently watched local people come and go in usual patterns, and glanced occasionally at passersby on the street, but learned nothing of value.

The only thing of interest was an attractive, honey-blond woman in a green slicker carrying a weighty plastic bag from the liquor store next door. She stepped up to the bar and waited for a word with the bartender, who nodded, then handed her a small black suitcase from behind the bar where she had evidently been holding it. He was too far away to hear the exchange between them, but noticed a look of puzzlement that crossed the blonde's face at something the bartender said before she shrugged and turned away. The suitcase was similar to one he thought the redhead carried, but so were a thousand others used by travelers these days.

Still, knowing his quarry had at times used other people as cover, he was unwilling to let the incident pass without investigation. As the woman left the Harbor Bar with the bag, he drained his beer, left enough to cover his bill, collected his jacket and duffel, and followed just a minute or two behind her. By the time he reached the street, however, she had vanished into the dark as completely as the redhead he had glimpsed at the ferry terminal.

This meant one of two things: either she had gone somewhere very close, or she was out there beyond his line of sight, still moving away to wherever she was headed. With long-legged strides, he reached the nearest corner and glanced quickly up and down the street. Nothing. As fast as he could without being forced to run with the duffel, he circled the block with no result, then hiked to the lower end of Dolphin Street, thinking the woman's goal could have been a boat in the harbor.

Everything there was calm and quiet.

He stood for a few minutes looking out at the dark water and the lights that glimmered over its small waves, two on an incoming fishing boat moving slowly back to safe haven. The sound of some kind of machinery working inside the seafood processing plant to his right drifted into his ears, mixed with the growl of the homing boat's engine and a car passing on Nordic Drive behind him. Someone shouted something unintelligible in the distance. The briny smell of seawater rose from below the barnacle-encrusted pilings of the dock, along with hints of the petroleum fuels that drove and oils that lubricated the boats.

Looking to the east, he wished for a moon, but the sky was still heavy with clotted cloud. How fine it would have been, he thought, to have a full moon rising over that long, crystal white range of coastal mountains, to have illuminated that great barrier cast up by the tectonic movement of unfathomable plates beneath the ocean into sharp peaks with deep valleys full of never-melting ice age remnants.

With a sigh, he turned, knowing he had a phone call to make and still needed to find shelter for the night. Suddenly he longed, not for just a temporary place to recharge his body and mind, but somewhere that belonged to him, somewhere quiet and solitary where he could rest and not be obsessed as he had been for a long time now. With a consuming grief he yearned for . . . Sucking air through his teeth like an accident victim in deep pain, he reminded himself that particular loss belonged to another life and time. But the specific yearning immediately stirred a renewal of hot anger at the circumstances that had made such an existence untenable and had driven him so far. Directly, he blamed the woman he was determined to find tomorrow. Tonight, she had eluded him and the chance was slim that the suitcase had belonged to her anyway.

Remembering that he had passed a hotel as he circled the block, he climbed back up Dolphin Street to the Tides Inn, where he took a room for the night on the upper level. Long habit reminded him to ask if a redhead had checked in that day, but the answer was negative.

CHAPTER TEN

IT WASN'T RAINING AT JUST AFTER EIGHT O'CLOCK THE next morning, when Jessie left the room and started up the hill to the hotel office to take advantage of their coffee.

Noticing that there was some blue sky between clots of the heavy-looking clouds that were floating steadily seaward overhead, she stopped on the corner and looked down at the harbor, where a band of sunshine brightened the white and blue of a fishing boat that was moving away from the dock of a processing plant at the foot of Dolphin Street. A few hopeful seagulls circled shrieking in its wake, ever optimistic at the possibility of snatching a meal. A member of the crew stepped out and tossed a few of what might have been breakfast scraps over the stern from a bucket, bringing the scavenging hoard diving down to land and bob on the water as they gulped up anything edible before it could sink.

Jessie took a deep breath of the cool salty air and raised her face to sunshine that swept suddenly across the corner on which she stood. The day looked promising for a smooth afternoon boat ride across Frederick Sound. Not particularly caring for heavy seas in combination with small boats, she hoped so, as she turned back to her errand.

In the office she dropped a handful of sugar and creamer packets into a pocket, filled two paper cups, added lids, and turned away, both hands full, to find the same woman she had met the day before behind the desk.

"You must feel the same way I do about your morning coffee," the woman said with a smile. "Takes me at least two cups to get going."

Feeling a hint of guilt at taking more than one cup, Jessie found herself making an unnecessary justification. "A friend of mine stopped by to visit last night," she said hastily, knowing she shouldn't explain why Karen had shared her room. "Ah—it got late and she stayed over. I hope that's okay. If there's a charge—"

"Don't worry about it," the clerk interrupted. "What's one extra person anyway? Did you sleep well?"

Jessie agreed that she had and took the coffee back to the lower level room, feeling slightly conspiratorial.

Karen, in the shower when she left, was now dressed in the same jeans she had worn the day before, but had replaced the yellow-and-white shirt with a green one. She turned from brushing her auburn hair and gratefully took the coffee Jessie offered.

"Thanks. You are a honey. Now I can get my heart started."

"Here's sugar and creamer," Jessie said, emptying her pocket. "No real cream or milk, I'm afraid."

"Not a problem. I take mine black anyway." She sat down on the tangled sheets and blankets of a restless night and sipped appreciatively at the dark brew. "Ahhhh—at least it's not weak as dishwater."

Jessie mirrored the action from the opposite bed.

"Have you decided what to do today?"

Karen's pleased expression faded into concerned frustration.

"I thought maybe I could risk a flight out of here and go back to Seattle," she said, shaking her head. "While you were upstairs I called Alaska Airlines and there are only two flights out of here, one at noon and one just after five in the afternoon. Both of them have at least two stops, in Juneau, Wrangell, or Ketchikan, and none of those are places I'd want to be seen. But it's immaterial anyway. If he's here and watching, this tiny airport would be a total trap. I should have gone on to Seattle yesterday, but how was I to know . . . ?" She looked up, clinging to the warm cup with both hands as if it were a lifeline. "What the hell am I going to do, Jessie?"

"Well," Jessie said thoughtfully, "if we assume, as you say, that he *is* here . . ."

"I *have* to assume that. It's too dangerous not to."

"Well, if he is and is just covering the bases, he can't know for sure that you're here, can he?"

"I don't think so, but . . ."

"But he can't know where you are right now anyway. True?"

"I guess not, but he's very good at finding things out. Wig or not, I was seen at both the bar and the restaurant last night. If he asked—and he would—someone could tell him I'm here. You and I were together at the Northern Lights, so the waitress could describe you too."

"No one saw you come in here last night."

"Did you tell anyone where you were staying—like at the restaurant?"

"No . . ." Jessie hesitated, frowned, and remembered her conversation with the bartender the evening before.

"Wait—she did ask me where I was staying when she gave me directions to the restaurant. I might have mentioned the Tides Inn."

"Dammit. Then he'll figure it out—may have already."

Standing up so fast the coffee she was holding sloshed over onto the carpet, she set the dripping cup down on the bedside table, rubbed coffee from her hand on her jeans, and began to toss belongings into the suitcase. "I gotta get out of here."

"Whoa!" Jessie set down her own coffee. "I think we'd better have somewhere else in mind to go before hitting the street, don't you? There're not many places to disappear in a town this small."

"Any place else will be better than this. You don't know him."

She's right, Jessie thought, *I don't.*

"Karen!" She demanded attention. "Stop what you're doing and *think!*"

"I *am* thinking," Karen said, without pausing in her panicked rush to collect her things.

As she snatched up her jacket from a chair by the television and slipped her arms into the sleeves to yank it on, Jessie stood up and grasped the collar so the half-on jacket confined Karen's arms and she was forced to stand still and listen. She struggled but, realizing she couldn't free herself, stopped and looked over a shoulder to face Jessie, tense and resentful, still ready to bolt if given an opportunity.

"You can't just dash out of here without a plan," Jessie told her in what she hoped was a calming, steadying voice. "That's crazy and will only lead to trouble. Sit down and let's make one. If he's here, he'll be looking for you. What if you run right into him?"

Slowly the fight went out of Karen; she sighed, gave in,

and allowed Jessie to move her to a seat on the bed before letting go.

They sat looking at each other for a long moment without a word.

"I'm sorry I got you into this," Karen said finally.

"Well, I'm not overjoyed myself," Jessie admitted. "But it looks like we're together in this situation, one way or another, now. Can't cry over spilled—coffee?"

A tiny glint of amusement reached Karen's eyes and the corners of her mouth turned up slightly as she glanced at the liquid pool around the cup that she had awkwardly set down.

"Well, I can't say I'm sorry to be with you, instead of on my own," she said, looking back. "Okay—you're right—a plan."

At first it seemed to Jessie that they were safer staying where they were—behind a locked door, in a room with a telephone connection to the Petersburg police, should they be necessary. "It would at least buy you time while they sorted it out," she suggested.

"They couldn't get here fast enough," Karen disagreed. "Besides, you've got a cell phone."

Jessie nodded, knowing also that if Karen's stalker broke in they might not be able to reach the phone in time to make a call.

"You've got to tell me more about this guy," she said. "What's his name? What's he look like? What's he liable to do if he shows up? I need to know what to expect if I'm going to be any help, and you haven't told me much."

"First, he's liable to kick in the door," Karen told her, anxiously glancing at its lock, which suddenly seemed inadequate protection.

As she went on to describe Joe Cooper, Jessie began to

picture a wide-shouldered construction worker of average height, but more than average strength and determination. According to Karen he was clean-shaven, had pale blue eyes—"so light they sort of look right through you"—short brown hair under a habitual baseball cap, and usually dressed in jeans and sweatshirts. Used to the rain of Ketchikan this time of year, he would probably be wearing a canvas jacket, she said, or some other waterproof coat, and leather boots.

"Okay. I've got an idea what this Joe Cooper looks like. Now, what's he act like?" Jessie asked.

"Silent and watchful—notices everything. And I mean *silent*—not just quiet. It was a large part of our problem— I could never get him to talk—about much of anything. He gets very still and you haven't a clue what he's thinking. But he's got a hot temper, which I guess you've already figured out. He's like a bulldog—never lets go of something he's got hold of and thinks belongs to him—me, for instance."

"There must be some nice things about him. You did have a relationship."

"He can be very appealing at times," Karen said, remembering sadly. "He's almost like a little kid when something pleases him. He loves presents and he'll give you the moon in terms of *things*. But he just doesn't get it about emotional support. It's like somebody in high school told him what to do to make girls like him. You know: give her presents and flowers, take her to dinner, be nice to her mother, remember her birthday. But he doesn't see that a relationship doesn't work because of a one-size-fits-all checklist. When it didn't work for me, when I needed things he didn't understand, he got mad. When he got mad enough he started hitting me. He's big—and strong. Put me in the hospital once." She raised her chin so Jessie could see a two-inch scar on her jawline. "There's another on the back of my head where I hit the refrigerator handle. He was always *sorry*—but insisted it was my fault when he hit me. Please, Jessie. *Please,* can we go now?"

They went.

Before leaving, Jessie called to arrange a late checkout with the office, explaining that she wasn't sure when Jim Beal would arrive in his boat to take her to Five Finger Light. She also asked about transportation to meet him at the dock, when she knew which one.

"Not a problem," the woman at the desk told her. "We have a van and can take you there with your luggage as soon as you know where he'll come in. Or we could bring your luggage down and meet you, if you'll give us a call. Will he call you here?"

"No," Jessie told her. "I gave him my cell phone number, so when he calls I'll let you know what time and where. We'll be away from the room this morning anyway."

"No kidding," she heard Karen mutter, from where she was impatiently waiting by the door, suitcase in hand.

"Leave that bag here," Jessie suggested as she put down the phone.

"It's everything I own right now. What if I can't get back here to pick it up?"

"Then I'll bring it to you—wherever. Or the hotel can hold it for you."

Karen agreed. Rather than wear her wig, she had carefully wrapped her revealing auburn hair with a large green-and-brown scarf, crossing the ends in back and tying them over her forehead in front, then added a large pair of dark sunglasses. Slipping a wallet into a pocket of her denim jacket, she was ready.

Jessie shrugged on the green slicker over the clothes she had worn the day before, slung her daypack over one shoulder, and stepped out the door first to give the corridor a careful look. It was empty and quiet.

"It's okay. Come on."

Together they hurried along it to Dolphin Street, turned left, and went downhill to cross Nordic Drive toward the harbor beyond it. As they walked, Jessie was aware that Karen was once again glancing suspiciously at everything and everyone they passed, as she had in the restaurant and on their walk to the hotel the night before. It was as if the woman's whole body had assumed a fight-or-flight stance and at the first sign of a perceived threat she would dart off in whatever direction seemed most likely to offer escape.

How the hell did I get myself involved with this? Jessie asked herself. It was certainly not what she had planned as a leisurely morning of wandering through Petersburg's shops and galleries after breakfast. *Breakfast—we haven't had breakfast.* One cup of coffee hadn't been nearly enough and the idea of eggs, bacon, and hash browns made her regretfully aware of the empty feeling in her stomach.

"Aren't you hungry, Karen?" she asked.

"Starving. But I don't want to be cornered in a café or restaurant, so there isn't much choice, is there?"

"We passed a grocery back there on the corner. I could go and get us—well, something."

"Let's find a place to get out of sight first."

They continued until they were standing at the edge of the harbor next to the busy processing plant. There, along a dock piled high with wooden pallets, crab traps, and large blue seafood containers, they came to an empty space sheltered from sight that both agreed might be suitable, at least for the moment.

Karen abruptly sat down, folded her arms across her raised knees, and laid her forehead on them with a sigh.

"What?" Jessie asked.

"Nothing," she told Jessie in a muffled voice. "I am just so damn tired of running from the bastard."

"Stay here. I'll walk up and find us something to eat, okay?"

"Sure. Thanks." She lifted her head to gaze dispiritedly out into the harbor, where another commercial fishing boat was moving slowly toward the open water to the east.

"I'll be back in a few minutes." Jessie hesitated, and then made a commitment that had been steadily growing in her mind since the night before when Alex had asked if Karen was part of the renovation crew. "While I'm gone why don't you consider coming with me to Five Finger Lighthouse. You could help, be part of the work crew, and I think it's a place you could be safe and forget about this guy for the time being. Think about it, okay?"

"Really?" Brightening, Karen looked up at her. "You don't think they'd mind?"

"Yes, really. And no, I don't think they would," Jessie said, turning to go back to the grocery she had spotted on Nordic Drive, wondering if, once again, she had done something she might later regret.

CHAPTER ELEVEN

THE TRADING UNION, A GROCERY AND DEPARTMENT store, was on the northeast corner of the intersection they had crossed coming down, its front door facing the main street. As Jessie approached from the harbor, a forklift made a quick turn off Nordic and came rolling toward her. A stack of round galvanized steel tubs, along with some other unidentifiable odds and ends of the fish processing business, were balanced on a wooden pallet that covered its forks. As she stepped out of the way to give it plenty of room, it slowed, then stopped, and, taking a close look, she recognized the driver as her hungover seatmate from the previous day's flight from Juneau. Though he still wore his billed cap, the jeans and jacket had been replaced with a black sweatshirt, well-worn and stained waterproof overalls, and a pair of grubby rubber boots.

"Hey," he said with a grin. "I know *you* from yesterday's plane ride. If you hadn't waked me up I might have been wondering what I was doing in Seattle and how to get back."

"Hi. Feeling better?" Jessie asked him, with a smile of her own.

"Yeah—amazing what a night's sleep and carb-heavy breakfast will do." He stripped off a glove and offered a hand. "I'm Tim Christiansen."

Even from Ketchikan he's another Scandinavian, Jessie thought with amusement as she shook hands and told him her name. "I thought you were going fishing."

"Boat engine got cranky. Captain's waiting on a part for the transmission that'll take the rest of the week to get here from the supplier in Portland. So I'm stuck ashore for the time being and filling time moving stuff from one place to another on this thing. Say, if you're in town for a while, I'm awake now and would be glad to buy you a beer later."

Jessie thanked him for the offer, but explained that she was waiting for a friend to ferry her to Five Finger Lighthouse, and told him why.

"Hey, that's cool. Knew there was somebody fixing up the lighthouse. Heard they were going to turn it into a bed and breakfast."

"And a whale-watching station, I think," Jessie told him.

"That's cool. Lot of whales in Frederick Sound this time of year."

They chatted for a few moments about the migration of the humpback whales on their way to southern waters, before Jessie turned back toward the grocery. As she walked away, he called out behind her.

"You think they could use more help? We won't go out fishing again until Sunday or Monday. But I've got a power-boat and could come out for a day or two, maybe tomorrow or the next day—sleep on the boat. Might even be able to scare up a friend to help."

"I'm sure they could," Jessie told him. "There's evidently a lot to be done and winter's just around the corner. Jim Beal will be here sometime around noon to pick me up, along with material to repair a shed roof, if you want to ask."

"I gotta run this thing around till sometime this afternoon," he said. "Why don't you tell him that I—or we—will just show up if we can?"

"I can do that," Jessie agreed. "Bring your own beer," she suggested over a shoulder as she headed for the grocery.

"You bet. See you." He revved up the forklift and was off again.

At the Trading Union she picked up a couple of bananas, a package of donuts, and two large cups of coffee to go. It wasn't the kind of breakfast she had anticipated, but would do to fill her empty stomach. Balancing the coffee, the rest dangling from a wrist in a plastic bag, she made her way back to the dock and around the piles of crab traps and seafood containers to the place she had left the other woman sitting.

It was empty. Karen was gone.

As Jessie stood openmouthed in surprise, her cell phone rang in the backpack over her shoulder. Scrambling to set down the coffee on the planks of the dock without spilling it, she dug out the phone and answered the summons on the fourth ring.

"Hello."

"Jessie?" a faraway-sounding male voice questioned.

"Yes. Jim?"

"Yup. I'm headed your way—about an hour out of Petersburg. Does that work for you?"

"Sure. Where should I meet you and have Hammer & Wikan deliver the groceries?"

"You didn't need to get groceries."

"Well, it's mostly just snacks and booze, but they said they'd bring it to wherever you would tie up. And the Tides Inn said they'd bring our luggage down in their van."

"'Our'? So Alex came too? Terrific!"

"No, not Alex. If it's all right with you, I've invited a new friend to come too. Her name's Karen and she's . . ." Jessie hesitated to try to explain about Karen over the phone. "If it's okay for her to come along, I'll tell you all about it when I see you, okay?"

"Sure. Bring her. The more the merrier and we can sure use the help."

"Well, in that case, there's a temporarily beached Petersburg fisherman who asked if you could use more help if he showed up at the island tomorrow in his own boat."

"Hey, are you running a lighthouse renovation recruiting office?" Jim asked, and she could hear the grin in his voice. "Any help offered is welcome. What's his name?"

"Tim Christiansen."

"Don't know him, but tell him yes thanks on his offer of help."

"Probably won't see him again, but I've a hunch he and a friend of his may show up. Now, where shall Karen and I meet you?" *If I can locate Karen,* she thought, glancing around for any sign of the redhead and seeing none.

"Let's say at the Harbor Master's office," Jim directed. "Anyone can tell you where that is—just a couple of blocks from the Tides Inn. I should be there—let's see . . ."

His pause gave her a mental picture of him scrutinizing his watch.

"Ah—about eleven thirty. Okay? And while I think about it, be on the lookout for an older guy, name of Curt Johnson.

A friend with a boat's giving him a lift to Petersburg and he'll meet us for the ride back to Five Fingers."

A glance at her own watch told Jessie it was almost half past ten already, later than she had thought. "That's fine. We'll watch for you on the dock side of the Harbor Master's office."

"Fine. See you soon."

Jessie called both Hammer & Wikan and the Tides Inn to give them directions on where to deliver the groceries and luggage, though she could only hope Karen would reappear to claim her black suitcase.

Finished with those chores, she put the cell phone away in her pack and looked around again for Karen, but saw no clue as to where the woman had gone, or why. Confused and a little irritated, she decided to wait where she was—at the place she had last seen her. It would seem natural to assume that if the woman meant to return, she would come back there.

Sitting down on a pile of three pallets and leaning against one of the large blue plastic boxes, Jessie retrieved a donut from the box she had bought, scattering powdered sugar across her knees. It tasted fine, but would, she decided, go better with a banana, so she half-peeled one and took alternate bites, washing them down with the rapidly cooling coffee.

Though clouds still drifted overhead, they were fewer and not so heavy in appearance. The sun came out between them to shine where Jessie sat and, soon finding herself too warm, she slipped off the green slicker. Tipping her head back, she closed her eyes, lulled to patience and relaxation as she waited with nothing else to do for the moment.

For the first time since meeting Karen Emerson the day before she was alone with time to think and found herself considering their encounter in the restaurant the previous evening and the story that had resulted in their sharing a room. She wondered if the stalker had somehow followed them from the hotel to the dock unseen, or if Karen had caught sight of him and felt it necessary to find a better hiding place. Worse yet, what if he had found her? She wished she knew what he looked like. The description Karen had given was fairly generic, fitting the dress and look of any number of manual laborers in the casual atmosphere, not only of Petersburg, but the rest of Alaska.

Never having seen him, I wouldn't know him if he walked right up to me, she thought uneasily, sitting up to glance around her, but seeing nothing but a raven farther out on the dock that was picking at a bit of something it hoped was edible. As the large black bird succeeded in collecting the scrap and taking off with it, two others flew in with piercing cries of harassment, hoping for a share of the prize. With a swoop of avoidance the first bird swung landward and all three quickly vanished from sight, though for a moment or two Jessie continued to hear their shrill demands dying away over the downtown area.

As if they never existed. She grinned. *Fractious characters.*

Leaning back, she once again closed her eyes. But as a passing cloud came between her and the sun, the warmth she was enjoying departed and she opened them again to stare unseeing at the waters of the harbor with a slight frown.

An idea that had slipped into her mind just before she fell asleep the night before, and which she had drowsily dismissed, had suddenly resurfaced. ". . . as if they never existed," she said to herself, repeating aloud her thought about the ravens, but hearing it in a different context. What if the man that Karen said was following her *didn't exist*? What if she was making him up?

Other questions swiftly followed. Why would she do such a thing? Hadn't she seemed sincerely frightened? Jessie was convinced that faking her fear was improbable. *But not impossible,* a small devil advocated. Not impossible then, she agreed, but unlikely.

But, if the man was real *and* in Petersburg, she had only Karen's word that he really was stalking her, only her description of him, only her side of the story. It was a tale Jessie had no way of verifying unless it was through this Joe Cooper, a person she'd never met, never even seen for that matter.

Why would she pick me? Jessie wondered. *Just because I was obviously on my own and a nonresident of Petersburg?*

And maybe I'm sitting here waiting for more sunshine, with nothing to do but imagine all of this, she told herself sternly. Looking at her watch again, she realized that it was after eleven o'clock and in less than half an hour Jim would expect her to be on the dock side of the Harbor Master's office, a block or so away. Time to get going. But what should she do about Karen, who wouldn't know where to find her?

Quickly pulling a pen from her daypack and tearing a page out of the memo book she carried, she scribbled a note:

> K.
> Have some to the Harbor Master's
> office to meet our ride. Come there
> ASAP. We can't wait long.
> J.

Leaving a corner of it tucked under the edge of a pallet so it could easily be seen, she took a minute to look carefully around again, without success, then walked away toward Nordic Drive. Someone on the street would be able to tell her where to find the Harbor Master's office, if she couldn't find it herself.

CHAPTER TWELVE

THERE WAS NO SIGN OF KAREN AS JESSIE MADE HER WAY along Nordic, though she looked carefully along the street and into each shop she passed on the way. She found the office a short block away at the foot of Excel Street, easily identifiable by a HARBOR MASTER sign that hung above a profusion of orange and yellow nasturtiums still in bloom in a wide planter. Walking around the corner, on the harbor side she found a bench where she could wait, sip at the now tepid coffee she had bought for Karen, and watch for Beal to arrive at one of the public docks below.

The rising tide, now close to high, had lifted the floating dock until the access ramps lay at a much shallower angle than those she had seen on the other dock from the window of the Northern Lights Restaurant the night before. A few people could be seen on or around the power- and sailboats that were tied up. One sailboat in a slip at the far end of the dock had evidently arrived recently, for Jessie could see that a man and a woman were still working to furl and put covers on its sails. The sun had come out again and beyond the docks, public and otherwise, waves and the ripples created by the breeze were sparkling bright reflections around a charter boat that was motoring slowly seaward. Dozens of the ever-present gulls soared in circles overhead or perched on the ridgeline of every building in sight.

"Are you Jessie Arnold?" a voice suddenly asked behind her, jerking her from the half-sleepy, sun-warmed state into which she had drifted.

Turning, she found a young man in dark glasses waiting for her answer.

"Yes, I am. And you're . . ."

"Hammer & Wikan delivery," he filled in with a grin. "Got a couple of boxes of groceries. You want 'em here?"

"Yes—please," Jessie told him, jumping up to help, but he had already vanished around the corner of the building. Quickly reappearing with her two boxes on a hand truck, he unloaded them, waved off the tip she offered, and vanished, a cheerful whistle fading behind him.

She was still standing, amused at the speed of the delivery service, when a familiar face came around the same corner—Connie, from the previous day's taxi, already commenting on the delivery driver.

"That," she said, "was Jerry from the market. He brought your groceries— yes? I've got your luggage. You want it here too?"

"Hey, Connie. I thought the hotel was going to bring it."

"Well, they were. But I was there with a passenger, so I volunteered. Thought I'd send you off to your island with a friendly Petersburg goodbye and good luck."

This time Jessie helped carry her personal items around to a spot beside the groceries, along with a small box into which the hotel had packed the whiskey and beer.

Jessie was surprised to find that Connie had not delivered Karen's bag. "Was there a small black suitcase?" she asked.

"Oh, sorry. Almost forgot. They said to tell you the owner came to pick it up just a few minutes before I got there— jeans jacket, green shirt, green scarf over her hair?"

Jessie nodded, knowing it was Karen. But, again, why would she leave without any kind of explanation?

Well, she thought, *at least I don't have to worry about what to do with her bag.*

"Something wrong?" Connie asked at her frown.

"No. Not wrong," Jessie told her. "It's fine. I didn't expect it, but it solves a problem. I really appreciate you bringing this stuff."

Again she reached for her wallet in the daypack, but again the tip was turned down.

Connie bounced back around the car and into the driver's seat, slamming the door behind her.

"Have a great time at Five Finger Light," she called through the open window, shifting the still-protesting gears and taking off with a wave.

Feeling that everything was happening at once, Jessie walked back around the building to her growing collection of groceries and luggage just in time to spot the long-legged figure of Jim Beal practically loping up the ramp from the dock with a wide smile on his face, two women coming along behind him.

"Hey Jessie," he called. "Thought that pile of stuff must be yours."

Though she hadn't seen him in several years, there was no mistaking slender, six-foot Beal, who had assumed the character, costume, and thin mustache of a riverboat gambler for the Ton of Gold Reenactment celebrating the

Klondike Gold Rush Centennial. With an enthusiastic group of crew and passengers, some descendants of the original Klondike miners, she and Alex had sailed from Skagway on the *Spirit of '98,* Alaska Sightseeing/Cruise West's flagship, which resembled an antique coastal steamer. An old-time melodrama had been part of the entertainment, with both Jim and Laurie as players. What had not been entertaining was a gang of killers and thieves they had helped to thwart on the way down the Inside Passage to Seattle.

Amused that Beal had retained the gambler's mustache, Jessie teased as she stepped back from his affectionate hug, "Thought you'd be sporting a lighthouse keeper's scrub brush on your upper lip by now."

"Naw—this suits me. How the hell are you?"

"Great, but taking a break from running my mutts this winter, due to a bad knee. So I'm all yours as work crew, as long as I don't have to crawl."

"Ouch! What happened?"

"Fell down a mountain and twisted it enough to keep me off a sled."

"Bad luck," he sympathized, then turned to introduce the two women who had followed him up the dock, both carrying travel bags.

"This is Anna Neumeyer and Becky Galvin, friends of Laurie's and mine who've been visiting from Colorado. They're a law enforcement duo, so watch your step and don't say I didn't warn you. Becky's a secretary for the FBI and Anna's married to a Denver policeman. Ladies, this is Jessie Arnold, famous Iditarod sled dog racer who lives with an Alaska State Trooper. So I guess you're about even-steven with the law thing."

"Hi," Jessie told them both, laughing as they all three gave Jim semitolerant glances. "Coming to the island with us?"

They shook their heads and Anna answered, "Unfortunately, we're headed home on today's plane. But we've been out there since Saturday, so we don't feel too deprived. It's a terrific place."

"Is this your first trip?" Becky asked.

"It is. And I'm really looking forward to it."

"You'll love it. Be sure to look for the resident eagle. She has a baby this year."

"I'll do that," Jessie assured her. "When does your plane leave?"

"Not until almost four o'clock, so we're shopping Petersburg first."

"Maybe you can leave your bags in the Harbor Master's office," Jim suggested. "When you're ready to head for the airport, there's a phone here to call a cab."

"Here," said Jessie, digging Connie's crumpled card from a pocket. "Call this number. The driver's a hoot and the cab not to be believed. You'll like her and owe it to yourselves to have a laugh on the way to the airport."

When the pair had given Jim thank-you hugs and left their luggage, they vanished, waving a last goodbye before turning the corner of Nordic Drive in search of gift shops. Jim picked up both boxes of groceries at once. "Let's get your stuff on the boat. My roofing materials should be along anytime now. Where's your friend? And have you seen Curt anywhere?"

Not wanting to get into the whole story, Jessie was explaining simply that Karen might not be coming, but could show up, when she was interrupted by a husky voice from behind her.

"Hey you—keeper of the light. Need a hand with that stuff?"

"Curt! There you are." Jim put the boxes back down and reached to shake hands with the newcomer. "Good to see you! I was just wondering if I was going to have to track you down at the Harbor Bar. Oh, this is Jessie Arnold. Jessie—Curt Johnson."

"Naw. Did that last night."

He offered a hand to Jessie with a nod. His thick fingers felt rough with callus that she recognized from people she knew in the building trades—carpenters, mechanics.

If he hadn't been carrying a duffel over his shoulder, she wouldn't have remembered this older man as one of the pair she had seen the evening before. "I think I saw you and another man come off the dock by the Northern Lights last night, yes? I was having dinner there by the window around eight o'clock."

"Nope," he denied firmly, frowning and shaking his head. "Not me. I was in the bar, like I said."

Jessie didn't remember seeing him there, but supposed he could have come in after she left. Odd! The two men had been some distance away and it *had* been dark. Still, she was almost sure it was the same person and wondered, if so, why he would deny it.

Must be mistaken, she told herself, turning to pick up her own duffel.

Daypack over her shoulder, Jessie carried the duffel and the smaller box that held the lager and whiskey the length of the dock to where Beal's twenty-five-foot Seawolf power-boat was tied up in the last slip. There, they stowed everything inside the pilothouse and went back to wait for a delivery van to arrive from a local building materials supplier. This soon appeared and the driver assisted Jim and

Curt in loading rolls of roofing and the other supplies he would need to install it.

As the van drove away, Jim turned to Jessie. "Let's go grab some lunch before we leave. My stomach's gonna be howling before we get back to Five Finger."

"How long will it take?"

"A little over an hour with this load."

Still thinking Karen might show up, Jessie suggested that they go for food, while she waited. "She won't know where I am, or which boat is yours, if I leave, and she doesn't know you."

But by the time Jim and Curt returned with a sack full of burgers and fries, there had still been no sign of Karen.

On hearing it, Jim frowned. "Really shouldn't wait around much longer," he said. "I need to get back to the island just after high tide, so we can off-load more easily and get the boat secured so it doesn't beat itself up on the rocks if the wind comes up. We should really get going."

"Then let's do that," Jessie told him, making up her mind. "Karen'll be fine on her own. Maybe she changed her mind and just didn't want to say so. Let's go."

Nevertheless, as Beal pulled the boat out of its slip, with Curt next to him in the front of the boat, and headed into the Petersburg harbor, Jessie stood in the rear and scanned each dock that they passed, thinking she might see her overnight roommate on one of them. As each slid past empty of Karen, she felt both uneasy, as if she were abandoning someone who might need her help, and disappointed in Karen for leaving with no explanation for her absence. She might have worried that the woman's stalker had caught up with her if Connie had not told her that Karen had picked up her suitcase from the hotel.

Hoping it was just a case of bad manners, she knew that

she was also not totally unhappy to be relieved of the other woman's problems, though she sympathized with her situation. Her fears had called up old memories and feelings on which Jessie would rather have kept a tight lid. Alex crossed her mind, and she wondered fleetingly if her past experience played a larger part than she had realized in her relationship with him. Refusing to examine that idea in detail, at Jim's request she opened the sack, handed him and Curt their share, then settled down to her first, and very welcome, hot food of the day—still closely watching the shoreline east of the docks that they were slowly passing at the harbor cruising speed limit.

Which was how, below a large two-story house set back from the water, she noticed the redheaded figure on the shore wildly waving a green-and-brown scarf to attract attention.

"Stop, Jim," she called, standing up to wave and let Karen know she had been seen. "That's Karen. Can we pick her up?"

Beal cut the speed of the Seawolf to idle and looked toward shore in the direction Jessie was pointing.

"What the hell's she doing clear down there?" he asked. "It's at least a mile out of town."

"I don't know, but she clearly wants us to collect her. She's in some trouble, Jim, and it may be important that we do, if you think we can."

He agreed, swung the bow shoreward, and took the boat in, cutting power and coasting as close as possible to a shore of rounded stones of all sizes. As they came in he turned the wheel over to Curt to hold steady and came to the stern with a boat hook to fend them off if necessary. As they bumped and grated gently aground, leaving a space of about six feet, Karen grabbed her suitcase and waded in up to her knees, running shoes and all. Reaching the boat, she heaved the case up to Jessie and clung to the side, trying to figure out how to get herself aboard.

"Wait," said Beal, and used the boat hook to pole the craft around so she could reach the stern, which was lower and allowed her to push off and hoist herself onto it on her stomach. With help from Jessie, she swung her dripping feet inboard and stood up.

"Thanks," she managed, breathless, as they both watched her pant to regain her wind. Recovering enough to speak, she nodded to Beal. "You gotta be Jim, the lighthouse man."

"I am. And the guy inside is Curt, but I'll introduce you later," he told her before hurrying back to the controls. "I'll get us headed out again."

His glance, as he passed Jessie, told her he would expect a few answers at first opportunity and she knew she wanted answers of her own. Turning back to Karen, she was surprised to find her staring toward the front of the boat with an odd frown of concern.

"What?"

Karen swung back toward her and lost the frown.

"Nothing. You just didn't tell me there'd be anyone else along."

"Does it matter? You don't know him, do you?"

"No. Not at all."

Jessie let it go. Then, over the roar of the diesel engine and rush of water as the boat cut through it, she questioned Karen, who proceeded to strip off her soaked shoes and socks and wring out the lower legs of her jeans.

"What happened? Why did you leave the dock? I came back and you weren't there. Did you find my note?"

"Note? No. I didn't go back there. What happened was that I saw him, Jessie. I stood up to see if you were coming back and he was *right there*—talking to some guy on a forklift by that fish place with his back turned to me. So I ducked down and waited till he left, but I didn't see which way he went, so I couldn't come looking for you. I just got out of there." She paused to open her suitcase in search of dry socks and began to pull them on her cold feet. "He was so close and looking for me *in town,* Jessie. I was very careful—went straight back to the hotel and got my bag. Then I walked—in the opposite direction I thought he'd be looking—east, out of town on the residential streets above the beach. Well, it's rocks, so I guess technically it's not really beach—but the shore above where you found me anyway. All I could do was hope I'd see you in the boat and could wave so you'd see me. And that's what happened—right?"

She stopped and gave Jessie a long look.

It all made sense. So why, Jessie wondered, did she feel there was something that didn't add up about Karen's account of her disappearance? And why did she feel that her own response was being closely assessed and that there was something almost sly in the way the woman waited for acceptance?

"Is there anything to eat?" Karen asked suddenly. "I'm starving."

Reaching, Jessie offered her the uneaten half of her hamburger and fries. "You can finish this. It's cold, but it's edible and I'm not poison," she apologized, knowing she wouldn't finish it herself.

Her appetite had completely deserted her.

CHAPTER THIRTEEN

As Jim Beal had estimated, the run to Five Finger Lighthouse took just over an hour. Though scattered clouds continued to float overhead, the afternoon had turned warm and sunny and, to Jessie's satisfaction, the sea was calm.

The snow-covered peaks of the Coast Mountains, bright in the sunshine, dominated the skyline to the east with their immeasurable, permanent ice fields and the great fingers of flowing ice that extended from them in glaciers, filling and carving out valleys in the process. Where the mountains reached the sea they were lower, more rounded, and without snow, but thickly covered with billions of evergreens. These slopes dropped so abruptly straight down that they gave the impression that the bulk of them was hidden under water and any boat on the surface hung suspended in liquid space over a profound abyss.

Leaving Karen to finish her lunch, Jessie stepped into the pilothouse with Jim and Curt to see what was coming up ahead of the boat, but was soon sidetracked.

As they passed the marker at the end of the Petersburg

harbor, Jim, once again in control, swung the Seawolf north into the lower end of Frederick Sound and increased their speed to twenty-five knots. Curt had taken the second seat at the front and ignored her presence as he followed their progress on Beal's nautical chart. Taking a look over his shoulder, Jessie identified two small islands approaching on the left as the Sukoi Islets. The name sounded Japanese to her, but Jim explained that it was a Russian word for *dry* and that there had been fox farms on both isles in the early days of the twentieth century, but no potable water.

"There's a historical atlas in that rack," he told her, pointing. "It's a wealth of information, if you want to know the background of almost anything around here. There were fox farms by the dozen up and down the Inside Passage back then."

The large spiral-bound book, *Exploring Alaska & British Columbia*—approximately a foot wide and a foot and a half long—had been authored by a Stephen Hilson thirty years earlier. Sitting down at the dinette table she found reminiscent of one in a motor home, she opened the atlas to a page that showed Frederick Sound and noticed that "Not to be used for navigation" was printed on each page of the charts that had been outdated when the book was published, evidence that the meeting of land and sea was constantly changing and not to be taken for granted.

Examining the two huge pages spread before her, Jessie located Petersburg and the Sukoi Islets, with a notation that confirmed Jim's information on the fox farms. What represented water was printed in blue. Notations filled much of the empty space that was land, printed in dark brown on a tan background. Reading a few of those close to the islets, she found an interesting mix of information, from where Point Agassiz got its name—"Naturalist Louis Agassiz was an instructor at Harvard University during the mid-1800s"—to the "Reported site of the sinking of a three-masted Russian gunboat" in Thomas Bay. There were mentions of John Muir, black bear and salmon streams, waterfowl nesting grounds, a bay named for Admiral David Farragut, "old Indian settlements" discovered by Captain Vancouver's men in 1869, and "March 7, 1924—Ole Haynes and his companions shoot and kill alleged fox poacher Billy Gray in his tent."

"Hey!" she said to Beal. "This is fascinating. Where did you get it? Alex would love it. I wish we'd had a copy when we did the Ton of Gold Run."

"I'd looked for a copy of the original 1976 publication for years, but never found one, so I snapped this up when it was republished in 1997," he told her. "I think it's still available, if you want one. It's expensive, but worth every cent in fascinating reading."

Looking farther north on the chart to where Frederick Sound joined Stephens Passage, she located "The Five Fingers," the tiny islands where the lighthouse now stood. They lay directly east of another pair of islands, "The Brothers," and just below those was one tiny island simply called "Round Rock" that was designated as a "Sea Lion hauling grounds." Jessie smiled, picturing what it must look like.

"Your lighthouse island is practically nonexistent on this, Jim—a mere dot on the map. You have any sea lions?"

"Yeah, but small has its advantages. It's hard to get lost on three acres, even if it is in a huge amount of water. It's twenty miles to the nearest island to the south, but Cape Fanshaw is just over five to the east of us. The Brothers are pretty close—maybe twice that far. Still, on a clear day you can see for fifty miles up Stephens Passage and at least that far down Frederick Sound from up in the tower. We do have

one old sea lion who swims around the island almost every
day like he's checking things out, but . . ."

Attention caught elsewhere, he reached for a pair of
binoculars that hung close at hand and examined the waters
ahead of the boat before turning to Jessie with a grin.

"Whales," he told her. "Looks like three, and they're
pretty close. You can read the atlas at the lighthouse. Better
go out, if you want a good look at these."

The boat was moving into the widest area of Frederick
Sound and Jessie could see that he was right; it was a *huge*
amount of water. Following his advice, she went out onto the
stern of the boat and leaned over one side to see around the
left side of the pilothouse.

"What is it?" Karen asked from where she perched on the
flat cover of a stowage locker built into the side of the boat
that served double duty as a seat. She had been sitting there,
staring out at the mountains with a thoughtful expression,
while Jessie was in the pilothouse with Beal.

"Whales," Jessie told her without turning. "Just ahead."

At first there was nothing to indicate their presence.
Then, about the length of a city block away, there was a disturbance in the water as the rounded back of a humpback
broke the surface, coming up for air, and slowly the charac-
teristic dorsal fin that makes the whale look humpbacked
and gives it its name came into view. A cloud of spray
erupted as it blew, and Jessie knew that, though it couldn't be
heard over the boat's engine, it would be accompanied by a
whoosh sound. In the quiet air the spray hung like mist, and
before it drifted away on the breath of a gentle breeze, she
could see a hint of rainbow where the sunshine hit it just
right. The enormous mammal blew once again; then as it
continued to roll forward, the giant flukes of its tail rose
completely out of the water and slowly slid beneath the sur-

face as the animal departed into the depths. As it vanished beneath the sound's gentle swells a second, slightly smaller whale repeated the maneuver, but disappeared without exposing its flukes.

"Awesome," said Karen, who had come to stand beside Jessie to see.

Though they waited and watched until the stretch of ocean where they had seen the humpbacks rise lay far behind them, the whales did not appear again.

"Can't you just imagine them sliding silently through the water like submarines?" Karen asked.

Jessie nodded, still gazing back in the direction the whales had surfaced. "They aren't always silent and I'd love to hear them sing. I've heard recordings collected by researchers who put down hydrophones. But I read somewhere that if you're in the water nearby you can hear them pretty well because water is such a good sound transmitter. They don't sing much in Alaska, though, mostly in Hawaii, where they go in the winter."

Karen went back to her seat on the stowage locker, but Jessie stayed where she was, leaning on the rail to watch the colors change as a broad patch of cloud drifted across the sun, casting a shadow over the boat and the sea on which it traveled. Uncountable shades of watery hues and reflections turned to a steely gray that lacked the earlier impression of depth. Sunlight fell through a few thin openings in the cloud cover in concentrated beams to cast bright patches on the surface of the water so glaring they were hard to look at without squinting. Cloud shadows moved over the rounded hills of the large islands between the sound and the Pacific Ocean, the dense green tree cover once again reminding Jessie of soft fur or velvet, separated from the water by a thin line of tan beach, or, in some places, dark rock.

She loved the sea, though she had never lived close to it. Breathing in the briny scent of it pleased her, as did the ever-changing nature of ocean waters and their inhabitants. Seeing the whales had raised her spirits and taken her back to memories of the long run from Skagway to Seattle and how much she had enjoyed it. Remembering that trip made her miss Alex, who had been part of it, and wonder where he was now. Probably somewhere around halfway home, she decided, and reminded herself to call him later, or tomorrow. It would be a long, tiring, five-hundred-mile drive, but she figured that he had left Dawson early and should reach her house on Knik Road by seven or eight that night.

"Five Finger Light coming up," Jim called from the pilot-house.

Karen stood up and both women stepped inside to look ahead, but all they could see was a small island or two and some ridges of stone that barely broke the surface at just after high tide. The largest of the islands had a dense covering of tall firs above a vertical cliff of gray stone.

"Where?" asked Jessie. "I don't see a lighthouse."

"Just wait," he told her.

He piloted the boat along the west side below the cliff and suddenly the top of a white tower came into view beyond the trees. Swiftly more of it appeared until the whole building was revealed as a tower atop a square one-story building, also white.

"Oh," exclaimed Karen. "I expected a round tower."

"The lights along the Inside Passage aren't the round barber-pole towers most people visualize from pictures. The passage is mostly between mainland and islands and that limits the distance that lights need to shine—they don't have to project a beam a long ways out to sea. This one shines eighty-one feet above sea level in a sixty-eight-foot tower on the roof of that building you see under it, and that's more than enough. The lower part was the keeper's quarters— when it had keepers. Now the light's solar-powered, so—no keepers. Instead the Coast Guard monitors and cares for it on a regular basis."

"What's that?" Jessie asked, pointing at a large platform that stood between the lighthouse and the northern end of the island.

"Helipad. Sometimes the weather's too rough for landing in a boat or floatplane, but helicopters can still come in."

As they cruised past the west side of the island, several people came out a door on the north side of the building and Jessie recognized Laurie Trevino as one of them—waving. They vanished behind high rock and the helipad as Beal swung the boat around the north end and turned back to an area where the jagged stone that formed the island sloped down gradually into the sea in a long finger that protected a small cove.

Expecting a dock, Jessie was surprised to find they would unload directly onto a rough-looking ramp of rock. It looked like a risky task, but Laurie came carefully clambering down with three other people. Jim tossed a pair of bumpers over the side and hurled a line to a slim young man with tousled hair and a wide grin who stepped out to catch it and draw the boat close enough for passengers to off-load cargo and climb ashore.

"Hey there," he called. "Thought you'd be back earlier."

"And I thought you couldn't make it until tomorrow, Aaron," Jim replied. "I see you brought Whitney along with you. Where's Linda?"

"I took an extra day, but Linda couldn't make it. They called her in for some emergency case at the hospital. Said to tell you she's sorry."

"Where's your boat?"

"Came down with a friend on his way to Wrangell. So we're hoping to hitch a ride back to Juneau with you. Brad said to tell you he'd try to make it down tomorrow."

"I'll believe it when I see it," Jim told him with a chuckle. "He's always got a dozen irons in the fire."

Collecting her gear to leave the boat and listening to their conversation, Jessie hadn't paid much attention to Laurie and the others, but as she stepped carefully out and caught her balance she took a second look at the man who gave her a hand and smiled in pleased recognition of another acquaintance from the Klondike Centennial voyage. "Don Sawyer! How's Skagway and the Red Onion Saloon these days? Still haunted? You still bartending?"

"We assume it is and, yes, I am. We had a profitable summer with hordes of the usual tourists from those humongous cruise ships, who couldn't be convinced not to throw their money at us, as usual. Now I'm resting up by volunteering for some physical labor that's heavier than serving up beers."

"Hey Jessie. Glad you could make it," Laurie said, reaching to give her a quick hug of greeting. "Welcome to Five Finger Light. Let's get your stuff up top and we'll sort out introductions there. The guys will unload the building supplies."

"This is Karen," Jessie told her, waving a hand in the redhead's direction.

"Hi Karen." Laurie nodded, reaching for a box of supplies. "We'll do the formalities when we get this stuff up top."

It seemed to be shaping up as a good crew for the next four days of lighthouse restoration, Jessie decided with approval, as they helped carry bags and boxes of gear and food carefully up the sharp rocks to a wide cement platform between the boat and the lighthouse. She noticed, however, that Karen was being very quiet, saying little, watching much, as she helped. That made sense considering that she was acquainted with none of the people there.

She hoped it wouldn't take long for Karen to relax and enjoy the pleasant, easygoing company. But would it? She seemed to find some kind of threat in almost everything and to view everyone she met with suspicion.

CHAPTER FOURTEEN

JOE COOPER HAD STOOD PANTING BESIDE A LARGE TREE IN A small picnic area just east of the seafood processing plant and watched in frustration and anger as the woman he had come so close to catching heaved herself aboard the Seawolf. Even from that distance there had been no way of mistaking her red hair as she stripped off the scarf she had been wearing and waved it frantically to attract the attention of the people in the boat. Scowling in aggravation, he had berated himself as he turned to walk back the way he had come, contemplating his next step in this game of cat and mouse.

In a town as small as Petersburg, how could he have managed to miss her? *Because she was watching for you and you were following the other woman,* he told himself. But had that other woman been just a distraction that had attracted his attention, or a purposeful decoy? There was no way of knowing. The thing he needed to know now was *where* they were going in that boat.

Heading down the hill on Nordic Drive beside the processing plant, he considered the previous two hours.

He had left his duffel at the hotel and gone out, intending to find somewhere to have breakfast. Turning the corner from the hotel office, he had spotted the honey-blond woman he had seen the night before in the Harbor Bar as she came off one of the docks near the processing plant. Stepping back to avoid being seen, he had watched her move away from the harbor. Halfway to the main street, she had been intercepted by a man driving a forklift and they talked for a few minutes before he drove on and she went into the grocery on the corner.

Moving quickly down the hill, Cooper had stationed himself in a recessed doorway and waited to see her come out with something in a plastic grocery bag and two cups of coffee—*two!* This had been promising; that second cup had not been for the forklift operator, for she had walked straight back to the dock he had seen her leave and disappeared behind a pile of large fish boxes.

Crossing to the processing plant, he had plucked two empty plastic buckets from a stack of them and walked out along the dock at the side of the building far enough to see her sitting on a pile of pallets, leaning back on one of the large boxes. She had been talking on a cell phone and sipping coffee from one of the paper cups. The second cup of coffee had stood beside her on the pallet, but there was no one else to drink it. She had been alone.

Attempting to look as if he fit into the dockside scene, Cooper had crossed to a hose connected to a faucet on the side of the processing building and carefully rinsed out both perfectly clean buckets, dumping the water off the dock into the waters of the harbor below, one at a time, still covertly watching to see if anyone would show up to drink that second cup of coffee. No one had.

Seemingly finished with phone calls, the woman had

shrugged out of her green slicker, sat back, and helping herself to a donut and a banana from the plastic grocery bag, had begun to eat them.

With no excuse to linger, Cooper had walked back toward the street swinging the buckets until he was out of sight and had repositioned himself in the doorway.

When she didn't reappear in fifteen minutes, he had repeated the cleaning charade. As he mimed his job this time, however, she had been busily writing something on a piece of paper, which she had secured under the edge of a pallet like a small white flag. Then she had collected her things, including that second cup of coffee, and left the dock for Nordic Drive, where she turned right and headed off down the street, pausing to examine the contents of a shop window or two.

The note Cooper had hurried to retrieve as soon as she was out of sight had been valuable. It had told him where she was headed and that she wanted to meet "K." The initial couldn't be coincidental, he had told himself. It *must* stand for the woman he was hunting. Reference to the Harbor Master's office had let him know that the ride she mentioned must be a boat and the "ASAP," that she expected it soon. He had stuffed the note into a jacket pocket and jogged off toward the office indicated in the note.

There he had watched for Karen to show up, to no avail. Then, when the boat was loaded and it became clear that they were leaving without her, he had jogged up Nordic to the picnic area as they motored slowly eastward, constrained by the speed limit. So he had been there in time to swear as he saw them pass, hesitate, and turn shoreward to pick up the woman who had wildly signaled with the scarf she had used to cover her telltale red hair and waded out from shore to hand them a suitcase and be helped over the stern of the boat.

* * *

As he walked back into town, having once again watched his quarry evade him, and passed the grocery, he was startled when the forklift he had seen earlier swung back around the corner and stopped abruptly in front of him.

"Joe Cooper!" the driver called out as he stopped and climbed off, leaving the forklift idling. "What the hell are you doing in Petersburg, you old reprobate? Thought you'd left for the Lower Forty-eight."

"Ho, Tim," Cooper responded, recognizing a friend from Ketchikan, but avoiding the question. "Thought I saw you earlier, talking to some woman, but figured it was a mistake—that you would be out fishing. Who's your girlfriend?"

"Not mine—met her on a plane from Juneau yesterday. Besides, she's headed for a lighthouse in Frederick Sound. I'll be fishing again next week. Bart's waiting on parts for *Bertha*'s engine, so I'm just killing time in town."

"A lighthouse? Interesting."

"Yeah—a renovation crew. Hey, I'm going out there tomorrow. You might like to come along if you haven't got anything better to do."

Such a windfall seldom fell off the tree straight into Cooper's lap. Usually he had to climb the tree and go out on a limb to shake opportunities off, sometimes ripe, sometimes green. He kept a lid on his enthusiasm for the suggestion and responded mildly, "Might at that."

"You be around later? We could have some beers and catch up."

Cooper nodded. "What time are you off?"

"Five. Meet you at the Harbor Bar?"

"Sure."

"Okay. Gotta go. We'll talk about it then."

He fired up the forklift and was off up the street, leaving

a bemused Cooper shaking his head at the serendipitous way things sometimes happened.

Later that evening, when the sun was wearily sliding over the tall western hills, throwing a blanket of shadow over Petersburg as it went—the blue hour when the lights along the streets glowed unrealistically bright in contrast to the growing dark—he skillfully finagled Tim Christiansen into agreeing that they need not wait till morning, but might as well head for Frederick Sound without delay.

"We could anchor up somewhere away from town where it's quiet and peaceful—sleep on that neat little speedboat of yours. It'll save me a night's rent at the hotel and we can have time to ourselves—show up at the lighthouse tomorrow morning."

So sometime later, under a sky strewn with stars between floating clouds, they had made the run across the sound and reached the south end of Five Finger Island, but decided they should wait until morning to motor on around and make themselves known to the work crew. After an hour of drinking beer and renewing acquaintance, Cooper waited until Tim, tired after a day's work, had drifted off to sleep in his bunk. Then he quietly rose from where he had purposely elected to sleep on the back deck, shrugged on a jacket, and, timing the gentle rocking of the boat carefully, stepped off onto the shore and walked away.

He did not notice that in the dark he had taken Tim's jacket instead of his own.

CHAPTER FIFTEEN

WHEN WORK ENDED FOR THE DAY, AFTER A COCKTAIL hour outside to watch the sun go down in a spectacular show of red, purple, and gold, it was an amiable working crew of nine who sat down together for dinner that evening around the large table that took up a considerable amount of space in the common room of Five Finger Lighthouse. A kerosene lamp and several candles provided pleasant light, so they could do without the rumble of the big generator downstairs, which supplied power for lights, water pump, and anything else requiring electricity that did not run on batteries or propane, like the kitchen stove and refrigerator.

Laurie had prepared prodigious amounts of spaghetti, green salad, and garlic bread, on which they made significant inroads, washing it down with a good cabernet. The conversation was spirited as they continued to get acquainted and hear what had been accomplished that day by the five who had remained at Five Finger Light while Jim made his run to Petersburg.

Jessie sat next to Don Sawyer, who had brought along his girlfriend, Sandra Collier, a watercolor artist from Skagway, petite and energetic, with a mop of sandy gold, naturally curly hair that stood out like a corona around her head.

"So wouldn't you know they've got me painting the roof," she announced, reporting her work in progress.

"Never would have guessed," he teased, pointing out the streak of bright red on her forehead and up one sleeve of her gray sweatshirt. "I know you tend to get colorfully involved in your work, but—"

"And how much old paint did you get scraped off those windowsills you're planning to repair?" she interrupted in response.

"Not enough, but a good start," he told her. "There must be half a dozen coats on there. We may have to replace a couple of them though."

"Well, we got the generator fixed," young Coast Guardsman Aaron Rudolph commented from a seat at a nearby desk. Being left-handed, he had been knocking elbows with right-handed Curt Johnson, who turned out to be an electrician acquaintance of Jim's, and had solved the problem by moving.

"From your mouth to God's ear," said Curt, who had slipped off a sweatshirt covered with grime and motor oil and stripped to his cleaner white T-shirt before sitting down. "We'll check it again tomorrow morning and hope the lighthouse ghost hasn't been at it again."

"Is there supposed to be a ghost?" Whitney Mitchell asked with interest, returning from the kitchen with a second bottle of wine. Tall and slim with the fitness of a dancer, she was a friend of Laurie's and another of the thespians who played in the Perseverance Theatre on Douglas Island across a bridge from Juneau. The way she moved reminded Jessie of a showgirl she had once seen strut a stage in Las Vegas.

"No, Whitney," Jim told her. "He's being facetious."

"Don't count on it," Curt responded. "Jim said he had it

fixed yesterday and it was running fine. But when he went down to start that thing this morning? Besides me, who but a ghost was in the basement last night?"

"Probably one of those awful bug things." Sandra shivered. "What *are* those things anyway? They look like some kind of cockroach."

"They're not," Laurie assured her. "Cockroaches are insects and have hard shells and six legs. These are isopods and they have sixteen legs. We took one to Bruce Wing, the biologist at the Auke Bay NOAA Lab in Juneau, and he told us all about them. He said they're invertebrates, related to things with sections, like pill bugs and centipedes. They usually come out at night or on overcast days and live mostly in the rocks above the high tide line, where they stay moist in the ocean spray and find algae to eat, right, Jim?"

"Yeah, and this is just one kind. There are dozens of different kinds that live both in salt- and freshwater. If they get dry and the rain leaves a puddle, they crawl right in, but they also like dark, damp places. There's a horde of them down in the old fuel and water tanks under the cement platform out there." He waved a hand toward the windows on the east side of the room.

"There are tanks under there?" Don asked with interest.

"The fuel tank's been emptied and cleaned, but we still use the one for water. It's huge. Full, it holds thirty thousand gallons. We can climb down and I'll give you a tour tomorrow, if you like."

"Not me!" Sandra flatly stated. "If those evil *pod* things live down there and like it, I'll take your word for it, thank you very much. I hate creepy-crawlies."

"Me too," Aaron agreed. "Can't *stand* 'em! Give me lizards, mice, even snakes. But you can have the bugs. Even if these aren't bugs, they seem like 'em. Yuck."

Jim laughed. "They won't hurt you. Kids chase them, like Sally Lightfoots, but these don't fight back when they're caught."

Karen, who had said almost nothing since they arrived that afternoon, was quietly listening to the exchanges from her seat to Jessie's left.

"What do you do, Karen?" Laurie asked in a moment of silence.

"Oh, a lot of things, but not necessarily well," she answered. "I'm a pretty good cook, though."

"Terrific. You can help me in the kitchen then. But listen up, people. Those who cook do *not* clean up. Got that?"

As a chorus of groans and laughter answered her, Jessie saw Jim assess Karen's unrevealing answer to Laurie's question with an inquisitive look, which Karen, attention elsewhere, didn't notice.

Tucking it away in her mind for the moment as the conversation turned back to the renovation projects, Jessie leaned close to Don and said quietly, "I can't come to Southeast Alaska without remembering your cousin."

Sawyer's cousin, who had been part of the crew aboard the *Spirit of '98,* had been murdered and thrown from the stern of the ship during the voyage.

He nodded. "I think about Donna too—especially in Peril Strait, where she went over. I've been through there a couple of times since."

"How's her boy doing?"

"Josh?" A smile spread across his face. "He's great. He's in third grade this fall—plays soccer and loves video games. I went down to Vancouver and kept Christmas with him and Donna's mother this year. He's a pistol, that kid."

"Hey Jim. Do we start on that boathouse roof tomorrow?" Aaron asked, having emptied his plate for the second time and pulled his chair back to the table.

"Thought we might, unless it rains."

"Rain is not allowed," Sandra solemnly announced. "I have propitiated the weather gods with burned offerings tossed into the sea, begging their compassion in providing good weather."

"But only after you forgot to make offerings to the gods of memory to remind you to remove those cookies from the oven *before* they were *burned*," Whitney reminded her with a grin.

Curt leaned back in his chair. "They were probably gobbled up by that sea lion we saw this afternoon."

"Where *are* those cookies?" Jim asked Laurie.

"Coming up. Anyone want coffee? Tea? More wine?"

Preferences were voiced and Whitney, Aaron, and Jessie stood up to clear the table while Laurie went to make coffee and get the cookies. Karen started to help, but Jessie waved her back into her chair. "Three's enough. You can take a turn tomorrow."

Laurie brought a large Ziploc bag to the table for the leftover green salad. "Sandra, would you fill this and take it to one of those shelves downstairs where it's cool? Just put it in that box with the rest of the veggies."

"Sure." She rose and came around the table. "Anything else to go down?"

"Something to come up," Jim suggested, holding up the empty wine bottle. "Another one of these would be good. Look for a box to the left of the door in that storage area."

Sandra disappeared down the inside stairs, passing Jessie who was collecting a last stack of plates and silverware for the kitchen sink, where Aaron was already up to both his elbows in soapy water. Jim got up and came around the table.

"See you outside for a minute?" he asked quietly, passing Jessie.

"Hey! You're stealing my cleanup crew," Laurie chastised him.

"Plenty of replacements," he told her without pausing on his way out the door.

Jessie followed, knowing she would now be called upon to provide answers to his questions concerning Karen.

Just outside the door was a waist-high, L-shaped cement wall that formed a sort of open porch perhaps ten feet wide and somewhat longer. Anyone going around the left end of it would immediately arrive at the top of the stairway leading to the lower level platform onto which they had climbed from the rocks upon landing. Instead of going down it, Jim strolled across to a set of wooden steps that led up to the helipad. Sitting down on one of them, he pulled a pipe from a pocket and proceeded to pack it with tobacco and light it with a wooden kitchen match. The fragrance of the tobacco caught Jessie off guard, as it was the same blend Alex periodically smoked. She sat down on a lower step, closed her eyes, and inhaled appreciatively.

"Familiar, huh?" Jim's voice held a smile. "It should be, I guess. Alex turned me onto it on the centennial trip. Wish he'd been able to come along."

"Me too," Jessie said, thinking she would call Alex later.

"Now, tell me about this friend of yours," Jim said, but was interrupted as Sandra appeared at the lighthouse door with the bottle he had requested.

"Jim," she called hesitantly, a frown of concern on her face. "Here's the wine, but . . ."

"That's it, Sandra," he told her. "Would you ask Curt to open it?"

"Sure, but . . ."

"Something wrong?"

"Ah—well—just a question about something in the basement, but it'll keep."

"I'll be in soon," he told her, and turned to Jessie as Sandra vanished into the kitchen. "There's something familiar about Karen that I can't quite put a finger on. What's her story?"

"Familiar?"

"Yeah. Like I met her somewhere, casually—maybe. But I can't think where or when. And I keep feeling that, if I had, I'd remember that hair easily enough. Where'd you find her?"

Jessie could just see his frown of puzzlement in the dull glow from the pipe as he drew on it.

"She's a puzzle all right," she agreed. "Actually, she sort of *found me*—joined me for dinner last night at the Northern Lights in Petersburg. Came right up and asked if I'd mind, since she was by herself and in trouble." She went on to tell him the whole of Karen's story, as she knew it, right up to her asking Karen to join them at the lighthouse and their collecting her off the beach as they left town in the Seawolf.

Jim was quiet for a few moments when she finished, reflecting on the tale. She waited without further clarification for his response, which came slowly.

"A stalker? Hm-m. No wonder she wanted out of Petersburg. Hard to hide in a town that small."

"Yes. And she seems genuinely terrified of him."

"What she *seems* is pretty hard to read," he rejoined, thoughtfully. "Lot going on in that head and she's pretty cautious about what she reveals."

He took another draw on the pipe and puffed smoke into the air over his head. "You ever see him?"

"Not once."

"You believe her?"

It was the question Jessie had been asking herself—one

that stifled her answer for a moment or two. She leaned back, raised her face, and took a deep breath, hesitating, considering.

It was full dark. Here and there, through a break in the clouds, a star would twinkle through, disappearing quickly as another cloud floated in to conceal it. Every ten seconds the light that had come on automatically overhead in the tower was now sweeping its long beam across the underside of the low cloud cover that had drifted in. It would, she knew, be only a flash in the distance, but next to the lighthouse she could see its full circle.

Warning, she thought, *warning. Here be dragons.*

Finally—the danger unidentified, unsubstantiated in her mind—she spoke, still tracking what Jim had told them was a solar-powered aerobeacon as it cast its slim line of caution around above their heads.

"I—think so, but I just don't know. There's something . . ." She let this thought trail off unfinished.

"Yes," he said pensively. "There is, isn't there."

What had crossed Jessie's mind more than once earlier now came together in words. "She could bear watching."

"She's *doing* a lot of careful watching. And she doesn't seem to like Curt for some reason. You notice how carefully she stays away from him?"

"I hadn't, but I'll pay more attention."

"Good. So will I."

Neither of them took what they had shared any further, for the moment. In unspoken agreement they rose and headed toward the lighthouse where, inside, they could hear that Aaron, finished with the dishes, had retrieved a guitar and was trying to elicit a sing-along from a group too satisfied with food to dredge up much vocal energy.

"Keep me up to speed, if there's anything?" Jim asked as they reached the door.

"Sure. And you."

"Of course."

Jessie found her uneasiness somewhat alleviated by having Jim's company in an evaluation of Karen Emerson.

Sandra was snuggled next to Don on the sofa, her question seemingly forgotten in listening to Aaron's music and humorous lyrics.

And there were cookies—*unburned*—on the table.

CHAPTER SIXTEEN

IN DAWSON CITY, ALEX HAD BEEN UP BEFORE THE SUN, ready early to cross the Yukon River on the ferry on Tuesday morning. He had enjoyed spending time with Del and Clair Delafosse and was more than pleased with the amount that had been accomplished in organizing the plan between the Alaska State Troopers and Royal Canadian Mounted Police in a joint effort to improve border security between the two countries. But he had been glad to be heading home with Jessie's lead dog Tank, head on paws, drowsing beside him on the seat of the pickup truck, both satisfied with the breakfast Clair had insisted on feeding them before they left.

"You can't make a run to the border on an empty stomach, or just coffee," she had told him, brooking no argument as she bustled around in the kitchen over sausage, eggs, and Del's favorite buttermilk pancakes.

"For heaven's sake don't discourage her," Del had begged. "I could eat them every day. But soon she and the twins won't be able to reach the stove, let alone that skillet, and I'll be out of luck until they're born because when I make pancakes they just don't turn out the same. After that, with three mouths to feed, it's anybody's guess."

Alex had grinned as he drove away from the river, remembering that Clair had also packed him a lunch that he probably wouldn't need to break into for hours yet.

"Even you were fed a hearty breakfast, weren't you," he asked, reaching over to rub Tank's ears. "Going to be strange going home to an empty house, though, isn't it? Jessie won't be back until Sunday, so we'll have to make do with each other's company."

Recognizing the name of his owner, Tank had raised his head to give Jensen a questioning look. He and Jessie went almost everywhere together and were seldom separated for more than a day or two at most. But Jensen knew that if the dog had been able to make a list of favorite people, he would have come in second. It was good to know that he'd been missed during the months he was away in Idaho, as he was very fond of this canine friend and glad of his being along on this trip.

It had been clear and sunny, a good morning for crossing the Top of the World Highway. As they had started down into Alaska, having crossed the border at Boundary, he had been able to see for miles to the distant purple, blue, and white of mountain ranges to the west. It was a favorite part of the trip, so he had stopped twice at viewpoints, once on the Canadian side, once on the Alaskan.

Just after noon he had cruised into Tok, where he had pulled in to fill the tank with gas, and a thermos with coffee, and to let Tank out of the truck again for a rest stop. From there he had taken the Tok Cutoff south, stopping an hour later at a wide spot in the road where he augmented his lunch with scenery: Mount Sanford rising in splendid

16,237-foot isolation from the Wrangell-St. Elias National Park. Another hour's drive had brought them to Glennallen at four o'clock. He felt almost home as he drove out on the Glenn Highway, which had taken him directly to Palmer and the turnoff to Wasilla.

And home they were not long after six, having made good time and stopped for groceries, Alex knowing that, while he could feed Tank easily enough, with Jessie gone he would have to cook his own dinner-for-one. If he had not had Tank along, he might have eaten out, but the dog had been in the truck all day and he didn't want to leave him waiting in front of some restaurant.

Going up the long driveway from Knik Road, he saw there was a light in Jessie's new log house. The few dogs she had kept in her kennel, not yet being totally used to Jensen's truck again, had begun to bark, but quieted when he let Tank out. They had clearly been fed and cared for by Billy Steward while he was gone, so he figured correctly that the boy had left the light on for him in the house. Taking his travel bag and the single sack of groceries, he went up the stairs and unlocked the door, Tank trotting along behind.

It was immediately apparent from the delicious smell that wafted into his nose that there would be no need to cook after all. A peek into the oven revealed a tempting casserole keeping warm, and a note propped against a covered bowl of salad on the table told him he had Billy's mother to thank.

"Bless her generous heart," he said, looking down at Tank who, sitting expectantly nearby, cocked his head and gave friend Alex a doggy grin.

"Okay, your dinner's coming up."

There was even a fire carefully banked in the cast-iron

stove, to which he added a log or two until it was crackling a cheerful welcome. Then he fed Tank, who afterward wandered over to curl up on the rag rug in front of it, hoping he wouldn't be put out just yet. Glad to be home, Alex got himself a Killian's and let dinner wait a bit while he drank it. Leaving Tank snoozing where he was, he filled a plate with noodle stroganoff and salad, put some Toby Keith on the DVD player for company, and settled down for his meal.

When the phone rang just after nine, Alex had put Tank back on his tether in the dog yard and was half asleep on the sofa in front of the television, where he had settled in hopes of staying awake until Jessie called, as promised.

"Hey," she said in answer to his hello. "You two made it home okay then."

"In good time and fine fettle. It was warm, sunny—a great drive. I could see almost to Magadan from the Top of the World this morning and Mount Sanford was cloudless."

"Well, almost to Siberia's a bit of an exaggeration, but I know what you mean. How's Tank?"

"He's fine. Just put him out in the yard for the night. How's the island?"

"You spoil him rotten. The island's terrific. We had a sunny day too, and a smooth ride from Petersburg *Whales! We saw whales*, Alex."

He could hear her delight at the sighting.

"Bet you see a lot more."

"That's what Jim said. Here on the island they have a resident sea lion and an eagle with a baby just learning to fly." She paused, and then went on. "Everyone says hello and—I wish you were here. I miss you."

It was worth the long trip from Canada just to hear her say it.

"I miss you too. This house is awfully empty without you in it. Oh—Billy's mom sent over a casserole, so I didn't have to cook."

"Ah, so that's why you miss me? Cooking!" she teased.

"Not tonight! But there are a few other things I miss you for."

There was a gentle giggle from Jessie before she said, "Save that thought. I'll be home Sunday, as planned."

"Terrific. Now, tell me about this woman you met in Petersburg, who stayed at the hotel with you."

Jessie told him everything she had told Jim, plus a few speculations of her own, and, like Jim, there was a few seconds' pause from Alex when she finished.

"And you think there's really some guy stalking her?"

"Well—I haven't seen him, but she's frightened of someone."

Jensen's law enforcement persona kicked in with his next comment. "If this guy exists, you should consider that he might figure you're in his way."

"How would he ever find us out here?"

"Don't people in Petersburg know where you were headed? The hotel people, maybe—a few others? Small towns tend to share information and he might ask the right— well, the wrong person—mightn't he?"

Jessie was quiet for a long breath of consideration before answering.

"It's possible, I guess, but don't you think that's a stretch?"

"Depends on how determined he is. You should have taken the problem to the Petersburg police."

"I suggested that. Karen refused."

"Well, I think you'd better keep a sharp lookout and take care. Tell Jim I said so, okay?"

"Okay."

"And call me often, so I know you're safe? Or I'll call you."

"Yes, I will. I have to take the cell phone outside, away from the lighthouse, to get a signal. I'm outside now. So if you try and can't reach me, don't worry. I'm probably just inside somewhere."

"I'll remember that, but keep it with you, okay?"

"Sure. If I can't reach you in the evening, I'll try you at work during the day."

They talked for a few more minutes, but after she hung up Jessie stood in the dark, looking out over the water to the west of the helipad, where she had gone to make the call. It was very still and though the sea was calm, she could hear the gentle sloshing of small waves on the rocks below. Far away across the sound the lights of a boat moved steadily southwest, probably headed for Petersburg at this late hour. A breeze crept in to rustle the brush under the helipad just enough to hear until it was covered by a burst of laughter that drifted out from the group still gathered around the table in the lighthouse.

The clouds had lifted and seemed to be breaking up, for stars now gleamed through several large patches. Something splashed in the water a good distance from the north point, its identity hidden in the dark. Did whales feed at night? Jessie wondered. Or did they sleep, perhaps floating head down, suspended in watery space, rising now and then to the surface to breathe, liquid resistance to their huge weight allowing them to fall slowly back to rest in the deep? It was an agreeable, enchanting sort of thought. Astronauts who slept weightlessly suspended in space must have some idea how whales feel.

She yawned at the idea of sleep, more tired than she had

realized and ready to find a bed of her own soon. It would be nice, when she was back home on Sunday night, to curl up next to Alex in her big brass bed, tell him all about her week's adventures, and hear about his.

"Jessie?" Laurie called from the door of the lighthouse.

"Here."

Her hostess came across and up to join her on the helipad.

"It's a great night, isn't it?"

"Hm-m," Jessie agreed.

"Looks like we might have a sunny day tomorrow, from the weather report. The guys can get started on the boat-house roof. That'll make Jim happy. He worried about it all last winter."

"I'm glad you invited me," Jessie told Laurie. "I've never been on an island this small in the middle of so much water. It's a fine place to be—sort of magical and otherworldly—peaceful."

"It is, isn't it? We're glad you could come. Too bad Alex had to work."

"He was disappointed, but—maybe another time. He got home from Dawson tonight and said to tell you all hello." Then, recalling Laurie's invitation by phone, "You had something you wanted to talk to him about, didn't you?"

There was a long moment of thoughtful silence and Laurie dropped her head to stare at the wooden pad beneath her feet. She crossed her arms, hugging herself, and when she raised her face Jessie was close enough to see that she was frowning.

"Yes," she said, "there was, but . . . oh, it's probably silly and just our—well, mostly *my*—imagination. But several times since we got the place we've had the feeling that someone else had been here when we weren't—things a little out of place, a door unlocked—and we always lock up before leaving—the coffeepot used and left unwashed—just small stuff. You know—things you could be mistaken about. So the first time or two we told ourselves that's what it was. But last time we found a wrench on the table that Jim knew he'd put away downstairs."

"Anything missing?"

Laurie shook her head, still frowning. "Not that we could tell."

"Jim said the Coast Guard comes to maintain the light. Could it be them?"

"Two guys came by last month when we were here for a week and we asked, but they said not and I believe them. They were concerned that someone might mess with the light, or the solar panel. Said they'd keep a lookout, but they're here less often than we are. I thought Alex might have some suggestions if he came."

"He might anyway. I'll ask him the next time we talk."

"Thanks, Jessie. It's probably not that important, but I hate the invaded feeling. It makes me uneasy all the time I'm here—and worried when I'm not. Kind of spoils the magic, you know."

"It could be someone local who just likes lighthouses and can't resist. This place could be a temptation for almost anyone passing."

"We thought about that, and someone local makes sense because a tourist on the way up or down the passage wouldn't come back several times, would they?"

"Let me see what Alex thinks."

"I'd appreciate that—a lot."

They stood together for a few more quiet moments, absorbing the gifts of the night from that particular island in the middle of such a wide piece of ocean. Then, in unspoken agreement, they went back to join the others in finding places for sleeping.

Though much was held in promise in terms of satisfying restoration work and the relaxation of a good company of friends, they hadn't a notion just how decidedly things could—and would—change in the next few hours.

CHAPTER SEVENTEEN

JESSIE WAS INTERESTED IN THE WAY FIVE FINGER LIGHT-house stood high above the sea, its foundation fastened securely onto the living stone that formed the island. According to the proud new owners, a station had been established there in 1902, but it was a wooden building that burned and was replaced in 1935 with the current concrete structure. Though the lighthouse was built to last and was solid, it was, after all, seventy years old, had been exposed for decades to the destructive forces of waves and weather in a broad expanse of saltwater, and required constant maintenance, which had been minimal since it was automated and lost its keepers. So there was much to do for the renovation crew that had gathered to effect what repairs were possible in a week's time.

A quick tour before dinner had shown Jessie that the lighthouse was quite simple in layout. Coming in the door from the north one walked immediately into the large kitchen, where a hallway branched off to the right and passed a bathroom on its way to two small bedrooms in the northwest corner of the square building. If one went on through the kitchen one arrived in the common room, which took up the whole of the southeast corner. What had been a small radio room opened from it to the right and, beyond that, another hallway branched off, passed a fourth small bedroom that was now used for storage, and wound up in the largest bedroom in the rear southwest corner.

In the center of the one-story building, through a door in the second hallway, a stairway rose up in short flights and landings around the square walls all the way to a room near the top of the sixty-eight-foot tower. At that point the stairway ended and a visitor must climb a metal set of circular steps with a brass rail; the steps led up into the round glass cupola that allowed the high-powered light to shine out into the darkness every night. From there, the wide expanse of Frederick Sound was spread out below, with the two nearest islands, the Brothers, almost directly west.

Opposite the bathroom in the hallway that led from the kitchen to the small bedrooms, a door opened onto a flight of stairs leading down to a large lower room. There, wide doors opened out onto the platform below and alongside the building to the east. This large room housed not only the huge generator to which Curt had earlier referred and a control console full of dials and switches, but also had storage for everything from all kinds of tools and materials necessary to the maintenance of the lighthouse, water and propane tanks, fire extinguishers, carts, ladders, to a washing machine and dryer, even a small skiff. In a couple of narrow annex rooms just off this lower room was shelving for fresh vegetables and beverages to be kept cool—including Jim's rather extensive wine collection. Almost anything necessary to living on the island was kept there.

But most interesting to Jessie was that on one wall of this

basement the last full-time crew had left their names (including the dog) and where they were from:

LAST 365 DAY
1983 CREW 1984
BM1 M.L. Harding—Washington
MK2 J.P. Breneman—Lancaster PA
FN R.A. Gere—Washington
SN M.J. Rausch—CO
Dog Neva

With only three useful bedrooms in the one-story building that, before the light was automated, had been occupied by a keeper and three or four assistants, the nine members of the current work crew were somewhat creative about sleeping spaces. Jim and Laurie had long ago set up a queen-sized bed for themselves in the largest of the bedrooms. Hoping that Alex would come with Jessie, Laurie had assigned one of the smaller bedrooms to them. Now she gave one of the single beds to Karen instead. It was, they learned, where Anna and Becky, now on their way home to Colorado, had slept.

"But you didn't expect me," Karen protested. "And I don't want to take someone's bed. I really don't mind sleeping on the floor."

But Jessie claimed that space, having brought her own sleeping bag and an inflatable mattress, and insisting, truthfully, that she was used to sleeping on all kinds of surfaces when she was out training or racing her dogs. So with Karen in one bed, Whitney, who had been sleeping on the couch in the common room, moved in to occupy the second, and they were three. After establishing their sleeping arrangements, they went back to the common room for a few minutes.

Don Sawyer and Sandra had moved into the other small bedroom in that hallway when they arrived, while both Curt and Aaron had elected to make their beds, like Jessie, on the floor. Curt, however, was sleeping in the lower room with his generator and Aaron had chosen the first wide landing on the way up to the tower, where a door could be opened onto the roof that Sandra had been painting red.

"That paint better be dry before you step out there and make prints in it," she called after him, as he and Curt said their goodnights and headed for the stairs, one up, one down, Aaron taking his guitar with him.

"He likes to sit out on the roof and sing to the whales at bedtime," Don explained to Karen. "They never answer, but it makes good music for the rest of us to go to sleep by. He's pretty good."

Jessie stood behind a chair looking around the room with interest, in the soft glow of an oil lamp and several candles that had been lighted in preference to running the noisy generator downstairs. A bright plastic tablecloth covered the broad table, now partially occupied with scattered coffee cups, wineglasses, and a single plate empty of all but cookie crumbs. The desk where Aaron had eaten his dinner took up one corner, with an office chair in front of it. A couple of lounge chairs stood under the east-facing windows. In an alcove on the south wall stood the afghan-covered couch that Whitney had used as a bed. Over it on the wall was a dartboard and next to it a shadowbox frame that held a sample of several nautical knots. Pinned up beside a window hung a chart showing various kinds of saltwater fish. Here and there maps, charts, fishing gear, a barometer, and other oddments covered the walls.

Turning, Jessie ran a finger along a collection of books, fiction and nonfiction, on three shelves of a case recessed in the wall under a map of the lower part of Alaska. Some she recognized; others were new to her, including an interesting-looking volume in a three-hole binder labeled "Historic Lighthouse Preservation Handbook."

"That's got everything you need or want to know about fixing up old lighthouses," Jim said. "It's put out by the government and includes all kinds of lighthouses anywhere in the United States."

"Interesting. I'd like to take a look at it tomorrow," Jessie said, yawning again. "Right now, I'm for bed."

So was everyone else, and things were soon very quiet at Five Finger Light. Even Aaron had stopped his songs and gone to bed.

Without the residual light of a town nearby, it was very dark in the small bedroom and Jessie could see nothing at all when something woke her much later in the night. Assuming she had heard someone headed for the bathroom, she rolled over and had started to drift off again when a soft, faraway resonance caught her attention. Almost too faint to be heard, it sounded like an engine, but who would be running an engine in the middle of the night? It couldn't be Curt's generator downstairs, for that would have been much louder. Sitting up, she reached for the small pencil flashlight she had tucked under her pillow, a habit she had acquired on the sled dog trail. Switching it on, she shielded the glow with her fingers and pointed it in the direction of one of the two beds in the room.

Whitney, covered except for the top of her head, made a quilted lump in hers and was snoring gently.

Jessie swung the narrow beam of light past the door, which was unexpectedly open, to Karen's.

It was empty.

Turning off the light, she lay back down and waited to see if Karen would come back from down the hall.

But what must have been ten minutes later, she still hadn't appeared.

The engine sound Jessie thought she had heard had died away completely and she told herself that it could have been a passing boat in the distance, but somehow felt it was not that far away.

Knowing she wouldn't go back to sleep without solving the puzzle of the sound and the missing woman, Jessie got up, slipped on her jeans under the large-sized T-shirt in which she slept, put on her shoes without socks, and went out into the hall with the flashlight once more shielded by her fingers. As she passed Karen's bed she laid a hand on the sheets and found them cold. How long had the woman been gone anyway?

The outside door in the kitchen was open a crack.

What could be going on? Listening carefully, she heard no voices.

Turning off the light, she walked quietly out onto the porch and stood looking around. As her sight adjusted to the darkness, she could see the solid shapes of objects on the island against the pale light reflected from the sea beyond it—the wall of the lighthouse, shrubs and brush, the roof of a shed on the lower platform, the raised helipad to her left, and a tree or two against the starry sky. A small scraping sound from the helipad attracted her notice. Carefully, she crossed to its steps, on which she and Jim had settled earlier, and went halfway up to be able to see across the top of the wide flat surface. Something moved directly across from where she stood. Climbing on up, she walked to the center and saw that it was the shape of a person sitting on the edge facing west.

"Karen?"

"Oh!" The figure swung around, surprised. "Didn't hear you coming. You startled me."

"Don't fall off of there," Jessie warned. "There are some big rocks a dozen feet below."

Karen had now turned halfway around, but didn't get up.

"I couldn't get to sleep," she said. "So I came out. It's a little claustrophobic knowing the weight of that huge tower is above you, don't you think?"

Jessie hadn't considered it and it made no difference to her now. "I think if it's stood there since the mid-1930s, it'll probably stand awhile longer," she said, a little amused.

Moving to the edge of the platform, she sat down beside Karen and leaned back on her hands to look up at the sky, now almost empty of clouds, but full of stars that were brighter and seemed closer without the conflict of artificial lights.

"Yes, I guess it'll stand," Karen said. "But it's nicer out here, don't you think, with the ocean all around and the stars? You can hear the waves splash on the rocks down there. Look up. There are millions of stars. I wish there was a moon, don't you?"

Why, she asked herself, did she have the uneasy feeling that Karen was talking more than usual to cover something?

"Well, it's nice. Did you hear an engine a little while ago?"

"An engine? No."

"You must have heard it. I could hear it from inside the building."

"Oh. Well—there was some kind of a boat that went past a little while ago, but it was a long ways away."

There were no lights from a boat to be seen now, Jessie noticed.

"Which direction did it go?"

"That way." Karen swung an arm imprecisely toward the south. "Its lights went out of sight behind the trees at that end of the island."

Must have been going faster than she thought. The engine had not sounded up to speed, but almost at an idle. "What kind of a boat?"

"I don't know. All I could see was its lights. Fishing boat, I guess."

Jessie wished she could see Karen's face to read her expression, but it was too dark.

All kinds of vessels—ferries, freighters, oil tankers, fishing boats, private pleasure boats, cruise ships, and others—went up and down the Inside Passage at all hours of the day or night, and she knew they were required to have running lights after dark. The larger ones, however, at this point did not make their way through Frederick Sound, for there was no passageway large enough to accommodate them. They took the outside route, or ran up through Chatham Strait on their way to Sitka, Juneau, or points farther north. The only boats that took the route through Frederick Sound must pass through the Wrangell Narrows, which were much too shallow and constricted for anything larger than fishing boats, power- or sailing craft. She remembered that the *Spirit of '98,* 192 feet long and 40 feet wide, had had a shallow enough draft to pass through the Narrows—one of the characteristics that made traveling on it such a pleasure, because it could carry its passengers to places those on huge cruise ships would never experience or even know they had missed.

Karen shifted her weight from hip to hip, as if she was uncomfortable sitting on the hard wooden surface of the helipad with her knees hanging over the low, six-inch rail at the edge of it.

But, Jessie wondered, was that the real reason for her discomfort?

"Think I'll go back to bed," Karen said, standing up. "You coming?"

"In a minute," Jessie told her. "You go ahead."

She thought about loaning Karen her flashlight, but didn't.

If she found her way out here in the dark, she can find her way back, she told herself, and realized she was annoyed and somewhat disturbed by Karen's middle-of-the-night skulking. *If it had been anyone else—Jim, or Laurie, or Don—I wouldn't feel that way, would I? But she lied, didn't she?*

By herself in the dark, she wondered why Karen would lie about hearing a boat, for she was nearly convinced that it had been an attempt at a falsehood the woman hoped to get away with. A shred of doubt lingered, however, for it could, as she had claimed, have been a passing fishing boat—seen and dismissed. Some worked late. Some didn't return to port until they had a good catch, but anchored up at night, or motored to a new and, hopefully, better location to be ready to drop their nets in the morning. There was nothing to be proved, or gained, by accusation—or speculation, for that matter.

Tired of conjecture, Jessie lay back on the helipad platform and looked up at the sky. On the island, with the mountains so far away, it was full of stars almost to the horizon. There was a cool breeze coming off the always-icy waters of the sound, but watching so many stars was almost as pleasant as lying on her sled bag during a race to see them through the northern lights that swirled slowly across overhead—and warmer. Picking out the Big Dipper, so closely associated with Alaska's identity that it was portrayed on the state flag, she mentally extended the line of the two pointer stars on the front of its bowl and, approximately six times that distance across the sky, found Polaris, the North Star, at the tip of the Little Dipper's handle. In the Far North the two constellations are circumpolar and always visible in the sky, so they were old familiar friends to Jessie.

Time to go back to bed, she decided, turned on her flashlight to make sure she didn't fall going down the steps of the platform, and went back to the lighthouse.

Sometime later the distant sound of an engine occurred again as part of a dream, but she had forgotten it by morning.

Chapter Eighteen

"WANT TO TAKE A LOOK AT THE ISLAND BEFORE WE GO TO work?" Laurie asked as they finished the last of the breakfast dishes the next morning.

"Sure," Jessie agreed, curious to see the southern end beyond the two acres of trees that grew tall in the patch of woods behind the lighthouse.

She had been awake early, but not as early as Karen, whose bed had once again been empty. Heading for the bathroom, Jessie had found it locked and heard the shower running, but in a few minutes Karen had come out in clean clothes, her wet hair wrapped in a towel. Tucking the roll of clothes she had been wearing into her suitcase, she had left the room with a brush in her hand, evidently headed outside, though Jessie had found her helping Laurie with breakfast a little while later, when she had finished her own quick shower.

The day was sunny, as predicted, and after eating, Sandra had gone up to the roof of the square building that supported the tower to finish the painting job started the day before, taking a CD player with headphones along for entertainment. "Music gets me into a painting rhythm," she told Jessie as she headed for the stairs.

Jim, Aaron, and Don—who had temporarily abandoned scraping the paint off windowsills—were removing old roofing on the boathouse in preparation for putting down the new materials Jim had picked up in Petersburg. Curt was once again tinkering with the huge generator. It had started that morning, but he evidently felt it still needed tweaking to operate to his satisfaction. Whitney and Karen were considering what to make for lunch, but Whitney gave that up to join Laurie and Jessie on their walk. Karen said she would stay to boil some eggs for a potato salad.

Taking off the denim jacket she had been wearing in the morning chill, Jessie took it to the bedroom, tossed it on her sleeping bag, and picked up the daypack that held her camera gear. To lighten its weight, she took out some toilet items and slipped her wallet under her pillow.

The three went down the stairs outside the north porch and crossed the broad concrete platform, waving a greeting to Curt through the large open doors of the lower operations room. Pointing down, Laurie called their attention to a round manhole cover in the cement pavement close to the doors. "That's how you climb down to the tanks for water and fuel," she told them.

They went on across to a dogleg flight of wooden steps between the boathouse and the carpenter shop that was next to the lighthouse.

"Playing tour leader again?" Jim asked Laurie, as they passed.

"Jessie hasn't seen the rest of the island," Laurie reminded him. "And Whitney wants to take another look at the fossils in the rocks at the other end."

"Don't get lost, or fall off the cliff," Aaron called, with a grin. "There's still work to be done."

"There'll always be work to be done," sighed Laurie.

"Ah, but you love it, don't you?"

She had to admit that she did.

From the top of the steps, single file, the three followed a trail that ran up across a grassy area and entered the woods. Once in the trees, the ground cover changed completely to lush ferns, shrubs, and a variety of underbrush that rose out of a deep bed of needles, sticks, and leaves fallen, for uncountable decades, from the trees of the small forest to join and sometimes bury the tangle created by branches and dead trees. It smelled damp and slightly moldy with decaying vegetation. But there were several kinds of berries on the bushes and a few flowers here and there where some space in the trees let enough sun through.

Not long after they entered the woods, Whitney stopped Jessie by clutching her elbow. "You gotta see this," she said, turning her around to face a tree they had passed beside the trail. Fastened to it was a roughly carved wooden mask with a face that resembled an artifact made by some coastal native Alaskan—but only resembled. Though unsmiling, the piece projected a sense of humor, as if it were amused at its own appearance. Three rain-bedraggled feathers had been stuck between it and the bark of the tree, adding to the insouciant attitude of parody.

"Who made it?" Jessie asked.

"A friend with a sense of humor," Laurie told her. "But I couldn't resist adding the feathers."

Amused, Jessie had them stand next to it while she took a picture.

The narrow trail ran like a ribbon, up and down, twisting

and twining around trees and stumps. To the left the ground fell steeply away to a wide jumble of huge rocks and tide pools between the forest and the shore. To the right, trees marched sharply up to the highest point on the island, where Laurie said the face of the cliff they had seen from the boat on arrival fell perhaps fifty feet straight down, onto fallen rock or into the sea.

Stopping them on the trail a bit farther on, Laurie pointed up to an untidy heap of small branches and twigs that filled the top of one tall spruce.

"There's an eaglet in that nest," she told Jessie, "but you won't see it unless it climbs out on the edge and tries to flap its wings. It's just learning to fly. We could see the mother when we get to the south end though. She fishes off the rocks just offshore and carries her catch back to her baby."

They walked on along the path and Jessie noticed that, especially in one place, several of the trees were festooned with gray green moss reminiscent of similar growth she had seen on trees in pictures of Southern plantation houses.

"They look like very old men with beards," she commented, eliciting a smile from Whitney.

"Yeah," she agreed. "Pretty ancient guys, aren't they?"

"Careful," Laurie pointed out. "There's a hole on your left."

Looking down, Jessie saw that under the large root of one tall tree the ground had fallen away to create a space large and deep enough to swallow a person up to the waist, completely if they crouched down. Cautiously, she stepped around it.

The trail began to go steadily down and they eventually came to a bend that turned them right and steeply up again. At the top they came out on a point of rock and grassy ground clear of the trees, where they could not only see for miles over Frederick Sound, but down onto the rock that formed the foundation of the island. Out in the water beyond them was a narrow ridge of rocks that stood above the water and on which the eagle predictably perched, watching for unwary fish to feed her youngster. As they watched, she suddenly swept down, talons extended, to snatch her prey from beneath the waves. Wide wings flapping strongly, she bore it up until they watched her disappear into the trees toward the nest they had seen, taking lunch to the eaglet.

Jessie turned back and stood looking out across the sound to the faraway hills on other islands that were so large they looked like mainland.

"Is that the island that you can see across the harbor from Petersburg?" she asked Laurie.

"Kupreanof Island—yes."

"Russian name."

"Well, the Russians owned it all until Seward insisted that we buy it, didn't they? Sitka was their base for hunting seals and sea otters, and it isn't far away. They probably gave everything in sight Russian names."

Jessie thought back to high school and remembered that sometime just after the Civil War the United States had bought the territory twice as large as Texas from Russia for just over two and a half cents an acre—a figure that had impressed her so she never forgot it.

"That means that this island back then was worth seven and a half cents. Can you imagine?"

"Let's go down where the fossils are," Whitney suggested, and led the way back down the trail a short distance to where it branched off to the right. When they had gone through a stand of tall brush and grass, she turned off to a rough wall where layers of rock flaked away to reveal dim plant fossils, and began to pry them apart. Laurie stopped to help.

Jessie walked on out to an open space that sloped off into the ocean in long fingers of stone with a small amount of sand between. The tide was coming in, so not much of the area was visible, but as she stood looking down at the small stones and shells left by the previous flood she noticed some distinct marks that looked as if something had been dragged along. Glancing around she saw nothing close at hand that could be responsible. The marks were quickly being erased by the incoming waves as she turned and called Laurie to come and see.

"Any idea what made those?" she asked.

Laurie examined what was left of the marks and shook her head. "No, but we do have an old sea lion that frequently hangs around at this end of the island. Maybe he crawled out here."

But the marks did not seem the kind to be made by an animal to Jessie. She thought they looked more likely to have been caused by the bow of a boat. She remembered the engine sound she had heard in the night and wondered about it as the last of the abrasions in the sand were eradicated by a particularly high-reaching wave.

Laurie went back to fossil-picking with Whitney, leaving Jessie to her speculations. But when she turned to look back at them she saw that Karen had evidently decided to come after all and was standing, hands in jeans' pockets, looking across at her. How long she had been monitoring her interaction with Laurie, Jessie had no idea, but Karen instantly shifted her attention to the fossil bed when she saw that Jessie was aware of her.

"Hi," Laurie greeted her. "Change your mind?"

"Yeah. Left the eggs in cold water and decided it was too nice to be indoors, so I tagged along. This place is . . ." Her words trailed into silence and she stood up straight, looking out at the water beyond where Jessie was standing. "Hey," she said. "Is that the sea lion?"

Laurie and Whitney stood up to see and Jessie turned seaward, in the direction Karen was pointing.

A few yards offshore a sea lion *was* swimming, with its reddish brown head above water, attentively watching the humans on the shore.

"Hey, that's cool," Karen said, hopping quickly rock to rock to come down to the tide line.

As this second human drew near, the sea lion turned and began to swim back around a high point of rock that had earlier hidden it from sight. Karen did more hopping till she reached that rock and began to climb it, clearly wanting to see more of the large animal. As she was high enough to see over, she suddenly sat down on the stone ridge that formed the crest.

"Oh God," she said in a strangled voice. *"Oh—my—God."*

"What?" Jessie asked, immediately starting after her, followed by Laurie, whose attention had also been attracted.

But Karen only looked back at them wide-eyed, pointed toward the other side, and said nothing more as Jessie scrambled to the top and looked over.

At the edge of the incoming tide, so close the feet moved gently in rhythm with the incoming waves, the body of a man lay facedown, half in the water, half out. Even from a distance they could see that the hair on the back of his head was soaked, like the shoulders of his gray jacket, with blood. The rocks on which he lay were splattered brownish crimson, but slowly, relentlessly, the eternal motion of the sea was washing them clean.

Laurie reached the crest just behind Jessie and the three,

speechless, stared down at the unexpected sight below for a long minute.

"Jesus!" Laurie breathed.

"Who is it?" Jessie asked her.

"I have no idea," she almost whispered, hoarsely.

"What's wrong?" Whitney called, looking up from below.

"There's a dead man down here," Jessie told her, turning to look back.

"A dead man? Did I hear you right?" Whitney started to come up to join them.

"No." Jessie waved her off. "Don't come up. Go back to the lighthouse as fast as you can and bring the guys. Tell them to bring a tarp of some kind. The tide's coming in, so we'll stay and make sure he doesn't float away."

"An accident? Did he fall?"

"I don't . . . know," Jessie said, hesitantly. "Just hurry. We need help."

As Whitney headed for the path at a run, Laurie and Jessie climbed carefully down over the steep rocks and went across to where the body lay. There they stood looking down at the crushed carnage that had been the back of his skull, which appeared even more devastating up close than it had seemed from above.

"I guess he could have floated in from somewhere," Laurie said, frowning. "People do fall off boats sometimes, right? But what could have . . ."

"It's not likely he floated here," Jessie told her. "This man hasn't been dead long. Bodies don't float at first; they sink and stay down until they decompose enough to rise. Besides, there wouldn't be so much blood on him. It would have washed away if he'd been in water. And there wouldn't be any splashed on the rocks like that."

"Do you think he could have fallen on the rocks?" Laurie asked, almost hopefully.

Jessie shook her head, glancing up at them to where Karen was still silently looking down from the top with a blank expression. "If he had fallen and hit the back of his head, he would probably be lying faceup, don't you think?"

Laurie had to agree.

"You think somebody could have . . . ?" She broke off what she had been about to say—what they were both thinking—and swallowed hard. "Who is he? How did he get here and who could have . . . ?"

"Well, he clearly didn't walk here."

"Maybe there was a boat that drifted away when the tide came in. You pointed out those marks in the sand."

"I did." Jessie nodded. "But, unless there was someone else, wouldn't the boat be floating somewhere in sight? The tide was just reaching those marks and it's coming in, not going out, so that means they were made when it was lower, yes?"

"That would depend on when this . . . happened . . . and how the tide was running through the sound, I think, don't you? I think at certain times it could carry a boat quite a long ways and in unexpected directions."

But Jessie was unwilling to play guessing games, or reveal the ideas that were running through her mind. Crouching next to the body, she slipped two fingers onto the pulse point under the jaw to make absolutely sure it *was* a corpse, not someone injured and unconscious who just looked like one. There was no sign of life and the body was unpleasantly cold and stiff. She wished she could remember how long after a person died rigor mortis occurred. She decided to ask Alex the next time they talked.

Karen groaned, slid weakly down on her side of the point, and threw up her breakfast on the rocks. There she remained, shivering and pale, clearly refusing to help, or even to look back again at what she had discovered.

Fifteen minutes later, when Whitney brought Jim, Don, and Aaron back with her, Laurie and Jessie were still standing guard on the rocks near the body and Karen huddled miserably near where she had lost her breakfast. The water was now high enough to reach the bloody rocks and cause the lower half of the corpse to sway slightly in the rising tide.

"Who is it? What the hell happened?" Jim asked, clambering carelessly over the rocks to reach them.

"We don't know," Jessie told him. "Karen spotted him when she climbed up to see the sea lion."

"Did he die here, or float in?"

She shrugged—then frowned. "I'd bet from the amount of blood on the rocks that he died here. There was quite a lot on the rocks, but it's almost gone now—washed away. But it must have happened after high tide last night, or he might have floated off then, mightn't he?" She hesitated, then, "There may have been a boat."

"How do you know?"

"There were marks—over there." She pointed to the area beyond the ridge of rock they had climbed over. "They're gone now—washed off like his blood is washing away here."

"Who is it?" This question came from Aaron, who was carrying a blue plastic tarp under one arm.

She shook her head. "We haven't turned him over. Just didn't want the tide to take him."

"Well, we'd better get him out before it does," Jim said. "Find a place above the tide line and spread that tarp you're carrying, will you, Aaron?"

Aaron and Don stepped up to help lift the body out of the

water and lay it gently on the tarp, carefully rolling him over onto his back in the process. Jim looked up sharply as Jessie gasped.

"You know him?"

"Yes," she said. "Well, not really *know* him. I met him on the plane from Juneau, then again later in Petersburg. His name is Tim . . . something Scandinavian. He's the one I told you about—the one who said he'd come out to help—who had his own boat? He said he had a friend he was going to bring along with him. Remember?"

"Yes. And he was coming today, right?"

She nodded. "That's what he said."

"Well—I doubt this is what he meant. We'd better call somebody—police, Coast Guard."

"I've seen him before too," Whitney said, having given the dead man a careful look. "He was part of a rowdy fishing crew that was in the Triangle Bar in Juneau last Saturday night."

She turned and stepped away to look out over the sound, frowning thoughtfully.

"Do we leave him here, or take him back to the light-house?" Aaron asked.

"Someone will want to investigate, so I guess we'd better leave him here. But he's got to be moved, so let's wrap him in the tarp and take him farther away from the water. The tide is almost full, so it won't come up much more, but we might as well be cautious."

They carried him up the slope to a narrow sandy space between two ridges of rock and laid him down where no tide could, or would, disturb him, except possibly during a storm and none were predicted. Weighting down the edges of the tarp with stones so it could not blow off if a wind came up, they left him there.

It was a concerned, confused, and sober group that hiked back to the lighthouse to make the call, talking little, thinking much.

As, white-faced, Karen stumbled clumsily along ahead of her on the trail, Jessie couldn't help remembering how she had heard the sound of a distant engine and come wide awake in the night to find her missing from her bed.

CHAPTER NINETEEN

JIM BEAL PICKED UP HIS CELL PHONE FROM THE DESK IN the common room and took it outside the lighthouse, where he could get a better signal, to call the Petersburg police.

Jessie watched as Karen, still pale and silent, made an abrupt right turn and left the group as they came through the kitchen door. She disappeared into her bedroom, closing the door behind her. Her state of shock seemed to Jessie to be somewhat out of proportion to the situation, so after a few minutes' consultation with Laurie, who was also concerned, she went to see if she could find out what was going on.

She knocked softly on the door, but getting no response, opened it and went in anyway, closing it behind her.

Karen had curled herself into a fetal position on the bed and lay motionless, face to the wall.

"Karen?" Jessie said, walking across to sit down on the foot of the bed. "What's going on, Karen? Talk to me. Did you know the man?"

"Go away."

"I'm not going to do that. I'd like to help with—well—

whatever's upsetting you so badly. But I can't do that unless you talk to me about it."

Abruptly, Karen turned over and scooted up until she could lean against a pillow and the wall to glare balefully at Jessie.

"You *know* what it is," she said heatedly. "It's obvious that the son of a bitch has figured out where I am and is after me again. Now I have no place to go. I'm stuck here, on an island with no escape. Can't you see that? It's your fault."

Obvious? My fault? Jessie was speechless, astonished at the intensity of the statement and the animosity directed at *her. Isn't anything ever* her *fault?*

She stared at Karen for a few minutes in silence, an impression surfacing that had once or twice nibbled at her consciousness and either been ignored or dismissed. The woman had never laid out many details of *why* her stalker was so determined to catch up with her. Jessie had never seen him. Did he exist? Had Karen done something to justify his anger and resolve? *Nothing,* she claimed, was her fault. Karen simply, without saying so, refused responsibility by blaming everything on the man that she feared—and now she included Jessie. It couldn't have been completely one-sided. Relationships never were.

And because of my own past experience, I've been willing to believe exactly what she told me and be helpful, Jessie thought, frowning. *Well, what's sauce for the goose can be sauce for—for me too. Sometimes a slap in the face gets faster results than a sympathetic pat.*

Standing up, she leaned over Karen. She didn't slap her, but released some anger of her own in giving her shoulder a hard shake.

"Look," she snapped. "I've had just about all I'm going to take of your histrionic pity party and bad habit of shifting

responsibility to others. It's not my fault that you're here. You chose to come. At my suggestion? Yes. But you *chose*— waved us down from the beach after disappearing into the woodwork without so much as a word to let me know you were safe. To be honest, I had taken a deep breath of relief at being off the hook when you didn't show up at the dock. I—"

"So you don't want me here after all," Karen interrupted in a shrill voice. "You and your so-called *friends!*" She spit out the last word as sneering accusation. "I should have known better than to trust you. I know better than to trust anybody."

"Well, *that's* becoming perfectly clear," Jessie couldn't keep from hurling back.

"Oh-h, I hate—"

The door opened behind Jessie and Laurie stepped into the room.

"Sorry," she said. "Everyone in the common room can hear the two of you yelling. Can I help?"

Karen immediately turned over to once again face the wall in stubborn refusal. Jessie, uncomfortable with her own behavior, swung around to apologize, but Laurie held up a preventive hand. "No, it's all right. But there's something else."

She glanced at Karen, who was ignoring them both, then back to Jessie with eyebrows raised in question.

Jessie shrugged and shook her head, defeated for the moment.

"What else, Laurie?"

"You have a cell phone, don't you? Jim's isn't working and Aaron can't find his."

"Yes." She checked her jeans' pocket and then the day-pack she had been carrying. No phone. Then she remembered she had put the phone in her jacket pocket. After promising Alex to keep it with her, in her rush to leave for the other end of the island she had unintentionally left it behind. Grabbing up the jacket, she searched each and every pocket, with no results. The cell phone was gone. Without it she wouldn't be able to call Alex and he would think she was just having cell phone problems.

"I had it in this pocket," she said, showing Laurie. "It was in there when I left to walk with you."

Suspicion dawning, she swung around toward the bed and its stubbornly antisocial occupant, who had stayed behind.

"Karen, do you have my cell phone?" she demanded.

Silence.

"Karen!"

"Of course not," the woman retorted in a childish whine, without moving. "Why would I want your stupid phone?"

Without another word, the two women left Karen to her angry sulking, closing the door behind them.

In the common room the rest had gathered around the table where Jim's phone lay; he had taken it apart to see if he could find out why it didn't work.

"You can see that someone's messed with it and put it back together," he growled in disgust. "Unrepairable."

"So there's no way to contact anyone?" Whitney asked. "What about the lighthouse radio?"

"It no longer works ship to shore, just ship to ship," Jim explained. "With so many people using cell phones, they shut it down awhile back. Now it's for marine use only."

"But it works, right?"

"Yes—to a boat."

"Couldn't you call some boat that has a working cell phone and have them make the call?"

"Good idea," Jim told her. "Hadn't thought of that."

He got up from a chair at the table and crossed to the small radio room that opened off the common room, where the whole group had assembled with work the last thing on their minds. In less than a minute they could hear him swear as he came back to stand in the doorway.

"Not functional. It's been smashed with something heavy, and hard enough to trash it."

There was a moment of astonished silence. Then Don Sawyer ventured, "You mean someone broke it on purpose?" He hesitated, considering the ramifications. "Why would—? Who the hell would—? When? But we've been in and out of here all morning."

"It didn't have to *be* this morning," Laurie reminded him. "We mostly use the cell phone—so no one's had a reason to check the radio at all this trip. It could even have been done before we got here."

"So we have no way to contact the outside world at all?"

"That's about the size of it," Jim agreed. "Unless we find your cell phone, that is—or Jessie's."

"*Jim,*" Laurie reminded him. "There's a radio on the boat."

"That's *right.*" He smiled. "Problem solved. But first I want to see about our disappearing cell phones, if possible."

He turned to Jessie, with a nod toward the room where Karen had retreated. "You think she's got them? She was the only one in here after the other three of you left to go to the south end of the island. We were working on the new roof, Curt was in the basement, and Sandra was upstairs painting."

"I really don't know, Jim. It wouldn't surprise me, but, on the other hand, I think finding the dead man put her on the verge of panic. She's blaming everybody but herself for her situation. I've given up trying to second-guess her, but I have a lot of unanswered questions."

"What do you mean—'her situation'?" Curt, who had abandoned the generator and come upstairs to sit silently listening, asked suddenly.

"What happened to your eye?" Don asked, looking in his direction for the first time.

Everyone looked to see an angrily swollen mouse had partially closed Curt's right eye.

"Nothing major," he said, shaking his head in annoyance. "Clobbered myself when a wrench slipped and I didn't have sense enough to duck." With a lopsided, embarrassed grin he shifted the focus back to Karen. "You said 'situation.' Is there something we need to know about the woman?"

Jessie turned to Jim, in whom she had confided, asking the question with raised eyebrows.

"It's a long story of personal stuff, Curt," Jim told him. "Maybe later, okay? Let things ride for the time being about Karen's situation while I think about it. But I *do* think we should search her things for both Aaron's and Jessie's phones. This thing of mine's no good to us." He tossed it across to land on the desk with a thump.

There was a long silence as everyone considered the situation in which they found themselves. It was obvious that no one relished the idea of rummaging around in Karen's belongings.

"Okay," said Aaron, at last, standing up, "I'll help. But what are we going to do about—the dead man?"

"He's okay where he is for the time being," Don said. "We don't want to bring him back here—do we?"

"It seems kind of wrong to leave him clear down at the other end of the island somehow, doesn't it? We could put him in the carpenter shed," Aaron suggested. He glanced around the room and frowned uneasily. "I'm sorry, but what we're all thinking might as well be said. It looks like someone on this island hit him with something heavy—probably a rock. We don't know who that someone was, do we? But whoever it is might just go back and shove him on out into the sound—get rid of him."

There was a moment of awed, motionless silence as they all stared at him in astonishment.

Then Whitney, lips stiff with indignation, stepped forward and slapped a hand on the tabletop. "Hey now. What the hell makes you think one of *us* killed him? You've got no right to make that kind of assumption. It could just as well have been *you* as any of us. I won't be . . ."

"Whoa, Whitney," Jim broke in. "Aaron's not accusing you—or anyone else directly."

"The hell he's not!"

"No, he's not. Think about it. You may have slept soundly all night last night. But I'm sure some of us didn't. I woke up enough to hear one person moving and, later, the voices of at least two people outside during the night."

Jessie was tempted to tell him who those two had been, remembering finding Karen on the helipad and their conversation, but kept her own counsel and filed the information for later. Everyone in the room did not need to know everything. But it was interesting that someone besides Karen had also been up in the night—unless it was Karen going out that Jim had heard.

Jim continued. "We didn't all sleep close together, you know. Aaron was alone on the roof. Curt slept in the basement. I have no idea if any of the rest of us were up, but someone could have been. The toilet was flushed twice. Did you hear it?"

Whitney shrugged and shook her head.

"I thought not. And you were sleeping closest to the bathroom. So let's don't any of us get crazy about this, okay?

Let's do what we can and let law enforcement take care of investigating when they get here."

"I still think we should bring that guy back here to the carpenter shop," Aaron said.

"I think so too," Jim agreed. "We'll do it after we search Karen's stuff for the cell phones, or make a call from the boat if we have to. Come on, Aaron. Might as well get it over with. Laurie, will you and Jessie see if you can get Karen out of there? It would make it easier."

Much against Karen's wishes, they did—insisting that she come out on her own, or be carried out. It did not win them any confidence points with her, but she seemed to have managed to regain some self-control and dignity. She marched stoically out of the lighthouse and up onto the heli-pad, where she sat, as Jessie had found her the night before, facing west, with her legs hanging over the low rail, and refused to speak to anyone.

As soon as she had vacated the room, Jim and Aaron went in to make their search, while the rest waited in the common room. It was very quiet for a few minutes. Then Don stood up suddenly.

"Sandra must still be painting the roof. With those head-phones on, she won't have heard a thing, but she's been up there a long time and I'd better go bring her down."

He disappeared toward the stairs that went up from the second hallway and they heard his footsteps as he hurriedly climbed them.

Jim and Aaron came back shaking their heads at not having found either of the two missing cell phones among Karen's possessions. What they did find made Jim not only glad, but also relieved that he had insisted on making the search. He came out—Aaron trailing behind with a worried expression—and called Laurie and Jessie back into the common room from where they had been keeping busy in the kitchen. Lifting the bottom of the blue Five Finger Lighthouse sweatshirt he was wearing, he removed a pistol from the waistband of his jeans and laid it down on the table without a word.

"Da-amn!" said Curt, sitting up straight in his chair on the far side of the room. "That's an interesting item. But no cell phones?"

"What would she have that for?" Whitney asked, eyes wide.

Jim shook his head. "I don't know, but it's loaded. You have any idea, Jessie?"

"No. I didn't know she had it." Curious, but she found that Karen's having a gun came as no real surprise. Would anything Karen did astound her? She wondered apprehensively. *Shouldn't take people for granted,* she told herself, and thought about calling Alex for advice before remembering that she now had no way of calling him at all.

Taking the revolver from the table, she noticed there were only four rounds left in the cylinder, and a quick sniff rewarded her with the acrid smell of cordite. This gun had been fired recently.

The heavy silence from those watching lasted for a long moment that was broken by the sound of Don's steps on the stairs. He came frowning into the room as Jessie laid the gun down again without revealing what she had learned.

"Sandra's not up there," he told them. "Anybody know where she is?"

No one did.

"Where the hell'd that come from?" he demanded in concern, spotting the handgun on the table.

Jim told him.

"Damn!" he said, spinning toward the kitchen door, ob-

viously on his way to wring a few answers from Karen. "Well, I'm going to get some information."

Jim caught him by the arm and swung him back.

"Hey, Don. Wait a minute and think about it. This thing was in Karen's suitcase, not her hand. What could it have to do with Sandra? She probably finished on the roof and went off to the south end looking for the rest of us. We must have missed her on our way back."

"How *could* we have missed her?"

"Pretty easily if she climbed the hill to look at the eagle's nest, or went around the rocky east side. Nobody was saying much. We could have passed without her hearing. Let's go around in the boat—make that call to the authorities on the way—and look for her before you start on Karen. If we don't find her going over, we'll make a careful search on the way back. We'll find her. Okay? Where's she gonna go on three acres anyway?"

"Okay," Don agreed, after a moment's hesitation. "We can collect that poor guy from the south end—get that over with at the same time."

"Right."

Jim took the handgun and, as they passed through the kitchen, raised the lid of a small freezer next to a closet and dropped it in. Then they all went out and down the stairs to the lower platform. Several glanced in the direction of the helipad, where Karen still sat, mutely staring west into Frederick Sound, but she didn't even turn her head, ignoring them completely.

They walked across to the edge of the platform that overlooked the small cove protecting Jim's powerboat.

Where is *the boat?* Jessie wondered, looking down, for the sheltered space where she had last seen it tied up was empty.

Then Jim began to swear—long and concentrated curses that included words even the dog mushers she knew seldom incorporated into their vocabulary.

Peering carefully into the water, she was just able to make out the shape of the Seawolf—resting on the bottom of the small cove.

CHAPTER TWENTY

ALEX JENSEN WOKE EARLY ON WEDNESDAY MORNING AND rolled over sleepily in the big brass bed toward the east window that filled with sunshine—when there was sunshine. On this particular morning he could see that the light filtering in between the half-drawn curtains was pale gray, which, combined with the sound of water dripping from the roof outside, signaled a rainy day. He could also see that he was alone in the big brass bed high in the loft bedroom of Jessie Arnold's new log house on Knik Road and remembered that she had gone off to work on the lighthouse.

In no hurry to leave the just-right morning warmth of the bed, he rolled onto his back, laced his fingers behind his head, and stared upward at the sloped ceiling, considering what he should do with this day off from his job with the Alaska State Troopers. Billy Steward, who helped Jessie care for her dogs, would be along soon. They had planned to spend the morning cleaning boxes for the few dogs left in the kennel but, not being a job for wet weather, that would only happen if the rain stopped. There were several errands to run and a pile of wood that needed splitting and stacking for winter fires in the potbellied stove downstairs. Soon, however, his mind wandered off to other things, specifically how familiar, yet different, it seemed to be back in Alaska in this new house. This replacement for Jessie's cabin that had burned had been constructed in the old footprint—new and better, but a little strange in its dissimilarities, and he was still getting used to it.

His relationship with Jessie was different too. In the last month they had fallen quite easily into old, comfortable habits and patterns of living in the same space, sharing many activities, but leaving each other plenty of room when appropriate.

He smiled, recalling that Jessie's assessment of personal space was usually *We're not joined at the hip, after all.*

But there were tentative spaces in their togetherness that he noticed and that had nothing to do with habits or patterns, but rather with the trust that had been a bit bruised in their separation. She would call tonight, he remembered, and their conversation could add another block of confidence to their togetherness. At least it pleased him to think so.

Now, he decided, tossing back the covers and swinging his long legs out of bed, it was time to let the coffee mumble itself into the pot while he showered. Then he had some bacon and eggs planned for the empty spot under his ribs.

He kept himself busy all day. The rain stopped midmorning, Billy showed up, and they worked together in the dog yard until close to noon. In the afternoon, though he wasn't on duty, he stopped by his office to let his commander know how well the meeting in Whitehorse had gone and the cooperation they could expect from the RCMP. As he walked back to his pickup after their conversation, he thought how much it satisfied him to be back and working in

Alaska, even with winter about to show up on the doorstep. Coming back had allowed him to realize that he actually felt more at home in the Far North than he did in Idaho, where he had been born and raised. It was another thing that pleased him.

From there he made another stop at the grocery store for general supplies he had not wanted to take the time to purchase the night before on his way home. Wandering through the aisles, he collected a cart full of items just because they appealed to him: crackers, cheese, smoked oysters, some apple-flavored sausage that he liked for breakfast, a couple of cans of stew—which he returned to the shelf upon deciding he could make a better stew of his own and picking up the meat and vegetables to do so. In the bakery section, he tossed in a loaf of his favorite sourdough bread that he had not been able to find during his time in Idaho, then went to the deli for some chopped green and black olives to mix with cream cheese. He went happily up and down the aisles and had almost a full cart when he finally decided he was ready to go through checkout. Slipping into the liquor store on his way out, he renewed Jessie's flagging supply of Killian's lager before pushing the cart with his purchases to the truck, through the rain that had started again, and setting out for home.

Home. The sound of the word—the very taste of it— pleased him as well.

Back at home, he brought Tank into the house for company while he browned the beef and chopped vegetables for his stew, then set it to simmering on the back of the stove, planning a late dinner complete with the sourdough bread he would heat in the oven. He turned on the six o'clock news and settled with a cold Killian's to watch it. Tank padded across to lie down with his muzzle companionably on one of Alex's stockinged feet, closed his eyes in contentment when the man rubbed his ears, then raised his head so he could have his chin scratched as well.

"You *are* spoiled," Alex told him. "You should be out breaking trail somewhere, not lying around here. But you can stay in until Jessie calls. Okay?"

By nine, when he had eaten dinner, cleaned up the kitchen, and watched a movie on HBO that he had seen before, she still hadn't called.

Flipping through the channels, he found nothing that caught his interest, so he turned on some music instead and found a book he hadn't read. By the end of the second chapter he realized that he had no idea which name belonged to which character, threw the book aside, turned off the music, and went to stand at the front window and stare out into the darkness that surrounded the house. A car went by on Knik Road, its headlights illuminating the pavement and making silhouettes of the trees at the end of the driveway.

She isn't going to call tonight, he thought suddenly.

Perhaps he should follow that car down the road to Oscar's Other Place, a hangout for local residents, many of them mushers. *I could have a brew or two and scare up a game of pool.*

But the idea didn't appeal enough to make the effort.

"Damn! Why doesn't she call?"

Tank raised his head to give Alex an inquiring look.

"No, not you."

Irritated with himself *and* a little with Jessie, he made up his mind, crossed the room, and dialed the number of her cell phone. It did little for his frustration level when an automated voice informed him that the party he was attempting to reach was unavailable—but he could leave a message.

"Leave a message!" he grumbled, putting the phone down more forcefully than necessary. "I don't *think* so!"

Tank jumped, startled by the sound, sat up and gave him another questioning look.

Then, suddenly, the humor of his behavior occurred to him and he found himself chuckling ruefully. *You're acting like an adolescent schoolboy,* he told himself.

There could be any number of reasons Jessie hadn't—or couldn't have—called him. She had said the signal was iffy inside the lighthouse. Maybe it was raining in Frederick Sound, as it was here. If it was, who would want to stand around outside to talk on the phone? She couldn't know— and wouldn't, if he could help it—that he was being entirely unreasonable about a phone call.

"And you," he told Tank, "are to keep your mouth shut about my fit of juvenile nonsense. Right?"

Turning the television back on, he found that *Comes a Horseman,* a movie with Jane Fonda, James Caan, and Richard Farnsworth—an actor he particularly liked—was just starting. Making himself a cup of tea and retrieving a package of Double Stuf Oreos—an item obtained in the afternoon shopping expedition—he settled to enjoy all three.

When the movie was over at eleven o'clock, he took Tank back to the dog yard, went upstairs to bed and quickly to sleep.

"What the hell *is* happening here?" Don Sawyer asked, when Jim had stopped swearing and climbed down over the rocks to the level of the cove, where he sat, furious and silent, staring into the water at his sunken boat.

For a long minute no one answered. They all stood looking down in astonishment and a sense of reality suspended.

Aaron sat down on the edge of the concrete platform with

his legs dangling into space over the cove and shook his head, but said nothing.

"Why did it sink?" Whitney asked finally. "Did something get left open that should have been closed?"

Jim looked up from where he was squatting on the rocks to peer into the water. "A sea cock, you mean," he said. "I don't see any structural damage from here, so that's what it looks like. I checked everything before we left Juneau, so someone was on the boat after we left it and opened one or more on purpose—meaning this was no accident. Someone wanted it to go down and took measures to ensure that it happened, damn him—or *her*." He glared up toward the helipad next to the lighthouse above them, where they had left Karen stubbornly sitting.

"But why? And when?"

Jessie was asking herself the same question. At between ten and twenty feet below the concrete platform the boat, nestled into the small cove, would have been out of sight from the lighthouse unless you went right to the edge and looked down.

"I would guess it was done sometime in the night," she said thoughtfully. "During the day there would be the risk of being seen coming or going down there. Anybody got any other ideas about when or, particularly, *why?*"

There was another long minute of silence as they took that in.

"To me, the only thing that makes any sense of this, *and* the cell phones, is to make sure we can't leave the island—or get in touch with anyone who could take us off," Jessie continued. "I have no idea why—or who—but I'd be willing to bet that, whatever the reason, it's not pleasant, and that it may be somehow connected to the dead man we found this morning."

What she didn't say, though it crossed her mind, was that

if there was one dead person there just might be two. And a sunken boat would be a very handy place to hide another body, namely Sandra's.

"Whatever caused all this," she continued, ignoring the shocked and puzzled looks on the faces around her, as the others absorbed her ideas, "I think it's definitely time to make a thorough search for Sandra and call her name often and loudly. She could have fallen somewhere and hurt herself, you know, so we need to *look* everywhere, not just call out."

Jim stood up and began to climb back to the platform, casting a last disgusted glance at his submerged boat.

"There could be some connection, I guess, Jessie. But you are right that Sandra might be hurt somewhere we haven't looked. The one thing we can do is make a serious effort to find her. There's not much we can do about the Seawolf. It's not going anywhere.

"Let's split up into two groups. Jessie, you, Whitney, and Don take the east shore this time and look in every tide pool and between all the big rocks out there. Aaron and Curt can come with me through the woods and look in the brush on both sides of the trail. Laurie, why don't you stay and keep an eye on Karen, but search the lighthouse again thoroughly—every cupboard and hidey-hole in the basement too. And there's the sheds and boathouse."

"Sure," Laurie agreed. "I can do that. The lighthouse first, then the outbuildings, and, when I'm through with those, I'll look through the brush under the helipad and over the rocks beyond it, okay?"

"That's a lot for one person to do," Curt suggested. "Especially the north end rocks and brush that'll take some climbing around to do well. How about if I search the lighthouse and Laurie does the helipad and the north end? If Sandra shows up on her own she'll wonder where everyone's gone. So it might be good to have one of us here, yes?"

Jim nodded. "Good idea. Thanks. Whitney, you come with Aaron and me. It's going to be more time-consuming to search the woods. Jessie and Don can take the rocks and pools. If she's out there, we'll find her, Don."

"And if she's not?" Don asked in a tense voice that held a deep note of apprehension.

"She has to be." Whitney attempted to reassure him.

The silence of the group implied that they had their doubts. Jim took a deep breath and broke it with an honest assessment.

"Then at least we'll know it, Don. But she *could* have fallen somewhere and be lying unconscious, you know. Let's do this and do it right before we get ahead of ourselves. If any of you find her, yell, so the rest of us know it, okay?"

Don nodded glumly and glanced at Jessie as he turned toward the rocky east shore.

"Wait a second," she told him and trotted up the stairs, through the kitchen and into the bedroom, where she collected her jacket and the daypack that held her camera gear and a first aid kit, just in case.

When she went back through the kitchen to join Don, Curt was already at work, opening storage cupboards in the hallway.

"Good hunting," he told her, and she nodded as she passed.

"You, too," she called back, hurrying to where Don fidgeted, waiting anxiously to get started. Remembering the condition of the handgun, it crossed her mind that if they found Sandra they might not find her alive.

* * *

"I guess we leave the dead man where he is?" Aaron asked, as he and Jim started up the stairs to the wooded area for their part of the search.

Jim nodded. "For the time being at least. He's not going anywhere any more than the Seawolf and he's okay where he is for now."

CHAPTER TWENTY-ONE

IT WAS A SILENT AND CONCERNED GROUP THAT RETURNED to the lighthouse early that afternoon. Tired and dirty from climbing through overgrown brush and fallen logs, possessed of a few scrapes and bruises from clambering over slippery rocks, wet from splashing into tide pools, they had all trooped up the stairs and into the common room where, except for Don, they collapsed dejectedly into chairs, confused and dispirited at their lack of success. Don paced the floor, unable to sit still, but just as unable to think of anywhere else to look for the missing Sandra. Without a word they had passed Karen, still sitting on the helipad, but some resentful looks were cast in her direction as they went in the door.

Almost everyone was hungry, so Laurie and Aaron organized the ingredients for sandwiches and heated some canned soup, while Jessie set the table and took orders for drinks.

"Beer," Jim growled, twisting his mustache in a parody of some pirate captain. "Grog for me men, wench," he demanded, in an attempt to lighten the somber mood around the table. But it fell flat and he gave up and slumped back into his chair.

"Jessie," he said to her as she handed him a bottle of the Killian's she had brought along, "while we eat I think you should share with the group what you told me last night about Karen."

"Yes," Don agreed, turning suddenly to take a chair at the table. "We haven't asked her if she knows anything about Sandra and she was here for a while after you left to go to the south end this morning—before you found that guy. I'd be willing to bet she's got something to do with Sandra being missing, dammit."

Jessie nodded. "Sure. I can tell you. But I really doubt that Karen's in any way responsible for Sandra's disappearance. What possible reason would she have? You can't jump to conclusions without proof, Don. She's upset with all of us right now, you know? And she may not have done anything but let her panic get away with her."

"And I'll believe that when I have proof of it," he stated grudgingly.

It could be true, she thought, but wasn't at all sure about any of it.

Neither were the others, when she finished telling them about her meeting with Karen in Petersburg, the stalker the woman claimed was after her, and everything else that had taken place since. They said little, but it was clear they held little trust or sympathy for Karen as a result of her behavior.

Don insisted on going back out to renew the search.

"There may be somewhere we missed," he argued stubbornly. "I'll just go and have another look around by myself."

With nothing else to do that afternoon and no way to solve their communication and transportation problems, the rest went back to work, keeping an eye out for any vessel that passed close enough to signal, but none did. Aaron and

Curt, who volunteered to leave his precious generator for the time being, climbed back up to finish stripping the old roofing material off the boathouse. Jessie, Whitney, and Laurie attacked more of the old paint Don had been scraping from the window frames.

Jim focused on trying to think of a way to raise the Seawolf from its watery bed in the cove, using a crane on the edge of the platform with which they had retrieved the new roofing materials. It soon proved unworkable, so he moved on to other ideas, all of which came to nothing at the end of the day.

"The blasted thing is down there for good. Well—at least for the time being, I guess," Jim said in frustration and regret, giving up at last. "I'll have to get someone with a barge and a lot more power out here from Petersburg. And the Seawolf's practically a brand-new boat, confound it all. I can just imagine the damage seawater's doing to those engines."

Sometime during the afternoon, with their attention elsewhere, Karen slipped back into the bedroom where she closed the door and once again curled up on the bed facing the wall. She had not touched the sandwich Jessie had taken out to her, nor would she talk to anyone, but she took a bottle of water with her from the refrigerator.

They left her alone.

They did not bring the body of the dead man back from the other end of the island, though Don checked on it in the course of his search, made sure it was safe, and came back as it was growing dark, looking even more glum and distracted. There were speculations of various kinds among the members of the group about Sandra's disappearance, but with little to go on nothing led to answers or solutions, just to more questions.

"I simply don't understand how she could just be gone,"

Laurie said quietly to Jessie, as they prepared dinner for the rest of the group. "Without a boat, there's no way she could have left the island."

"Unless someone took her, or unless . . ." Jessie began, and swallowed the rest of that thought. "I can't help thinking of that guy we found. Someone was responsible, Laurie."

"That crossed my mind too. But why Sandra, and how . . . ?"

"And more important, who?"

They let it go for the moment.

"There's leftover salad from last night downstairs. Would you bring it up, Jessie?"

"Shall I bring some more lettuce and stuff to add to it?"

"Not if you think there's enough. Nobody's very hungry. There're a couple of kinds of dressing down there too. Be careful on the stairs. It'll be dark down there, but there's a light switch outside the storeroom."

Finding light switches for the stairs and the basement workspace at the bottom of the stairway, Jessie stopped and took a long look around the large room. Besides Curt's favorite generator, it was full of a collection of tanks, pumps, gears, and dials—large machines that in the past had kept electricity, heat, and water running in the lighthouse—many of which were now obsolete. There were tools of all kinds and storage materials necessary to the renovation. On the south side stood a washer and dryer, and an assortment of odds and ends, from paint buckets to sawhorses. Curt's sleeping bag was rolled up in one corner on a narrow mattress, pillow on top, reminding her of how dedicated he was to getting that generator into tip-top condition. With a smile, she remembered Alex's approval of an engineer on another boat trip through this same area. He had called the man one of the true "sons of Martha," and quoted parts of a Kipling poem of that name about men who work with machines:

> . . . *it is their care that the gear engages; it is their care that the switches lock . . . it is their care that the wheels run truly . . .*

Curt, with his mechanical focus, was certainly another of Martha's sons.

Turning, she made her way into the back of the basement and found the light switch Laurie had mentioned. The cement foundation of the lighthouse had been solidly built onto the living rock of the island. That base of stone could be seen sloping upward toward the west at a steep angle, and to the right in front of it was a narrow storeroom that Laurie and Jim had claimed as a cooler for drinks, vegetables, eggs, cheese, cured meats, anything that would keep without freezing. Halfway along it, next to a set of shelves, lay a large cardboard box of lettuce, carrots, onions, celery, and other vegetables. Half crooked, as if it had been dropped on top of it, was the large plastic bowl half full of salad from the night before and covered with plastic wrap.

As Jessie stepped forward to retrieve it, something crunched grittily between her shoe and the concrete. Stepping back, she glanced down at a small spot of white just larger than a quarter on the floor. Spilled sugar, she thought, or salt. But both of those, she knew, were kept in tins upstairs in the kitchen, where they would stay dry. What was this then? Curious, as always, she bent, moistened an index finger with her tongue, reached down to touch the white spot, and examined the powdery crystalline stuff that clung to her fingertip. Baking powder? she wondered, or, perhaps, soda?

The basement floor was an odd place for either of those as well. As she lifted the finger to her mouth and tentatively tasted, the idea of rat poison entered her mind—too late.

Alex would definitely not have approved the action. But immediately she remembered his description of the taste of cocaine: medicinally bitter, with a numbing, tingling sensation on the tongue. Could it be anything else? That was possible but, she thought, unlikely. Would Jim and Laurie keep cocaine in the basement cooler of their lighthouse? If so, where was the rest of it? The idea stopped her cold. After all, how well did she know them from one trip together down the Inside Passage? They were theatrical types, but typecasting theater people as drug users was as absurd as stereotyping all churchgoers as chicken-on-Sunday folks. Besides, they weren't the only people who might have brought an illegal substance with them to the island. There were five others—counting Sandra, but not counting herself—who could be responsible, and Jim and Laurie could be completely unaware. Thinking back, she couldn't recall anyone exhibiting signs of drug use, though Curt was the one who spent the most time in this lower part of the building—another assumption she was unwilling to make.

Giving herself a mental shake, she remembered that Laurie would be wondering what was taking her so long in the collection of one bowl of salad. A glance at it told her there was plenty left for tonight's dinner, so she took it, picked up a large bottle of dressing, pulled the box forward enough to cover the substance on the floor, turned out the light, and went back upstairs, thinking hard as she did so.

Could this have anything to do with Sandra's disappearance? That was probably a stretch, but she couldn't help equating the two things in her mind, probably, she thought, because they happened in close proximity. Still, given the circumstances, asking Jim wouldn't be a bad idea, though she thought it could wait till a more opportune time than around the dinner table.

There was a little more discouraged discussion, but no new ideas, over the meal that no one really enjoyed. Don merely shoved food around on his plate, but drank two glasses of wine.

"Look," Jim said, when they had finished and it had grown dark enough for the light in the tower to automatically begin its nightly revolutions. "I can't think of anything else we can do tonight. So let's get some sleep and we'll work out something in the morning. Tomorrow some boat will pass that we can flag down from the tower."

They agreed, and Whitney went to take care of cleaning up the kitchen, leaving the rest still sitting disconsolately around the table as if feeling more secure as a group. Laurie had made Don a cup of tea and Aaron was listening closely as Curt explained details from the preservation handbook on how to restore some part of the lighthouse.

Encouraged by a tilt of Jessie's head toward the door, Jim nodded and joined her outside. Starting automatically for the helipad steps, he turned and followed her down the stairs to the lower platform and into the basement cooler room when she beckoned.

"What? Something about Sandra?"

"No—well, I don't think so, just something I found that I think you should see."

Moving the box she had used to cover the white substance on the cement floor, she pointed it out to him.

"Do you know what this is?"

"Probably flour somebody spilled. Why?"

"Take just enough to taste it, Jim."

He did, and his questioning expression quickly shifted to a deep frown of concern and anger.

"Is it what I think it is?" Jessie asked.

"Cocaine?"

"I think so too. Yours? Tell me the truth, Jim. I need to know."

"Not a chance! Neither Laurie nor I would have anything to do with the stuff," he assured her and went on indignantly. "And somebody brought this shit onto *our* island?"

It was hard not to believe him.

"Remember when Sandra wanted to tell you something last night? We were talking about Karen and she came up from the basement with that bottle of wine you asked for."

"I had forgotten all about it. I never got back to her."

"Could this be part of that?"

"I don't know, but it's possible, I suppose. But Sandra's not the type to be mixed up with drugs. I am sure of that."

"Any idea who could be?"

"Not a clue, but I don't like it one bit. They're all still up there. Shall we go ask?"

Jessie shook her head reluctantly, frowning.

"I don't think so. We might not get anywhere by asking, when they can just deny it. Everyone is worn out tonight, so let's not toss another piece of trouble at them. Let's think it over, get some rest ourselves, and see what we can find out tomorrow. We might learn more if we just wait and watch."

Unhappily, Jim agreed, but said he intended to tell Laurie in confidence. They went back upstairs, after tossing the paper towel that they used to wipe up what was left of the drug from the floor into the trash.

Not long afterward they all went to bed, worn out with the day's extraordinary events. Curt and Aaron disappeared first to their singular sleeping spaces, with Jim and Laurie following soon after.

Jessie yawned and turned to Whitney. "I'm inclined to move out here tonight and leave Karen the bedroom. You?"

"Good idea. I'll get my things out of there."

"Take our room, why don't you?" Don suggested. "I'd rather stay out here, if you don't mind."

Making sure he meant it, Jessie and Whitney collected their things and appropriated Don and Sandra's room, as suggested. Karen was either already asleep, or wanted them to think so, for she didn't move while they were there. Jessie left the doors to their new room and to Karen's open a crack, hoping to hear if she once again went out in the night.

Everything was dark and quiet when she realized that she had not called Alex as promised. But without her cell phone there was nothing to be done about it. She could only hope that he would remember what she had said about connection problems and that she had always been capable of taking care of herself. Still, she would have liked to talk to him.

She heard Don quietly moving in the common room; then the kitchen door was opened and closed as he went outside. She hoped he wasn't going out hunting again in the dark.

It bothered her that she didn't know what was going on. You could deal with what you knew and understood. The unknown left you off balance and, possibly, unable to defend yourself. There *was* a dead man, after all, and someone had killed him. Who—and why? And where in the world was Sandra? Not knowing made her absence even more worrisome.

An odd sound brought her suddenly out of the half-doze

she had been drifting into. Listening carefully, she had to smile when she identified it as coming from the bed next to her. Her last thought before falling asleep was to wonder if Whitney knew that she snored.

CHAPTER TWENTY-TWO

BETWEEN THE LIGHTHOUSE AND THE WOODS THAT TOOK up the southern two-thirds of Five Finger Island, at the edge of the hill that fell away to the concrete platform below, Joe Cooper had stayed quietly hidden in the tall grass and watched the lights go out inside the east-facing windows. Another light had glowed briefly in one of the rear windows, but that too had been quickly extinguished and all had grown dark and still.

Earlier, a younger man had come out onto the lighthouse roof below the tower for a few minutes, but he hadn't stayed long. Before the light in the basement section was turned off, an older man had walked out to the edge of the platform and stood for a minute or two looking into the small cove where the boat lay sunk beneath the water. Going back, he closed the two large doors and that light momentarily went off as well.

When all was dark and quiet, Cooper rose from where he had spent the last hour and a half, stretched to rid himself of the slight stiffness that had resulted from lying on damp ground, and made his way not toward the trail through the trees, but around to the rocky eastern shore, taking care not to betray his presence by too much rustling of the dry fall grasses through which he passed.

Though he had not seen the woman, he was satisfied that she was there, knowing that he had time to decide when to do something about it. With their boat beyond use, with the exception of something totally unexpected and unlucky, none of them were going anywhere.

For a time he stopped and stood beside a tree above the first of the rocks, looking east across the water at the pale white of the snow that topped the peaks above the dark wooded slopes below, reluctant for some reason he couldn't name to go back to where he had tethered and left Tim's boat to rock gently in the sea.

Bitter regret swept over him again about Tim. It had been a shock to return from a reconnaissance the night before and find him, not comfortably asleep in his bunk as expected, but outside on the rocks, with the back of his skull crushed. In examining the body with a light obtained from the boat, he had realized his error in the selection of jackets, for Tim's blood had been spilled, not on his own tan coat, but across Cooper's gray one. So it was possible that, having mistaken one for the other, the killer either believed Cooper dead, or had recognized her blunder and would still be hunting him. *Her!* It had to have been her. Who of the rest knew him or would have wanted him dead? None.

Furious, he had returned to the lighthouse end of the island where, without hesitation, though he heard distant voices from the helipad, he had quietly ventured out onto the platform, down onto the rocks that formed the cove, and, with a little mechanical tinkering, made sure the Seawolf would remain where it was, impossible to start, and that the radio was inoperable as well. Until he had satisfaction, none of them would leave the island or call for assistance.

On this second night, he had been astonished to see that the boat was no longer there and assumed for a few minutes that it had been fixed and someone had taken it away from the island. Then he had seen that it now rested on the bottom of the cove. Nothing he had done would have caused it to sink, but clearly someone had found a more effective way to render it unusable, which suited his purpose as well. Still it seemed wasteful to spoil such a fine craft that was, from what he had seen, practically brand-new. He had thought about it as he went back through the sheltering of the trees, questioning the necessity of the submersion and who had accomplished it.

Reaching Tim's boat, he wondered if he should motor out across the sound to the mainland, as he had the night before, to spend the rest of the night anchored up there, staring back across the wide stretch of waters between him and his objective. Instead he decided to stay where he had anchored the boat, on the east, least likely to be seen, side of the island. If she had been out and prowling last night, she might be again in this one. He could keep watch and hope, letting anger and resentment work at him until morning, for he was determined that this time she would not escape him.

They had once been three. Now because of her there were only two. Soon, however, he intended that there would be only one left in the game.

CHAPTER TWENTY-THREE

IT HAD BEEN A LONG AND STRESSFUL DAY, AND JESSIE, physically and mentally tired, slept more soundly than she intended once she had fretted herself to sleep with the unanswered questions that kept running through her mind. More than half asleep and groggy, she had no idea what had roused her sometime very late in the dark of what had been Don and Sandra's small bedroom. She lay facedown, eyes shut, listening without moving in the snug warmth of her sleeping bag.

She remembered that as she had drifted off she had heard Don quietly leave the common room, where he had evidently been unable to sleep, and go outside, closing the kitchen door behind him. Poor Don. It was evident that he sincerely cared for Sandra and she for him. They made a nice couple. It had to be terribly frustrating for him to find himself more or less at a dead end in terms of finding Sandra or learning what had happened to her, particularly with no way to contact anyone who could help mount a more extended search. Hearing him go out she had been tempted to go join him so he wouldn't be alone with his dark worries and speculations, but sleep had swallowed her while she was still wondering if he would welcome company, or not.

She had a feeling that she had almost subconsciously heard other stirrings during that period of sleep, but couldn't remember for sure and had no idea who or what had made them—Don, Karen, someone else?

She was considering going to see if Karen was still in her bed when, awake and listening in the dark, she heard someone bump a chair that moved with a small screech on the tile floor of the common room.

Probably Don coming back inside, she told herself, wondering what time it was. She could understand why he couldn't sleep for worrying. Sandra's absence disturbed her too. The most reasonable and discouraging answer was that she had somehow fallen into the sea and drowned, only to be swept away in the tide as it moved through the sound. The sinking of the Seawolf made it impossible to search the waters around the island.

Jessie thought again of the cocaine on the floor of the cooler. Happening within hours, it seemed that somehow it must all be connected—but how? With the Seawolf in her moorage, out of sight below the platform, there was no way of knowing when she had been sunk—or who had sunk her, for that matter—if it had not happened by accident somehow, which was a slim possibility. But a purposeful sinking must have been done by some member of the work crew. No, she decided, that wasn't the only possibility. Tim, the dead man at the other end of the island, could have accomplished it before being killed, whenever that had been, the night before. But why would he or any other person have sabotaged Jim's boat? There had to be a reason someone, part of the crew or not, wanted them to be stuck on the island without communication or possibility of escape. Why? And who . . .

There was suddenly another screech of the chair moving, then a muffled human sound from the common room—the sort of *hm-m* that is made with lips closed.

Hit his toe on it, Jessie thought.

Whitney sighed and turned over in her sleep, obscuring another small sound of motion in the common room.

Jessie rolled over and sat up in bed, listening intently. Something was going on out there with someone besides Don, for she could now hear the murmur of voices.

Well . . . as long as I'm awake anyway, she told herself, unzipped her sleeping bag, and swung her legs over the side of the bed onto the cool floor.

Quietly barefoot, she padded to the door and peered through the crack she had left open into the hallway. It was very dark, but as the beacon swept around in the tower overhead it cast enough vague secondary light through a rectangular kitchen window to make silhouettes of two figures coming toward her. She stood still and watched as the nearest figure opened the door to the stairway that led to the basement and disappeared through it, followed by the second person, and the door closed behind them. She thought the first had been Don, but the open door had concealed, and kept her from identifying, the second. Maybe it had been Curt, she decided. Hearing Don moving overhead, he must have invited him down to the basement to talk where their voices wouldn't wake those sleeping upstairs. If so, it was thoughtful of him to keep the bartender company. Nice guy, Curt, if a bit quiet and watchful.

Without further thought Jessie opened the door, slipped across to the door to Karen's room, and opened it as well.

Dummy! she told herself, realizing that without her flashlight she couldn't see if Karen was still there or not. Careful not to stub her own toes on the bed legs or Karen's suitcase, she crossed the room and stood still and silent, holding her breath to listen for that of the supposedly sleeping woman. Not a sound. With care, she laid a hand very lightly on the woman's bed and found nothing but a jumble of blanket and sheet. The bed was empty. Karen had clearly once again abandoned sleep to roam the night.

Hurrying back to her room, Jessie yanked on her jeans, crammed her feet into socks and running shoes, grabbed her jacket, a flashlight, and her daypack before starting out the door.

"Hey," Whitney said in a half-awake voice from her bed across the room. "Where ya goin'?"

"To see where Karen's gone," Jessie told her. "Go back to sleep. I'll be back shortly."

"N-kay," muttered Whitney, and Jessie heard her turn over and snuggle down again. "Have a good time."

A good time? Jessie questioned that as she closed the door behind her and headed down the hall to the kitchen door, willing to bet she wouldn't find Karen on the helipad this time, or inclined to make time pleasant. Leaving the flashlight off so as not to spoil her night vision, relying on the limited amount of ambient light from the tower, she stepped outside and closed the door behind her, heading for the helipad. Might as well start there.

As expected, it was empty. So where the hell had the woman gone this time? Remembering her reaction to the dead man, she doubted that Karen would go anywhere near him and would instead probably stay somewhere on this north end. Maybe she had gone downstairs to be with Curt and Don, who were obviously awake. It was worth a look.

Heading for the stairway that led to the lower platform, she heard a voice and stopped halfway down to listen, but heard only silence for a moment or two.

There was a sudden, half-familiar-sounding clank, as if

someone had set down something quite heavy, a metal tool or piece of equipment, and the voice continued, moving away from her now.

Once again she started quietly down the stairs, listening as she went, her running shoes making almost no sound on the cement steps.

Whoever was speaking turned and came toward her like a walking shadow in the dark and she realized that it was Curt's voice she was hearing. As if he were holding a low-toned conversation with someone, there were pauses between his sentences. But she could not determine what he was saying, and even listening intently she could not hear a response in those pauses. Maybe Don was answering from inside the basement, out of audible range. But who was Curt talking to?

As he approached some of his words became audible.

". . . told you. Yesterday morning . . . take care of . . . the tank."

As he neared the stairs Jessie caught a whole sentence or two.

"Yes—all four of them—the two couples. I'm going back for the others now."

What the hell was he talking about?

As he came closer, Jessie, astonished and confused by what she had heard, knew there was no time to figure it out, or to go back up the stairs without revealing her presence. She flattened herself into the deep shadow of the wall and stood still, scarcely breathing, expecting him to round the corner and confront her at any second. But he unexpectedly turned back and walked away again, his conversation fading into indistinct mutters with a few discernable words.

". . . the musher woman, and . . . Yeah . . . her too . . ."

Holding her position like a statue against the wall she immediately realized two disturbing things from what she had just heard. He was talking to someone *on a cell phone,* and *she* had to be the "musher woman" to whom he had referred.

Turning, she went swiftly and silently, two at a time, back up the stairs, started to go into the lighthouse, but hesitated, then altered that intention. His words lingered unpleasantly in her memory, calling to mind a dead man on the other end of the island that someone had "taken care of." Maybe it hadn't been Karen, as she had suspected. And where was the once again missing Karen? Had Curt "taken care of" her too? Who else? He had mentioned two couples. That had to be Don and Sandra, Laurie and Jim—the only couples in the group. What had he done with them?

It all spun confusingly in her mind. But one thing she did know for certain. Avoiding him was the most important thing she could do at the moment.

The lighthouse was a box of walls within which she did not want to be trapped. If he came up the outside stairs behind her he would block the kitchen door, leaving only the interior stair to the basement for escape. If he elected to use the interior stair from the basement to the hallway, she might be able to get out the kitchen door, but only if she were not in the bedroom beyond it where Whitney was sleeping, totally unprepared for confrontation and needing to be warned. Could she get in and out fast enough to wake and alert her? It was probably not worth trying, knowing she would wake groggily and want some kind of explanation that would take too much precious time given the situation.

And there was Aaron, who must be asleep and unknowing. There was no chance she was going up that narrow winding stairway in the tower—an absolute trap with no possible exit.

One thing she could do. Stepping quickly into the

kitchen, listening closely for any sound that would warn her of anyone's approach, she opened the freezer and felt around for the handgun Jim had found in Karen's suitcase. Hard, cold packages of meat and vegetables were all that met her searching fingers. The handgun was gone.

The scuff and sound of feet coming up the interior staircase decided her next move. Closing the freezer lid quietly, she slipped back out into the dark through the kitchen door she had left open, taking care to shut it as soundlessly as possible behind her.

Outside it was, as before, somewhat lighter, but not by much.

If he was coming up the interior stairs, she could use the outside ones. Quickly, quietly, she went down them to the concrete platform and across it past the basement doors, one of them half open to darkness inside. Between the lighthouse and the carpenter shop, in the dim reflection of starlight on water and from the overhead beacon she could make out the end of the wooden steps that led up to the trail through the woods.

Glad she had been able to escape, but concerned about the people she had left behind, she went quickly to the steps and quietly up them to the trail. Hurrying along it in the dark, she stumbled twice over the uneven ground—once falling to her knees. In the shelter of the trees, it was so black she couldn't even make out the trail. Not knowing if she was far enough away from the lighthouse to be out of sight, she risked taking out the small flashlight and directed its beam at the ground, filtering it through her fingers. Speed at this point might be more important than secrecy, and there was a fifty-fifty chance she wouldn't be the object of a singular search. She went hurriedly on, looking for some way off the path, somewhere to hide and watch.

As she trotted south she remembered another fearful time in the dark woods of an island. Then it had been an island in Kachemak Bay, where she had been trapped with a stalker and an old man who had drowned while trying to escape by boat in the violence of an October storm. She recalled the sickening terror of being hunted like an animal and knowing that she might not make it through the ordeal. But she had, thanks to her own determination and abilities, and Alex and his pilot friend, Caswell. This was different. Alex wasn't likely to show up here. He was not on the trail of a stalker as he had been back then, but at home thinking she was fine and just having the cell phone problems she had warned him were possible reasons why he might not hear from her and couldn't reach her.

And Curt evidently had her cell phone, or one of his own, and was using it. Anger burned in her, as she wondered exactly what he had meant about "taking care" of people.

About a third of the way along the trail she stopped, turned out the light and stood looking back toward the lighthouse, listening intently, hoping to hear or see if anyone was following. She saw nothing but the inky blackness, and there was nothing to hear but the waves of the outgoing tide lapping gently against unseen rocks to the east, the soft rustle of a breeze through the brush around her, and its whisper in the trees overhead. As far as she could tell, no one had seen her go or followed her.

Satisfied, she took a deep breath, turned the flashlight back on, and almost cried out in shock at the face that appeared in its light directly in front of her, waiting with a leer of anticipation for her to discover it. Staggering back, she almost dropped the light in the trail, but recovered and held onto it, focusing its beam on the face she had seen.

The face did not move or change expression and she realized in seconds that the object that had startled her was inanimate—the mask on the tree that Whitney had pointed out the previous morning. It was now no matter for light amusement.

As she stood staring at it, heart thumping, she gasped again and whirled at a rustle in the brush beside her as some small animal scurried away in the dark, probably as startled as she was.

Turning, she started on along the trail, shivering as the surge of adrenaline left her system. Beneath her jacket she wore only the large T-shirt she had slept in, and now she wished it were a sweater. It was cold and damp as well as dark and the trail seemed more uneven in the night.

Passing the hole that fell deeply away at one side of the track, she stepped carefully around it and continued until the trail turned right on its way up to the rocky point where they had watched the eagle fishing. Just past the turn she sat down on the huge twisted trunk of a fallen tree, switched off the light, and allowed herself time to rest and think. There was a corpse under a tarp not far away and she had no intention of joining his chill indifference to the night if she could help it.

There were stars twinkling through the branches of the trees, but they wouldn't last long. It would be morning, with its revealing light, in—how many hours? She assumed it must be two or three o'clock, but had left her watch back in the bedroom with the rest of her things. Was there anywhere on the island she could hide well enough to avoid being found when it grew light?

Five Finger was a very small island. Curt knew how many people were in the work crew and would know that one member of the group was missing, and who. As soon as the sun came up, if not sooner, he would likely be after her, searching the three acres carefully from end to end. So it would be wise to proceed with that in mind, wouldn't it?

Where was the rest of the crew? Had he taken them all to the basement—killed them? Why? Did it have anything to do with the cocaine she and Jim had examined on the cooler room floor? Then there was that person he was talking to on the cell phone. Who was it? Could Karen's disappearance mean she was involved, or had he "taken care of" her with the rest? If not, where was she?

Had anyone else escaped? Aaron? If they weren't dead, could she be of any help to the ones that had not? All she had were questions—too many questions and very few answers. How could she find out what was going on and who was responsible without revealing herself as most likely the only wild card in the deck?

CHAPTER TWENTY-FOUR

IT SEEMED VERY STILL AS JESSIE SAT ON THE LOG AND WON-
dered what to do next, but not being able to see in the dark
seemed to sharpen her sense of hearing. She became aware
of the light breeze sighing softly through the trees behind
her. It set the grasses whispering together between her and
the rocks where the fossils lay and those that Karen had
climbed to see the sea lion and found a dead man instead.
She could also hear the receding tide as it washed at the island's pebbly shingle and remembered how that morning it
had tirelessly swept away blood that stained the water with
scarlet threads. Now as it came and went it tumbled loose
stones that, partially submerged, knocked against each other
with an almost musical sound.

Slumping a little on the log, she sighed, trying to relax and
let go some of the stress that had built through her escape.

The breeze momentarily held its breath, but the rhythmic
sea continued to create the pleasant harmony of stones that
was almost a voice. Within that sound, her ears suddenly
caught another rhythm that had nothing to do with stones or
water. Very faint and from not far away there was a human

note in the music. Someone just within hearing distance was very quietly sobbing.

Jessie was instantly on her feet, poised and concentrating on what she had heard. The sound faded, stopped, and then softly returned between where she stood and the verge of the tide.

Leaving her daypack behind the log on which she had been sitting, she crept forward, holding the flashlight covered with her fingers except for one narrow beam aimed on the ground at her feet. This was no time to stumble or give her presence away. Slowly, carefully, she passed through the grasses, moving only when the breeze sighed through them, hesitating when it hesitated.

When she was beyond them and could look out over the rocks that angled gently down into the tide, she froze and stood waiting, listening. The sobbing had ceased, but a rock clacked against another rock as someone moved to her left. Whoever it was had to be close to where they had left the dead man wrapped in his shroud of blue plastic.

With no further attempt at silence, Jessie stepped quickly forward over the ridge of stone and aimed the full beam of her flashlight toward the enclosed body. It was no longer completely draped with blue weighted with stones. The face and upper half of the body lay exposed to the night, cold and silent. Kneeling beside it, tears streaming down her face as she turned blindly into the light, was Karen Emerson.

As if she were frozen, she stared into the light in Jessie's hand without moving, startled, but clearly not caring, or perhaps resigned to whoever was holding it.

"What are you doing *here,* Karen?" Jessie demanded.

The woman looked down at the man by her side, but

said nothing, just shook her head and wiped at her face with one hand.

Lowering the beam of light from Karen's face, Jessie stepped forward to stand beside her.

"What's *this* about? Do you know this man?"

Karen reached out to lay a hand protectively on the shoulder of the dead man.

"He was my friend," she said simply. "He helped me when I needed help."

"Why didn't you say you knew him when we found him?"

Before she stood up to answer, Karen pulled the blue tarp back up to cover the body and carefully replaced the stones that held it in place. Facing Jessie, she frowned and took her lower lip between her teeth in a long moment of assessment. There was a note of bitterness when she finally spoke.

"You're the one who said his name. *Tim.* But you didn't say his last name, so I wasn't sure it was the Tim I knew until I came back here to see for myself after you had all gone to sleep. It could have been someone else with the same first name, but it wasn't. It *is* my friend. What I want to know is how *you* could have known him."

The accusation was tossed like a gauntlet that lay in the space between them, concerning something Jessie didn't understand.

"If you knew him," she said slowly, thinking back, "why didn't you recognize him on the plane from Juneau when he was sitting in the seat next to you?"

"What?"

"It was a short flight, but he was right beside you, sleeping."

But as she spoke she remembered how the hungover fisherman had used the long bill of his cap to cover his face and gone to sleep before Karen came aboard the plane. Then, when they had landed, before she had nudged him awake as promised, Karen had been on her feet in the aisle, so intent on getting off quickly that she had crowded in front of other passengers, never glancing back. She attempted to explain this only to be met with disdain and disbelief.

"He couldn't have been there. If he had been I *would* have recognized my own *friend*."

"Well, he was. And you clearly didn't."

They stood staring at each other in the half-light of the flashlight Jessie now held pointed at the ground—both defensive, both unwilling to provide a way out of the impasse.

Jessie suddenly realized they had been talking in normal voices that would carry in the stillness of the night. Anyone searching might hear them or see the glow of the light in her hand. Abruptly, she switched it off and lowered her voice almost to a whisper.

"Hush! There's something happening that I don't like back at the lighthouse and we really don't want to be heard talking. How long have you been out here?" she asked.

"Why do you care?" Karen hissed back.

"Did you see anyone when you came?"

"Why would I?"

Impatient with Karen's belligerence, Jessie gave up, reached out to grip the woman's shoulder and give her a shake.

"Stop answering a question with a question. There are some nasty things going on—or do you already know that? Are you part of whatever's going on with somebody on a cell phone? Did you know someone else would show up here before we came?"

"No."

She shook her head, a motion Jessie found unconvincing,

noticing the glance of fearful assessment Karen included with it.

"What are you talking about?" the woman demanded, a familiar note of dread in her voice.

"Curt's got at least one of the cell phones—or one of his own. I overheard part of a conversation he was having with someone, probably off-island. Do you know who?"

Karen's body stiffened under her hand, but all the censure and hostility had fled her voice to let fear flood into a moan. "Oh my God. It's Joe. He's coming here and he'll find me."

As in the hotel room two days before, she went immediately into flight mode, pulling away and turning in confusion and panic, trying to settle on a direction in which to escape.

"Wait. *Wait!*" Jessie snapped just loud enough to be heard as she grabbed Karen's arm. "Think first, run after. Remember?"

Stones at the edge of the sand stopped rattling under Karen's feet as she was forced to stand still.

Seldom that Jessie recalled had she been confronted with anyone who made such a problem of herself at every turn. Exasperated, she heartily wished she had never had dinner with the woman to begin with—even more that she had kept her mouth shut and not invited her along to Five Finger Island. But she was not so much a concern as a complication to Jessie at the moment. What to do with her was the question. Left to her own devices she was likely, one way or another, to betray either or both of them to Curt.

The tempting thought of tying Karen up somehow and hiding her in the brush flitted through her mind, but not seriously, for she had nothing with which to tie her and short of knocking her on the head with a rock there was no way to keep her quiet enough even if she had.

"Look," Jessie told her. "They know who we are and how

many of us are here. Soon they'll come hunting. Hiding is better, and quieter, than running. So we've got to find somewhere to hide and there can't be many good places for one of us, let alone two, on an island this small. You got any ideas?"

Karen shook her head mutely, but she had stopped trying to pull away and seemed to be listening, though still panicked.

Jessie glanced around at the dark shapes of the stones and the trees beyond.

Not here, she thought. It was too open.

But he wouldn't look in the *open,* would he? If he came—and she knew that if Karen was right and her stalker was involved, for whatever reason, he *would* come—he would focus his most intensive search in more promising places, those with concealment potential.

Looking down at the body at their feet, she asked Karen, "Are you afraid to stay with this dead guy?"

"Stay?" Karen asked in a horrified whisper. "Joe'll see me in a second here next to him."

"But are you *afraid* of the dead guy?" Jessie insisted.

"Of course not. He can't hurt me, but Joe *can.* Let's go hide in the trees."

"Not just yet. Let me think a minute. This may be the safest place on the island for you right now."

When Jessie departed there was nothing at all to reveal Karen's presence, or hers. Their new tracks in the sand didn't hold prints, or matter, for the work crew had left plenty of footprints earlier in moving the body to its current resting place, and theirs only added to the churned-up appearance. Assured that Karen would stay completely still and quiet in the space they had scooped out in the sand, tossing excess sand into the water, Jessie slipped away and left her hidden beneath the tarp-wrapped corpse, once again covered with blue plastic that had been carefully secured with extra stones to hold its edges.

"I can't leave you the light," she had whispered to Karen. "It's the only one I have and I need it."

"Where are you going?"

"To find another hiding place. Then I'm going back as close as I can to the lighthouse without being seen. Maybe I can find out something about all this and what they've done with the rest of the work crew. I'll come back, unless I get caught or have to stay hidden. If you hear anyone be very still. If it's me, I'll let you know."

Karen agreed and in seconds Jessie had gone, a shadow to join the other shadows of the night.

She had been surprised by Karen's acceptance of her hiding place, expecting the very idea to give her the shudders after her alarmed display that afternoon upon finding the body. But there had been none of it. She had been oddly acquiescent in helping to move the dead man in his plastic shroud and to hollow out a space just large enough for her to lie down in. In clothing warmer than what Jessie had on, she had laid herself down and allowed the tarp with Tim's body to be dragged over her. None of the hostility of the afternoon had been in evidence—no resistance offered. It could be a result of her fear, but she had been so compliant that Jessie found herself wondering why and if it would last, or if Karen would be out and gone at the first opportunity. If she did slip out, she would be on her own, for there were more important things to be concerned about. As she walked, Jessie resolved to expend no more time or energy in Karen's direction for the time being, if at all.

Cautiously, using the light as little as possible, she made her way back to the log behind which she had left the daypack. Deciding it was time to stop carting around the pack, without which she could move more easily and quietly, she tried to think of a place to leave it for the time being. Somewhere along the trail between where she was and the lighthouse would be best.

She remembered the hole in the side of that trail and went immediately and cautiously to it. Partly covered by a large root of the tree that stood above it, with a few handfuls of dry leaves tossed in last, it made a secure, invisible hiding place for the daypack and its contents. Satisfied, she left it.

She thought about abandoning the trail and finding another way back to the lighthouse, but the west side of the island was nothing but the cliff that fell directly into the sea, and she recalled from the morning walk that the east side had no concealing trees and no beach on which to run if discovered. It was nothing but huge stones piled and tumbled as if some giant had taken them like a handful of pebbles and scattered them in heaps of jagged edges and sides too steep to maintain footing. One had to pick one's way with infinite care through a tidewater field of hazards—risking falls, sprains, broken bones, cuts, and bruises.

More slowly than she had come away on it, she started back over the remaining section of the trail toward the lighthouse. Prepared to meet someone coming in her direction, she took her time, stopped often to listen, and used the light only when absolutely necessary. That was hardly at all, for by slowing down she found she was more adept at making things out in the darkness under the trees. Night vision was better than the flashlight, which made it impossible to see anything outside the tunnel of light it created. When she came to the mask, showing as a pale shape against the dark trunk of its tree, she recognized it for what it was, smiled ruefully at her earlier fright, and brushed it with her fingertips as a sort of greeting as she passed.

Soon she could see, not light, but a lessening of the dark
between the trees at the edge of the small woods and knew
she was approaching the open grassy space between it and
the steps that led down to the concrete platform on the east
side of the lighthouse.

There at the edge of the trees she stopped and stood
completely still to watch and listen, alert and wary, for
what must have been ten minutes. Nothing moved and there
were no sounds to be heard over the sighing breeze and the
sea still softly rolling pebbles on the shore somewhere to
the east.

Almost ready to creep out as low and quietly as possible
to look down at the lower half of the lighthouse that could
not be seen from where she stood, she hesitated and was relieved not to have made that mistake when, high above, on
the railed walkway outside the glass of the tower, there appeared a small and singular glow that grew and died in no
more than a second.

Jessie waited and, when the light revolved to the north in
its ten-second cycle of warning for any mariners in the area,
she could just make out the silhouette of a figure on that
walkway. Motionless except for the rise and fall of his arm
as he smoked a cigarette, someone stood there looking down
in the direction of the woods.

As she watched, frozen still, he dropped the cigarette,
which scattered a spark or two as it landed on the walkway.
He stepped on the butt to extinguish it and went quickly
back inside the tower through a door in its side.

Had she been seen? There was no way of knowing, but
she thought not, for she had not left the sheltering darkness
of the trees. Still, caution was called for, so she moved slowly
a little back and sideways ten feet or so into the woods, creat-

ing a few small sounds in the brush as she did so, but confident that with the rustle of the breeze in the leaves for cover
only someone very close could have noticed.

Unfortunately, someone *was* very close and *did* notice.

CHAPTER TWENTY-FIVE

THE GLOVED HAND THAT WAS FIRMLY APPLIED TO JESSIE'S mouth was sudden, unexpected, and stifled her gasp of surprise. At the same time, a strong arm circled her waist without warning and yanked her back against her captor, making it impossible to move away. Instantly, she struggled to free herself, aiming kicks at the shins of whoever held her, but the semisoft soles of her running shoes did little to effect a release through the application of pain.

"Hold still," a man's harsh whisper instructed, close to her ear. "I'm on your side, dammit!"

Realizing that she had very little option, she stopped struggling, but remained tense and waited to see what would come next, hoping that by allowing him to assume compliance she might take advantage of any opportunity to liberate herself.

"Good," he told her, slowly moving them both farther back into the dark of the trees. "Now—if I take my hand off your mouth will you be quiet?"

As she considered sinking her teeth into the hand, with a limited nod Jessie let the person know she would keep still, then gave up the biting idea as she realized from its feel and smell that the glove was made of heavy leather.

Cautiously, the hand was removed from her face, but the arm around her waist remained, keeping her immobilized.

"What do you mean, you're on my side? Who the hell are you?" she demanded in an angry whisper. "I'm not going anywhere. Let *go* of me."

"Promise?"

"Yes, dammit. Who *are* you?"

Reaching with the hand that had covered her mouth, he took firm hold of her right wrist, relaxed the pressure around her waist, and released her.

Immediately whirling to face her captor, she twisted the arm that was secured in his grip.

"Ow!"

"Hold still," he told her, adjusting the grip. "And be quiet."

In the dark of the forest Jessie could see little, but from a limited initial assessment she could tell this was someone she didn't know and to her knowledge had never seen before. Was it the man she had heard on the cell phone? Until she knew otherwise she couldn't trust him, and tensed to look for any opportunity to escape.

Two or three inches taller than her five feet eight inches, she had to look up only slightly at his face. The dark shadows made it impossible to tell much about his coloring, but as the beacon swung over their heads again she could see that he wore jeans and a jacket that might have been gray or light brown over a dark sweatshirt. A small flash of that beam was reflected in his eyes, but did not disclose their color, just an interested appraisal of her that held no malice as far as she could tell. His face was as lean as his body, though he had broad shoulders and from his clothing and strength she guessed that he was accustomed to physical labor that did not entail time spent pushing paper around a desk in some office.

"Let's get away from here," he suggested in his hoarse whisper, cocking his head toward the trail and letting go of her arm, "and talk where we can't be overheard."

Rubbing at her wrist with the opposite hand, she nodded agreement without speaking and when he gestured for her to go first, swung that in direction and went as silently as possible through the brush till she reached the trail, hearing him move close and quiet with similar caution behind her.

If this man was part of whatever was going on, he certainly didn't act like it, she reasoned. If he were, wouldn't he have taken her to the lighthouse? If not, what was he doing here by himself in the woods, watching the tower from concealment, as she had been? On the other hand, could he be the person who had been on the other end of the phone conversation? It didn't seem likely, when they could simply have talked in person. She had a feeling that the phone call had been to someone off-island. How long had this person been lurking in these woods? Could they have somehow missed him in their thorough search for Sandra earlier, or had he arrived later? These were all questions to be answered.

In five minutes, when they reached the hole in the trail where she had stashed the daypack, she stopped and turned abruptly to face him and spoke in an annoyed half-whisper.

"Okay. This is far enough. Now, who the hell are *you* and what are you doing out here in the dark? How did you get onto the island? What—"

"Who are *you?* What are *you* doing out here in the dark?" he countered, with a slight note of indulgent humor in his voice that further infuriated her.

"I'm *supposed* to be here," she snapped. "You're *not.* Let's have some answers, dammit."

There was a long moment of silence and when he spoke there was no humor at all in his voice.

"I *was* invited along—by a friend, Tim Christiansen, who someone killed last night and whose body I think you've already found. I'm looking for Karen Emerson, as she's calling herself now. My name . . ."

But Jessie had already leaped ahead mentally and knew, with a sinking feeling, what he was about to say before he finished the sentence. ". . . is Joe Cooper. Who are *you?*"

Oh shit, she thought, and glared at him without answering, once again tense and ready in a fight-or-flight attitude.

So this was Karen's stalker, in person and just what she needed least. *Teach me to trust my instincts,* she decided in resignation.

"I'm Jessie Arnold," she told him.

"The Iditarod musher?"

"Yeah, that Jessie Arnold."

"I've seen you race," he commented, a note of respect creeping into the admission. "I was in Nome the year you got hurt close to the finish."

How bizarre, she thought, staring at him in confusion. *Here we stand—me and a stalker—in the dark, on an island full of trouble that I, at least, don't understand, with a boat that someone sank in the cove, the woman who's being stalked hiding under a dead man, and others disappearing into nowhere. And we're talking about* sled dog racing?

"Whatever," she said. What she wanted was relevant information. "How long have you been skulking around out here in the dark then?"

"Since it *got* dark," he answered, without hesitation. "When I arrived you were all inside having dinner."

"How could you know that?"

"I watched. From that hill above the boathouse you can

see into the lighthouse where you were sitting around the table."

"Were you here earlier in the day?" Jessie asked, wondering if he could be responsible for Sandra's disappearance.

"No. Why?"

"One of the group is missing—a woman from Skagway. We've searched the whole island, but she's nowhere to be found. Have you any idea where she is? And someone sank our only boat. Was that you?"

"No, and no again," he answered without hesitation. "Why didn't you call the Coast Guard, or the police? I expected that someone official would be out here by now because of Tim."

"The radio's been trashed and our cell phones stolen. We couldn't call anyone. But one of the work crew is somehow involved—and maybe you. And I'm still reserving judgment on that, by the way—since I heard Curt talking to someone else on what had to be a cell phone earlier, before I left the lighthouse. In fact it's why I left—in a hurry."

She could feel him staring silently at her for a long moment before he spoke.

"Who's Curt?"

"One of the work crew."

"And the woman who's missing?"

"Another."

"Well, I can make a guess where she is. I'd be willing to bet that she's with the others that the two of them—"

"*Two?*"

"Yes, I saw two. One was forcing some people to go down into a manhole on that platform between the lighthouse and the cove. He has a gun and I've watched him use it tonight to make them climb into it. But I didn't see Karen. Where is she?" he demanded, and waited.

Jessie maintained her listening silence, refusing to answer as she considered the *two* people he had seen. *Two?* She had only seen Curt. Had someone else arrived without her knowledge, like Cooper?

Before she could come to any conclusion he asked a different question. "What's under that platform? What's down there?"

She hesitated. It made sense of the phone mention of "the tank." And the clank of metal she had heard could have been the heavy cover for the manhole on the platform being dropped into position.

From her own past experience and having seen Karen's fear, she was inclined to be highly suspicious of this man. Though he sounded reasonable now, he was obviously hunting for Karen, had somehow managed to track her from Ketchikan to Seattle and all the way to this tiny island in the middle of the vast expanse of Frederick Sound. She had no intention of telling him anything that would lead him to the woman he was so diligently seeking. It seemed, however, that there was no reason not to tell him what she knew in answer to his last question. Maybe, if he thought Karen was confined with them, she could get him to help her rescue the rest.

"Tanks," she told him. "Large ones. At least one holds water and there's another that was used for fuel, when the lighthouse was manned. That manhole is the only way in or out of an access space that amounts to a perfect concrete prison. And you say he's made people go down there?"

"There's eight of you, right—not counting Karen? I've watched four being forced down there, so that leaves you and Karen, and whoever else. I'll ask you again, where is she?"

"I won't talk to you about Karen," Jessie told him shortly, thinking of Whitney and Aaron, who, besides Karen and herself, he had *not* seen forced into the tanks, but who probably had been by now. Curt had mentioned two couples, but said he was going back after the rest. But Cooper evidently knew that Karen wasn't in the tank, or he wouldn't be asking where she was.

There was an extended silence as Cooper stared at her, then said in a frustrated tone, "Well, I guess I can't blame you. She's told you all the bullshit she's made up about me and you have no way to know she's lying. She's very good at convincing others that she's an innocent victim. But I *will* find her, whether you tell me or not."

"How should I know anyway?" Jessie asked, keeping her knowledge to herself. He was right that she had no way to know which of them was telling the truth. *Better safe than sorry,* she thought, before saying, "I'm not her keeper. I took off on my own after I heard him talking on the phone. Besides, how do you know he hasn't caught her, and the others, and put them in the tank when you weren't watching? He knows how many of us there are."

"I doubt that he—" He stopped abruptly in mid-sentence and his focus shifted as he turned to look toward the trail behind him, in the direction of the lighthouse.

His body blocked her sight of the trail and she stepped aside to see what had caught his attention. In the absence of conversation, she could hear the sound of pounding feet coming rapidly in their direction, and the beam of a flashlight could be seen bouncing along ahead of whoever was running toward them.

"Let's get out of here," Cooper said and passed her to take off in a swift sprint toward the south end of the island.

Jessie wheeled and started to follow, but in her haste forgot about the hole that lay in the track. One foot slipped into it, tripping her into a full-length sprawl into the dirt of the trail, striking the side of her head on something hard as she hit the ground.

There was a moment or two of consciousness, of knowing someone had stopped beside her. Then she felt a hand roughly seize her shoulder and turn her over as everything faded. Then there was nothing at all.

CHAPTER TWENTY-SIX

WHEN JESSIE REGAINED AWARENESS, SHE WAS FLAT ON HER back and her first thought was to wonder why she was so cold. Opening her eyes, she saw nothing but blackness—listening, heard nothing but silence. She tried to move, but pain, sharp as lightning, stabbed through her head and compelled her to immobility with its savage grip. Helpless, she groaned, and someone spoke near her in the dark.

"She's coming to."

"I've got her." Don Sawyer's voice this time from just above her. "Lie still, Jessie. You've got a nasty lump on your head—maybe a concussion."

Closing her eyes again, she assessed the pulses of pain in her head.

"What . . ." she started to ask, but her voice came out like the air from a tired balloon, unfamiliar and whispery. The single word grated in her throat as dry as paper, making her cough, and with each paroxysm the pain struck again.

"Don't try to talk," Don's voice admonished. "It's okay. You're safe with us."

"But what . . . where . . . ?" It was easier this time, but just a breath of a question and she did as told and didn't move.

"I'll tell you, if you just be still and rest."

"Okay." Another breath.

"We're in the tanks under the platform. You remember the tanks Jim told us about—for water and fuel? Well, they've put us in the maintenance space between them."

"They?"

"Yeah—Curt and someone we didn't know. We don't know who the second one is, why we're here, or what they want. But Curt, at least, has a handgun. The bastard caught Sandra in the basement yesterday, when we were all at the other end of the island, and put her in here. She was scared to death in the dark by herself all the time we were looking for her, and that's why we couldn't find her. Then last night he made me and Jim and Laurie climb down. He was waiting when I came back in from outside sometime after midnight. After that, he got Aaron."

"Why?"

"We don't know."

"I saw you go down the basement stairs, but I couldn't see who was with you," Jessie told him softly. "Then I went out looking for Karen and heard Curt talking on a cell phone."

"So *that's* why he couldn't find you—or Karen. We wondered. He tried to get us to tell him where you'd gone, but none of us knew. Where is Karen—and Whitney? We haven't seen either of them."

When Jessie tried again to sit up her head hurt, but not so badly, so she stayed where she was for the moment.

"Karen's hiding," she said, as the pain faded again, "but I left Whitney sleeping in her bed. Where's Aaron?"

"I'm here," Aaron chimed in from somewhere nearby in the dark.

"Didn't you hear him on the phone?"

"Not a word. I was sleeping on the west side of the roof and didn't know anything till Curt woke me up with a gun in my face."

"How long have I been here?"

"They brought you over an hour ago. We've been really worried about you."

As he had named the members of the work crew, she could feel the concern of them all gathered around her in the dark.

"You make six," Don continued. "Karen and Whitney are still missing, like I said. So were you, until they opened that manhole cover and told us to come and get you, or they'd drop you. It's at least ten feet to the floor, so Jim and I reached up and eased you down."

"Thanks. I'm glad I didn't know it at the time. Is anyone else hurt?" she asked.

"Banged around a bit—mostly in getting down here. I've got a sore ankle, but nobody's really hurt like you. Did they hit you with something?" Jim asked out of the dark.

"I fell in the trail and hit my head, I think."

She could feel that she was lying on something hard and cold, with her neck across one of Don's thighs. He shifted his weight slightly at Jim's question and there was a flash of pain in her head, but quite a bit less this time—she could stand it without feeling she would pass out again. Carefully, slowly, she raised one hand to the side of her head. There was, as he had said, a sizable lump where she had hit something. She had no recollection what, but nothing felt broken, though her hair was sticky with drying blood from a cut about two inches long. Remembering the pool of Tim Christiansen's blood that the seawater had washed off the rocks, she was grateful that it had not been worse.

"They know how many of us there are and they'll hunt

until they find Whitney and Karen, I think—if they haven't found them already. But if they've been caught, why aren't they here with us? That handgun worries me." It was Jim's voice this time, near at hand, with a bitter note of anger in it.

"Why put us in here?"

"We have no idea, but they obviously wanted to get us out of the way for some reason. Curt wouldn't answer questions or tell us anything. But there's no way to get out, so we can't make trouble for them—though I'd like to make a *lot* of trouble for them."

"And you don't know who the second one is?"

"Nope. Did you get a look at him?"

She could remember nothing but standing in the trail talking to Joe Cooper. "No. I don't think it was Curt who was running on the trail and caught up with me, but I couldn't see him before I fell. It was dark—in the trees. But there's someone else out there—Karen's stalker."

"So he's real?" Jim asked, surprise raising his voice.

"Evidently. You thought she made him up?"

"It crossed my mind that she might have."

"Me too, but she didn't. I met him—Joe Cooper."

"Well, if Karen's still loose, maybe she'll be able to help us."

"She won't know where to look, will she? And she won't want to run into Cooper."

"Unless . . ." someone said, then stopped.

There was a tense pause full of consideration. Then Laurie spoke softly out of the darkness beside Jim and put words to the question Jessie could feel them thinking. "We can't help wondering, Jessie. Could she be in on this with them? Could he?"

It was something Jessie had not really considered, but her head ached too much to give it much serious thought. Still . . .

* * *

An hour later she felt better, still shaky and a little nauseous, but was on her feet and feeling her way carefully in the dark along the cement walls of the room beneath the lighthouse platform. The walls were cold and slimy, dripping with water in places. The whole space smelled dank and moldy. Periodically she felt one of the isopods that so revolted Sandra and Aaron move beneath her fingers or heard one crunch underfoot. The space seemed lousy with them. She imagined them everywhere, crawling on the walls, the floor, even the ceiling for all she knew, and hoped none would drop off into her hair.

It was a confusing space with standing water in some places and felt almost like a maze, with walls that started and stopped unexpectedly and turned corners that didn't make sense in the dark. The floor was uneven, with unexpected raised sections like some kind of footings for walls that no longer existed, or never had, and over which it was easy to stumble and fall if incautious. She couldn't seem to be able to get hold of a mental map of the place, even after going over it twice.

Though he hated "the bugs" as he called them, Aaron had tried to help, but had not done much better and finally went back to sit with the others. Jim, more familiar with the space, having seen and explored it with lights in the past, was more able to make his way through without running into walls or losing his footing on the parts of the floor that were wet and muddy. But even he had trouble with orientation in the dark.

"Isn't there any way out of here except for that round hole that goes up to the platform?" Jessie asked.

"Nope. And when we tried raising it awhile back we found that they must've dragged something heavy over it to keep it there. There's only room for two at a time to reach it anyway and, whatever it is, I doubt all of us together could shift it now."

"Any place we can see out?"

"There is one pipe through the wall on the cove side—maybe a drain, I don't know. But you can't see anything but a little light at the other end because it's either angled down on purpose or bent. I've never really paid attention because it didn't matter."

He took her over to peer through the pipe at the small amount of light that told them it was now daylight outside.

Crouching there, with the width of the room between the two of them and the rest, Jessie lowered her voice to ask Jim his opinion of something that had been running through her mind.

"Do you think the cocaine we found last night has anything to do with this?"

"I've been wondering that myself," he answered. "I haven't said anything, but maybe we should ask Sandra about it and get it out into the open. If none of them knows where it came from it might tell us something, even if there isn't much we can do about it."

"And if someone does? It's possible, you know?"

He sighed. "I don't know—just don't know."

Finished searching the walls, they felt their way back in the dark and sat down with the other four.

"Sandra," Jim said.

"Yes?"

"What was it you wanted to talk to me about last night—when you came back upstairs with that bottle of wine? You said it was about something in the basement, remember?"

There was a long moment of thoughtful silence from Sandra. Then, before she could answer, Don spoke up from beside her.

"She found something down there, Jim, that maybe you don't want shared with everyone. Something that—"

"I can tell it, Don." With a little good-humored irritation, Sandra interrupted him. "I should have said something earlier anyway."

"What," Jim asked, "did you find?"

"I didn't mean to snoop, Jim, honestly I didn't. I was just looking around. You know—it's interesting how the lighthouse is built, so I walked back in that narrow space that extends south from the cooling room to get the wine you asked for and then a little farther, just to see how it all fit together. It was kind of dark with just the light from the cooling room and I didn't have a flashlight, so I didn't see that something stuck out beyond the wine boxes, and stumbled on it.

"In the dark I couldn't tell what it was, but I felt around and there were two packages, one half on top of the other. Each one was over a foot square and maybe eight inches thick, and it felt like they were wrapped in some kind of plastic. I'd knocked the top one partway off and it was heavy and kind of soft when I picked it up to put it back. Then I felt that the corner was torn where I'd hit it with my foot, so I took it out into the light to see about that.

"When I saw what it was—and I've seen it before, so I knew what it was—well, I didn't know what to do. So I found some electrical tape in Curt's toolbox and used it to fix what I'd torn. Then I put it back and went upstairs. On the way up I debated whether to say anything, or not. When you were busy talking to Jessie, I decided to just keep my mouth shut, that it was none of my business. So that's what I did, except I told Don and we both thought it best to just keep still about it.

"I really didn't mean to get into anything that belongs to you, Jim—honestly. I'm sorry."

Jim's voice was tense coming out of the dark.

"I didn't know it was there. And it *doesn't* belong to me or Laurie. *No way*."

"What the hell did you think it was?" Aaron asked from a few feet away.

"Cocaine," Jim and Sandra said together.

"A *lot* of cocaine," Don added. "I went down and had a look, just to be sure, and there's more than just for recreational use."

Everyone was silent for a minute, considering the ramifications of that.

"How did you know I found it?" Sandra asked. "I put it back."

"You spilled just a little on the floor in the cooler," Jessie told her. "Probably when you took it out to look at it and fixed the wrapper. I found it later, when I went down for the salad, and showed it to Jim."

"You know," said Aaron, with a note of wicked humor in his voice, "you can tell us about it, if it *is* yours, Jim. We're all friends here, right? But it sounds like a lot of stuff for two people to me."

"Look, Aaron." Jim's voice was sharp with anger as he swung toward the younger man. "I don't care if you believe me or not, but that stuff does not belong to me and I'm really pissed that someone was careless enough to bring it to our island."

"Hey!" Aaron said, hearing the implied accusation in his words. "You got no reason to think . . ."

"Hey yourselves—both of you." Laurie broke in with an attempt at peacemaking. "There's nothing we can do about any of this now. There's nothing to show that anyone here had anything to do with it, so let's let it go for now and concentrate on figuring out if there's anything we can do about being down here, shall we? Any ideas?"

The silence that followed spoke louder to any practical solution to their confinement than the prior echoes of Jim's angry voice.

In her search of the space, Jessie had stumbled over several pieces of junk metal on the floor, including a couple of pieces of rebar approximately six feet long.

"Any possibility we could use some of that stuff to pound or scrape a hole in the wall?" she asked to fill the dispirited stillness.

Jim's laugh held no humor coming out of the blackness.

"That wall," he told her, "is more than a foot of solid concrete. I don't *think* so! Do you?"

Discouraged, head still throbbing, Jessie felt her way to one of the raised footings and, bugs or not, sat down and leaned back against a section of the wall, turning her face to one side so she didn't strike the lump on her head against the rough concrete. Even damp and slimy, it was cool against her cheek, the only relief she had; she longed for some of the Tylenol she carried in the daypack she had left in the hole in the trail.

She wished for water too. Damp as it was, there was nothing that was safe to drink and her mouth felt lined with cotton. It was absurd to be sitting next to a tank that was full of water they couldn't drink without boiling.

She hoped Karen would stay hidden and not do something foolish like try to come and find her. It still seemed out of character that the woman had been so willing to hide under the body of a man she called her friend. She had more than half-expected Karen to refuse with revulsion and had been surprised when she had not only agreed to the hiding place, but had helped to create it.

And where was Whitney?

It was very quiet in the maintenance space between the tanks, one full, the other empty. The six had gathered together near the overhead opening that they couldn't even see, except for the small amount of light that filtered through a few drainage holes, and were barely visible. Jessie could place them by the sound of their voices and movement— Sandra huddled next to Don, Jim and Laurie together nearby. Aaron had stretched himself out on his back on top of the footing beyond Jessie's feet, probably hoping the isopods would stay below it on the floor.

For a long time no one said anything. Then, out of the dark, came the singular and reverberating snore. Aaron, against odds, had dozed off and the evidence of this all but echoed off the unseen walls.

Sandra giggled, a slightly hysterical sound in the dark.

Laurie joined in.

And suddenly they were all laughing.

The unexpected noise of their mirth woke Aaron and his snoring stopped abruptly as he sat up.

"What's going on?"

The question simply boosted their amusement into hilarity and made an answer impossible.

"What's wrong with you people?" he asked.

Sandra, who had started it, finally regained enough self-control to sputter out, "You snore."

"Yeah. So?"

"No," Don told him, still chuckling. "She means you *really* snore. We thought there was a foghorn in here."

There was a pause, while they waited.

Jessie heard him recline himself again before his response came through the dark, with a grin in it.

"Why do you think I'm still single—and have been sleeping upstairs?"

The incident relieved a little of the tension and brought them back together as a group, but it was clear that there was nothing to do but wait for—whatever. There was not a sound from above them, but the heavy layers of concrete were such effective sound blocks that Jessie doubted they could have heard anything that was not loud and directly overhead. Even then it would be questionable.

Leaning back against the wall again, she wondered how Aaron could possibly sleep. What about Karen? How was she faring at the other end of the island? Would she remain in her hiding place when so much time had passed? Could she really be part of what was happening to the rest of the work crew—one with the two men who had entombed them in the dark of these tanks? Where was Joe Cooper? She wondered, suddenly remembering their conversation. He seemed tough and agile enough to have escaped in his sprint for the south end, especially if they didn't know he was on the island. But they might have heard him running. If they found him would he try to fight it out with would-be murderers? She recalled the gun that had been missing from the freezer upstairs, now probably in Curt's hands, and hoped not. But, knowing where they were, maybe he would be of some assistance to those in the tank.

This small island seemed so odd a place for what had happened to them all. What *was* behind it? Somehow the cocaine must be involved. Could Cooper be this unknown person Don and Jim had referred to, the one who was helping Curt? If so, why would he have run away? Was this merely a way for him to finally catch up with Karen? It seemed extreme but he had been very determined about it. Still, getting the rest of them out of the way had to be factored in as a possibility. Could he have killed Tim Christiansen himself and, if so, why?

Her head throbbed and she gave up trying to figure it out. Once again she wished for water, achingly thirsty though surrounded by the huge amount of water that was Frederick Sound—undrinkable as well, but water nevertheless.

She thought about what it must have been like for the early keepers of the light, back when the area was much less settled than it was now. Some of them must have been odd ducks, willing to spend years of their lives out of touch with the rest of the world, in a sort of voluntary solitary confinement. But they hadn't been alone, she remembered, thinking of the names of the last crew she had seen on the wall inside the lighthouse. At least they had had the opportunity to say *We were here* before they went away and left the place empty.

If the worst happened and their present captors went away and left the six of them trapped where they were, there would be no record of their presence until, eventually, someone found their remains. Even if someone came, who would think to look in the tanks? They could shout, but odds were they would not be heard unless someone was standing almost on top of them, if then. They could die where they were. It was possible.

Knowing that in the dark and silence she was letting her imagination take over, it still suddenly seemed important to leave something identifying—some record of her own existence.

Feeling a little hysterical and foolish, she got up and felt her way back to where she had noticed the pieces of scrap metal. On her hands and knees, she blindly searched the floor in the dark for one of them to use as a tool. She found chunks of concrete, an isopod or two, a puddle of undrinkable water. Then her hand struck a piece of slightly curved metal with a sharp edge on one end. Getting to her feet, she found her way back to the wall near the rest of the group.

Slowly, by feel in the blackness, she began to scrape on the wall. J-E-S-S-I-E W-A-S H-E-R-E. Then she scratched out the W-A-S and above it carved I-S.

Under it she added the date and finished by running her fingers over what she had written as if she were reading Braille.

Then she sat back down and stared silently into the dark.

CHAPTER TWENTY-SEVEN

ALEX WENT TO WORK ON THURSDAY MORNING GLAD TO have something to occupy his time, for Jessie did not call all morning. Before noon he had completed a report on his trip to Canada and the afternoon was spent clearing his desk of paperwork on several small cases now closed and ready for filing. One open burglary case he set aside until last, then called John Timmons, friend and assistant coroner at the crime lab in Anchorage, to see if he had a report on the evidence left at the scene—a small weekend cabin twenty miles out of Palmer that had been broken into and vandalized the week before.

"Still waiting for the report on the latents," Timmons told him. "The owner had a party the weekend before, so there're prints up the yin-yang to be identified. We're working our way through them, but slowly. By tomorrow—hopefully. Okay?"

Arriving at home, Alex spent a couple of hours outside in the shed splitting firewood for winter fires, with the kitchen window open so he could hear the phone if it rang. Throwing

himself into his work, he burned excess energy with an axe
to make stove-sized chunks out of the rounds of log and
stack them neatly under a roof next to the shed, where they
would stay dry. The swing of the axe felt good and he made
a significant and satisfying inroad on the large pile. It had
been a year since his last stint at wood splitting, however, so
he was aware that the exercise would make itself felt the
next day in his back and shoulder muscles. He decided that a
long hot shower would not be a bad idea before reheating
some of the previous night's stew for dinner. Next year, for
sure, they should acquire a splitter.

He was still drying himself off with a large towel when he
heard the phone ring.

At last, he thought. Quickly he wrapped the towel
around his waist as he moved to the bedside phone and
lifted the receiver.

"Jessie?"

"Not even close. Sorry to disappoint," the voice of Ben
Caswell, friend and pilot for the troopers, informed him.
"But maybe I can make it up to you. Linda's got enough
meat loaf over here to feed the entire cast of *Cheaper by the
Dozen.* Why don't you bring some of that beer you've got
going bad in your fridge with no one to drink it and come
help us out?"

Any other time the invitation to dinner would have sent
Alex straight out the door, for he knew that Linda Caswell
made a killer meat loaf. Not having heard from Jessie the
night before, however, he was reluctant to abandon the telephone when he was sure she would call the minute he left.

"You are surely hooked, old man," Cas ribbed him. "But
I'll bring you a sandwich tomorrow for lunch anyway, just to
remind you what you missed."

After that, and stew for dinner, it was a frustrating eve-

ning as far as the telephone was concerned. In three hours
there was only Caswell's single call.

At eight o'clock, Alex tried to call Jessie, but got the
same "unavailable" message as the night before. He tried
again three times, with the same lack of response. Finally, he
called the Petersburg police to ask if they were aware of any
problem in reception for cell phones in the area of Frederick
Sound.

The dispatcher assured him there was not. In fact, she reported, they had just had a cell phone call from a fisherman
in the sound who was requesting emergency medical assistance for an injured deckhand. "Sometimes they have trouble getting a signal out there," she told him, which he already
knew. "Keep trying and eventually someone will answer."

Alex hung up, wishing he had asked for Jim's number
and had another to try, but it was too late for that.

With Tank resting as usual on the braided rug in front of
the cast-iron stove, Alex tried to watch the television,
couldn't concentrate, turned it off and got up. While Tank
watched, he paced and fidgeted, irritated one minute, concerned the next. Something was not at all right. Jessie was
not inconsiderate. When she said she would do something
you could count on her doing it, or having a good reason
why she had not. With the phones working okay, he could
think of no good reason for her silence. *Unless she just
doesn't want to call,* a nagging internal voice taunted him.

Get serious! would have been his response in the days before he had left and gone to Idaho. Now he wasn't as absolutely sure. Maybe she really *didn't* want to talk to him
and this was her way of saying so—without having to say so.
Maybe he should just give her space and leave it alone till
she came home on Sunday.

But he couldn't. There was another voice, one he had

learned to trust. It kept telling him that he would be making a mistake to do so. *You know Jessie better than that,* it said. *Trust your instincts. Something's wrong.*

Sure of it, he picked up the phone and called his commander to request the next day off. Then he called Caswell.

"I'm headed south first thing in the morning," he told him, and why. "Do you know a pilot in Petersburg, or Juneau, who could fly me out to Frederick Sound on floats?"

"I can probably scare one up. Are you sure?"

"You think I'm crazy?"

"No. You're pretty good with hunches. It's a bit of déjà vu though, isn't it? Flying off to find Jessie on some island?"

"I thought of that—and didn't like the feel of it."

"You could call Wrangell or Ketchikan and have someone go check it out," Cas suggested.

"I don't want to fire up the guys unless I know for sure something's wrong."

"Want company?"

"Naw. I'll just go down and take a look. It's probably nothing and, if everything's fine, having someone else along would make it seem like *something.*"

But he didn't really feel it was nothing. *Something* was ringing warning bells in his consciousness and there was nothing for it but to go and see, however unreasonable it seemed on the surface.

By ten o'clock the next morning Alex was lifting Tank into a floatplane and climbing in after him from a dock north of Juneau, having been picked up by the friend from whom Cas had called in a favor the night before.

"Bill Knapp," he had said, shaking Alex's hand and touching the bill of his hat when they met.

Ex-military, Alex had thought as he returned the shorter man's welcome, and was glad of it.

"Hope you don't mind the dog," he had asked, and been assured there was no problem.

He had not originally intended to take along Jessie's lead dog, but decided at the last minute to include him, though for the commercial part of the trip it meant confining him in a portable kennel and checking him through like baggage, which he was sure Tank would not have appreciated, had he realized the implication.

Once in the floatplane without the kennel, Tank, who had often flown in small planes before and knew the drill, made himself comfortable behind the seats, muzzle on the sleeping bag Alex had tossed in, and snoozed.

Knapp taxied slowly away from the dock to avoid creating a wake and into the open water of Auke Bay, where he increased his speed until they lifted off over Coghlan Island. Once up, he made a left turn into Stephens Passage, which they would follow all the way to Frederick Sound, approximately seventy air miles away.

As the turn was made Alex looked over the pilot's shoulder to see the deep blue of the Mendenhall Glacier's crevasses and the permanent snows of the ice field glistening high above them in the morning sunshine. The Juneau airport passed below at the north end of Gastineau Channel and fell behind as Knapp skirted the end of Douglas Island to fly along its western side, periodically muttering into the microphone of his headset for clearance from the airport. Finished, he gestured toward a second headset and Alex put it on to be able to hear what was said to him over the roar of the small plane's engine.

"The weather's great for flying," Knapp assured him.

"We'll be able to land on Frederick Sound and pull up to the lighthouse with no problem. When it's choppy you can't get in out there. They've got no dock, so rough weather beats up floats on the rocks."

"You've been there before?"

"A time or two. It's a great location. You going to stay long?"

"A day or two," Alex said, wondering just how much Caswell had told this man about his reasons for wanting to reach Five Finger Light as soon as possible.

"Cas said there might be some kind of trouble out there," Knapp said, as if in answer to that thought.

"Nothing that I know of for sure," Alex answered carefully. "But my lady is out there. She said she would call and does what she says she will, but I haven't heard from her for two and a half days now. That's enough *not* like her to make me uneasy."

"Know what you mean," Knapp said, frowning. "My Cheryl wouldn't let that much time go by if she knew I was expecting to hear from her."

They flew on down Stephens Passage with one island after another coming into view. For a long time Admiralty slid by on the right, notable to the residents of Southeast Alaska for its large population of grizzlies, but Alex, watching, saw none on the beach. On its near side the long narrow finger of Glass Peninsula ran south for over thirty miles, with 3,316-foot Washburn Peak rising three-quarters of the way along it.

Knapp was a commercial pilot and not a law enforcement officer, but he, like Caswell, flew for the State Troopers on contract when needed. In an environment where there are few roads and almost every community must be reached either by air or sea, getting anywhere in a hurry most often means flying, in good weather or bad. As Southeast Alaska is not known for its sunny days, Alex, though concerned about Jessie, enjoyed the flight that gave him a rare window on an extremely beautiful part of the coast and was almost sorry when they reached Frederick Sound and Five Finger Island appeared far ahead of them.

"Whales," Knapp said suddenly, pointing down.

Leaning close to the window, Alex was able to pick out a pod of five humpbacks cruising along near the surface of the water, so small from that altitude that they looked like fat sardines. One after another they rose to blow and breathe, then one breached, throwing its huge body out of the sea and crashing down with a huge splash.

"Out there, across the sound."

Perhaps half a mile away another whale had risen and Alex sighted it just in time to watch the flukes appear as it dove. Beyond it he saw spray as two more blew—then another. The sound seemed full of whales.

"They're beginning to head for Hawaii for the winter," Knapp told him. "A few stay here, but most of them migrate south—like some of the rest of us would like to."

A fishing boat was running north in the middle of the sound, and as the pilot swung in low over Five Finger Island Alex saw a tug with a raft of logs on a line behind it chugging slowly south between the island and the distant mainland. But his attention was focused on the white deco-style lighthouse that rose high on its crest of stone, red-roofed and solid in appearance, with several outbuildings and what was evidently a helipad near it. He looked carefully for people, but saw none. Even what he could see of the woods and rocks were empty, except for what appeared to be a sea lion swimming a few yards off the south shore.

Knapp took his plane to the east, made a wide descending turn, and flew back toward the island, dropping down to skim the waves until the floats made solid contact with the water when they were still a fair distance away. It slowed the plane so he could taxi up to the rocks that rose to a wide platform in front of the building.

As they drifted to a stop Alex, used to flying with Caswell, was ready to step out, walk the float, and hop off onto the rocks with a tethering line, while Knapp held the plane close with gentle acceleration. As soon as he could see it was secure, the pilot shut down the idling engine, stepped out, and brought Tank ashore with him.

It seemed odd to Alex that not a soul had come out of the lighthouse to meet them. Someone should have heard the plane. Glancing around, he could see no restoration work being done either. It looked closed up and empty.

"You're sure they're here?" Knapp asked.

"Supposed to be. Let's go up and find out."

Climbing over the rocks, the three of them crossed the platform, empty except for a heavy cement mixer sitting in front of the closed lower doors. They went up the outside stairs to the door, which was also closed. Alex hammered on it with his fist, but there was no response. Turning the handle, he found it unlocked and walked on into the kitchen where he called out.

"Hello. Anyone here?"

There was no answer.

Hurriedly, they made a search of the rooms on that level, opening all the doors. In every room there was all the normal evidence of people staying there: clothing, sleeping bags, pillows, duffels, suitcases, towels, toothpaste. Finding the stairway to the room below, Alex went down for a quick look, but came immediately up again when no one answered his call.

Kneeling beside the dog on the kitchen floor, he addressed him. "Where's Jessie, Tank. Find Jessie."

Though the husky had followed them in their search, told to find his mistress he now trotted back to one of the bedrooms and barked once sharply. Following, Alex looked more closely and recognized things he knew belonged to Jessie. Sitting down beside Alex, Tank looked up expectantly for further orders.

"Good boy," Alex told him. "Well, he knows she *was* here. So where is she now—and everyone else that's supposed to be here working?"

"My guess?" said Knapp. "They've gone off for a side trip somewhere and will be back later. There used to be a fox farm over east on Fanshaw where they took me once. Maybe they've gone there—or out fishing."

"Maybe. There was no way to let Jess know I was coming. We'll wait, if that's okay with you."

"Sure. But there's gotta be a way to get up in the tower," Knapp suggested. "Wouldn't hurt to take a look from the top."

From the door in the second hall they climbed the tower stairs that followed its square walls with ninety-degree turns. When they reached the last sweeping curve of metal steps with its brass rail, they went up that as well, leaving Tank at its foot, and stood looking out on a full 360-degree panorama of Frederick Sound and its surrounding mountains and islands.

No one was visible anywhere that they could see, though the trees to the south obscured that part of the island.

But outside on the circular walkway, Alex found and picked up a single cigarette butt, mashed flat under an indifferent foot.

As far as they could tell, Five Finger Island was empty.

CHAPTER TWENTY-EIGHT

IT WAS WHEN THEY CAME DOWN FROM THE TOWER AND made another search of the lighthouse and the area around it for any clues they might have missed that Knapp discovered the sunken Seawolf at the bottom of the small cove and waved Alex over to take a look at it.

"There's something really wrong here," Knapp said, looking up from where he knelt at the edge of the platform. "How the hell did they get off the island with their boat down there?"

"We don't know for sure that they only had one boat, do we? Maybe they didn't leave the island. Just because the lighthouse is empty and the rest looked empty from the air doesn't mean that it is. They could be somewhere in the trees between here and the south end, so we'd better find out."

Knapp agreed. "And if they're not, we'll fly on to Petersburg and see if we can find out anything there. But I really think, if they're at the south end, that when I circled before landing they should have seen and heard the plane."

"Well, if we have to go to Petersburg and there's still

nothing," said Alex, with a note of anger and determination in his voice, "I call in every man I can get from the Troopers and Coast Guard till we know what's wrong, where they are, and why."

With a last look at the lighthouse and still calling out periodically in the hope that someone would hear and answer their shouts, they went up the steps by the boathouse toward the trees.

Tank perked up considerably when they started down the trail. Nose to ground, he trotted along quickly, wagging his tail when he stopped to wait for Alex and Knapp to catch up.

"Jessie's been through here and he knows it," Alex said, watching the dog carefully. A little farther on, he stopped to examine a mask attached to a tree they passed, but quickly continued.

The trail wound its way up and down and Tank disappeared around some brush that obscured part of it. When Alex called him, he didn't come back, but barked from where he was. Catching up, they found him nosing into a deep hole in the side of the track. He whined and looked up at Alex.

"What is it, fella? You find something?"

With Knapp watching, Alex knelt in the dirt, reached down into the leaves that covered the bottom, and was surprised to touch fabric. The stained daypack he lifted out of the hole had weight, and opening it he found personal items that he recognized—Jessie's.

As he swore, Tank barked in his ear, recognizing the scent of these things that belonged to his mistress.

Knowing that Jessie would not abandon her daypack, for the first time he felt a real sense of fear clinch its fist in his stomach.

"Okay," he told Knapp. "Now we get very serious about this thing."

Pushing on hurriedly, they reached the place where the trail made its right-hand turn.

"Someone's been through there," Knapp said, pointing to the grasses crushed by passing feet, and Tank all but leaped into the gap.

Coming out the other side they found themselves standing between rocky ridges where stones and sand sloped gradually down to the water. It was empty, very quiet and peaceful, with nothing but the cry of a gull as it rose from the rocks close to the tide line, startled at their sudden appearance.

Alex stepped up on a large rock and followed its flight over a short stone ridge that broke the shallow waves to the west. An eagle rested there, looking closely for an unsuspecting fish to swim close enough to snatch out of the water. As he watched, it shifted weight from one claw to the other and settled back to waiting stillness on its stone perch.

Carefully, he examined the space in front of him for any indication of human presence, but the tide had swept the sand between the rocks clean and level. Turning to the east, he could just see over another stone crest, beyond which a bit of blue too bright for nature caught his attention.

"Over here," he told Knapp, clambering up and over the rocks that hid the rest of what he thought was a plastic tarp.

On the sand that was only slightly damp, and not smooth and level but churned like the sand of a beach volleyball court, there was a tarp that had been doubled and spread over something. That something raised it slightly in a shape Alex was afraid he recognized from past experience. Rocks had been laid around that shape to secure its covering from the curious fingers of the intermittent breeze that blew in over the cold waters of the sound. A corner of the end farthest from the water flapped a bit as a gust lifted it, for the rocks that had held it appeared to have tumbled off into the surrounding sand.

When the two men had climbed down and stood next to it, Alex, with a sinking feeling, reached and folded back that corner to expose the body of the man who lay faceup beneath. Taking a deep breath of relief, Alex knelt for a closer look. He was not recently dead for, when Alex reached to lift one of his hands, there was none of the resistance of rigor mortis in the arm that had been neatly laid at his side. Nor did his flesh hold even a hint of warmth. He was as cold as the sand on which he lay.

"Dead at least a day, probably more," he told Knapp.

A smear of dark brown blood on the tarp led him to the shattered skull as cause of death.

"This is not where he died, so we can't know what position he was found in. It's possible that he fell and hit his head on one of these sharp rocks, so this could be an accidental death. Or someone could as easily have hit him with one. It will take some investigation to find out which. But it would definitely have taken more than one person to move him here and cover him so carefully. Time, I think, to use that radio in your plane to call in a forensics team along with the guys from Ketchikan."

Knapp agreed. But as Alex examined the body, he had been intently examining the sand around the tarp.

"This is an odd set of marks," he pointed out, when Alex sat back on his heels and tugged the tarp back over the unwelcome discovery. "It looks like someone slid out, then crawled away across the sand."

As Alex stood up to join him, he lifted the edge of the tarp behind the head of the dead man, and then they were both looking at a space large enough for another person to have been under him. Coming away from it were what Knapp had identified as drag or scrape marks; then there were hand and knee prints in sand just damp enough to hold their impressions.

"Someone was *under there?*" Knapp asked in repulsed astonishment.

"Looks like it. And not a bad hiding place for someone desperate enough," Alex returned, having seen many stranger and more distasteful things in his career in law enforcement. "What concerns me is who it may have been, and what could have been enough of a threat to encourage this as a hiding place. But what alarms me most is that the people who are supposed to be here are not—including Jessie. Let's get back to that radio."

Though they could not know it, Karen had evidently either been stubborn enough to ignore Jessie's instructions to stay in her hiding place, or she had been frightened or forced out by someone else.

Had Jessie known and been able to venture a guess, knowing what she did of Karen, it would probably have been the former.

In the dark of the tank, however, nobody was venturing guesses any longer as to what was going on, or who was responsible. Uncomfortable, hungry, thirsty, and growing more concerned and stressed by the hour, they had stopped moving around, even talking much, and simply sat together, mostly in silence, hoping for something to happen—*anything* to happen—but very much afraid that nothing would, or of what it would be if it did.

For a while they had periodically heard things or people moving overhead, but for at least two or three hours there had been no sound above them.

"I'm really worried about Whitney," Laurie fretted more than once. "Where is she, if she's not down here with us? And what's going on? I hope they haven't hurt her."

Aaron had grown more restless and irritable. As the hours passed he gave up sleep and found an open space clear enough so he could pace back and forth. Jessie imagined him glowering as, periodically, she heard him muttering numbers in counting his steps so he wouldn't run into a wall, and uncharacteristically swearing under his breath when he tripped once. Finally he gave it up and sat down again, but she could hear him moving nervously in the dark.

"It'll be all right, Aaron," she told him. "Somehow, it will."

He didn't answer.

Jim and Don struggled one more time in a feckless effort to shift the manhole cover that sealed them in, but it was as immovable as if it had been welded shut.

"God damned thing. What the hell have they put up there to hold it down?" Don asked.

"Could be any of a bunch of heavy things from the basement shop," Jim told him. "They could even have managed to move Curt's precious generator out onto the platform. It's on skids. But it wouldn't take much weight to hold that lid down, considering how little force we can apply upward with only two of us able to try at once and it almost beyond our reach."

"But we didn't hear anything that big, did we? Wouldn't we have heard them move something really heavy?"

"With our lack of leverage it wouldn't take much."

"Doesn't really matter, does it?" Sandra's flat, discouraged voice came from out of a corner where she waited for Don to come back. "Whatever it is, it's doing a great job."

They had no idea what time it was, no one having a watch with an illuminated dial. But they knew it was still daylight from the hint of it through the bent pipe and the holes in the lid on the manhole.

Jessie had fallen asleep for a few minutes at one point, but jerked awake when she unconsciously turned her head and the bump on it came in contact with the cold cement wall. She sat up and yawned, then stood up and stretched to relieve the ache in her back, Aaron's impatient fidgeting making her restive as well.

Sandra had spent most of the time half curled up in Don's lap and Jessie had heard him murmuring encouragement to her once or twice.

No one had spoken again about Karen—or Whitney.

"You know," Jim said suddenly from his reclining position on the footing beyond Jessie's feet, "I wish I knew how Curt's involved in this. I would never have believed this of him. I trusted him."

"I've been wondering that myself," Don said slowly. "The thought of that handgun makes me uneasy. He's a tough old guy, but . . ."

"You don't think . . ."

Laurie's tentative question trailed off. Then she took a deep breath and tried again.

"Well . . . Oh hell, I might as well say what we're all thinking. We haven't heard anything from up there for a long, long time. They may have decided to just leave us in here. Leave and not let us out, I mean."

There was a kind of gasping sob from Sandra at the brittle tone of Laurie's voice and the dreadfulness of what she was suggesting.

Even Jessie swallowed hard hearing it.

"We might as well say it," Laurie insisted, with a frightening sharp-as-glass edge to her voice. "And, if it's true, then in a few days, without food or, especially, water, none of us will be in any kind of shape to make a sound that could be heard, even if anyone does come looking for us, will we?"

The concept effectively silenced them all, no matter that it had undoubtedly crossed the mind of each independently and been refused consideration as unthinkable.

For several interminable minutes no one said a word.

Then Jessie heard Aaron suddenly sit up in the dark. There was a scrambling sound as he moved across to stand under the manhole through which they had all been forced into the tank.

In the tiny traces of daylight coming through the holes in the heavy lid, she could just make out the worried and angry expression on the face he had raised longingly toward it.

CHAPTER TWENTY-NINE

ON THEIR WAY BACK OVER THE TRAIL FROM THE SOUTH END of the island, Alex stopped so suddenly that Bill Knapp almost ran into him.

"Look," Alex directed, indicating a point on the rocky eastern shore that was visible through a space in the trees. "Where did that come from? It wasn't there earlier."

A powerboat was gently rocking in the waves, a line tethering it to one of the huge boulders, two white fenders strategically placed to keep the side from contact with the large stone.

"It wasn't there when we flew in," Knapp agreed. "We'd have seen it from the air."

"Funny place to tie up." Alex frowned. "As if whoever was in it didn't want to be seen from the lighthouse."

"Well, the plane may have left no space at the cove. You want to take a look?"

The trooper shook his head and started on along the trail at a jog. "Not now. Maybe after I call and get our guys on their way here from Ketchikan. Besides, whoever's driving that boat may be at the lighthouse when we get there."

"Right."

When they, and Tank, came trotting out of the trees and across the grassy area overlooking the platform, there was a man on it engaged in shoving at the cement mixer they had passed in their earlier search. At Alex's call he looked up to see them coming down the steps, moved behind it, and stopped them with a suspicious demand. "Who the hell are *you?*"

"Who are *you,* would be a better question," Alex told him, walking forward. "And where are the people who own this place, and the restoration crew that's supposed to be working here this week?"

"You first," Cooper told him, keeping the mixer between them defensively. "And make it quick."

Taking out his identification, Alex tossed it over. Cooper caught it one-handed and the gold shield inside the leather case shone in the sun as he flipped it open.

"This for real? A State Trooper—detective sergeant?"

"Believe it. And this is the pilot who brought me."

"Why?"

"Because nobody's heard anything from anyone here for the last couple of days and one of them's a very good friend of mine. Now—who are you and where are they?"

"Okay. I'll explain and we'll straighten that out, but first, come and help me move this thing. The people you're looking for have been under here in a tank for a long time without food or water and we need to get them out—now."

It was enough to bring Alex and Knapp to his aid, though they were both watching him closely as together they shoved aside the heavy cement mixer and lifted the manhole cover beneath it.

The grimy faces of several people blinked up at them from below, almost as blind in the sudden brilliance of the late afternoon sun as they had been in the dark.

"Alex Jensen, as I live and breathe, thank God. Are we glad to see *you*!" said Jim Beal, with a grin to accompany his squint, as he recognized one of his benefactors. "Welcome to Five Finger Lighthouse."

"Where's Curt—and the other guy?" Don Sawyer asked the minute he reached the platform above ground. "Have you found Whitney?"

"We've found no one but you—and a dead man on the other end of the island, if that's who you mean," Alex told him. "You know anything about that?"

"We found him yesterday, but it's not Curt. Curt's one of *them*. We'll tell you about it, but we need to find Whitney. He put us down there and he had a gun, but Whitney hasn't been with us."

"Two people took off in a boat that showed up just over an hour ago," Cooper told them. "They were too far away to identify, but I saw them go."

"Where were you?" Alex asked, turning to look him in the eye for an answer.

"Watching from the edge of the trees. I heard the boat engine on its way in and came from the south end to see what was going on. One of them was on board and another came out of the basement carrying something in a cardboard box and joined him in a hurry. When they left, I took my boat and followed. They were headed toward Petersburg—fast."

"Where was your boat?"

"Off the rocks on the east side, where it is now."

Alex nodded, satisfied with that answer. "Can you identify the other boat?"

"Yes."

"But you came back."

"Yeah—of course. There were people here who needed help."

"We'll talk," Alex said shortly, turning back to help Sandra out of the tank.

"We need to find Karen too," she reminded him. "She's the other person who's missing besides Whitney."

Alex, who was helping Cooper to lift her up through the manhole in the pavement, noticed that at Sandra's mention of the woman's name, Cooper froze for a second or two and gave Sandra a questioning glance before leaning to help Laurie up into the daylight. He made a mental note to find out why the man had reacted as he did. Who was he anyway? Evidently not part of the work crew. So why and how had he managed to show up and be in the right place to rescue the work crew from their prison? Someone had killed the man at the other end of the island and Cooper was as good a candidate as any until he knew more.

Tank trotted in anxious circles around the group that grew larger as person after person came up from their dark underground prison, until he was finally rewarded when the one person he wanted to see was next to last in being lifted out. The affectionate greeting he received was brief, however, as Jessie was swept aside by Alex into an enormous hug of affection that was accompanied by murmurs of relief and assurances. Finally he held her away to grin and say, "Figured I'd better find out why you hadn't called. Are you really okay?"

"I knew you'd be worried, but I'm fine. Just a bump on the head that may need a stitch or two, but a cleaning and some tape will probably take care of it."

"Let me see."

"It's stopped bleeding and will keep for now. Let's go up where there's water and food. Then I want to wash at least

my hands and face in the worst way. But there are still questions to be answered, and a couple of people are missing
who were not down there with us."

"Let's take care of these folks first, you mean?"

"Yes. Water first, please, and some Tylenol."

But, when asked her preference, it was a Killian's she se-
lected to go with the sandwich Alex threw together for her
from whatever supplies eager hands snatched from the refrigerator and spread out on the table of the common room.

When she was provided for and the rest were busy with
their own lunches, he went with Knapp, made his call to
Ketchikan, and was assured they would come as soon as
possible and forward to the Coast Guard, the information he
gave them on the boat Cooper had seen but it would take
time for anyone to arrive at Five Finger Light.

Understandably, none of those rescued from the dark
wanted to eat within the confinement of four walls. Instead,
they took their food to the helipad, where they washed it
down with plenty of liquids, while soaking up the heat and
light they had feared they might not see again. Between
bites, in no particular order, they gave their rescuers a brief
and rather disjointed account of their abduction and subse-
quent captivity, the finding of Tim Christiansen's body, their
problems with communications, and the discovery of the
sunken Seawolf the day before.

While they talked Cooper listened in silence, saying
nothing. He paid close attention, however, to the notice of
Alex, who was quietly watching *him*—with growing interest
and curiosity. No one, he thought to himself, had yet answered to his satisfaction the question of *why* they had been
imprisoned between the tanks, and none of them seemed to
know, or be willing to say.

They were a grimy group, coated with mud and the dirt

that had covered the walls and floor of the maintenance space between the tanks. Some had scrapes and bruises collected on their way in, or in falls or collisions with the rough cement walls during their internment. But soon, in twos and threes, everyone, including Alex, Knapp, and Cooper, spread out to mount a concerted search for the two members of the crew who were still missing.

Bill Knapp went with Don and Aaron to search through to the other end of the island and back for Whitney and for Karen, whom Jessie had identified as the person she had helped to hide under Tim Christiansen's body.

"Leave his body where it is," Alex told them. "There'll be an investigation and enough disturbance has already been done to that scene already. But Jessie says that Karen was frightened and may be reluctant to trust anyone. She and Whitney have to be out there somewhere, so make sure you're thorough."

Jessie went to take a look around the north end of the island and under the helipad. After a fruitless search, she was coming back when she noticed that Alex and Joe Cooper were standing together on the lower platform in earnest conversation. Alex nodded in answer to something, added a comment of his own, then tipped his head back in a hearty laugh at Cooper's response. They seemed to have reached some kind of understanding that eluded her, but they were both serious again when Jessie trotted down the stairs to join them, Tank close beside her, unwilling to be separated from his mistress.

"Good," Alex said to Cooper. "We'll work that out. It won't be a problem. I'll call . . ." He hesitated and turned to Jessie as she slipped in under his arm.

"Hi there. Find anything?"

"Nothing. Let's go up and see how Laurie's doing."

"Sure. Coming, Joe?"

Joe? Jessie considered the apparent change in the relationship between the two men as the three climbed the steps. Something had transpired that she didn't understand, but she was sure Alex would clarify later, and let it go as they entered the lighthouse.

Laurie and Sandra had decided to once again examine every closet and storage space in the lighthouse where Whitney might have been incarcerated.

"Alex." Laurie stopped him, as he, Jessie, and Cooper came in the door. She went to the nearby half-sized freezer and lifted its lid to rummage through the packages of frozen food. "We found a handgun in Karen's things and Jim put it in here, but it's gone, so someone took it out—probably Curt, from what Jessie says."

"Who knew it was there?" Alex asked sharply.

"All of us," Jessie told him. "We were all together when Jim put it there."

"Not all. Karen was in the bedroom," Jim reminded her, coming in from the common room.

"That's right, she was. But I think the door was open."

They looked at each other. It could have been any one of them—or not.

"So Curt *could* have taken it?" Alex questioned. "Or Karen—or Whitney, for that matter?"

Yes, that was possible.

"You know," Jim said, frowning at his own lack of attention, "I'd like to have a look at the space in the basement behind the wine—just to see if those packages Sandra told us about are still there."

"What packages?" Alex asked.

"Drugs," Jessie told him. "Someone had two good-sized

packages of cocaine stashed down there. It's probably what this is all about."

Thinking back to what he had learned in Whitehorse about drug smuggling across the international borders of Southeast Alaska, British Columbia, and the Pacific Northwest, a nasty picture was beginning to take shape in Alex's mind.

The cocaine, when Sandra, Jim, and Jessie showed Alex where the packages had been, was gone. But in its place they found an unexpected and unpleasant surprise. Curt's body lay there on the cold cement floor. He had been killed by a shot to his left temple.

There was a more welcome surprise when they were back upstairs and had gathered around the table to answer a few more questions from Alex.

The outside door was suddenly opened and Bill Knapp came in. After him, followed by Don and Aaron, Whitney limped into the kitchen, damp, dirty, and bedraggled, with dry leaves and grass in her hair and a bloody scrape across one muddy cheek.

CHAPTER THIRTY

"It was Curt," Whitney told them from a seat at the far end of the table, where she was drinking the water Jim handed her, while Laurie attempted to treat the cut on her cheek. She had pulled off the filthy sweatshirt she had been wearing over a T-shirt, now also stained, but not quite so dirty.

"When he woke me up, Curt told me he wanted one hostage within reach, just in case, and since I was the last one, he would keep me upstairs. He tied me up, gagged me, and left me on the bed. I had no idea where anyone else was, except that Jessie had gone out earlier to look for Karen. But after a while I heard Karen here, talking to Curt.

"Later someone else came in a boat. I heard it come into the cove and then heard them talking in the common room, but I never got a look at them. I struggled till I got loose, and then took off out the kitchen door when the three of them went to the basement. I heard a shot as I went up the boathouse stairs, but I didn't stop—just booked."

"Where did you go?" Alex asked.

"To the east side, where there are lots of deep spaces

between those big rocks. It was a mess going through them in the dark. I was in a hurry, so I slipped and fell more than once—that's where I did this," she said, putting a hand to her cheek. "Once after that I landed knee-deep in a tide pool. Ugh! Awful standing water that smelled rotten. Finally I found a good place between a big rock and the roots of a tree, crawled into it, curled up, and stayed there. I think I even went to sleep for a while.

"Later, I heard the boat motor start, so I stood up enough to see and watched it leave."

"Why didn't you come back then?"

"Well, there were only two people in it, so I figured it was possible that one of the three was still here and probably had a gun. What would you have done? I crawled back into my hiding place."

"Did you see anyone else—hear anything else—any other boats?"

"Nope. But when I heard Aaron and Don shouting my name just now, I figured it was safe to come out. So here I am—what's left of me. And I need a shower and something to eat. I'm starving."

Alex glanced across the table at Joe Cooper, who had been casually leaning back in his chair, but now slowly sat up to place both elbows on the table, fold one hand over the knuckles of the other, and rest his chin on them. Jessie, next to Alex, with Tank curled up under her chair, saw him give the trooper a quick inquiring look, which Alex answered with a slight nod of his head.

"So," Cooper asked Whitney in an offhand, indifferent tone, "you didn't hear my boat—or see me tie it up and come ashore on that side of the island? Then when the other boat left, come to take it and follow them out?"

She turned to assess him questioningly, stiffening enough

so that Laurie paused in her application of disinfectant to say, "Sorry. Did I hurt you?"

Whitney didn't answer, simply stared resentfully at Cooper. But something alert and wary moved in her narrowed eyes as she answered him.

"No. And I think I would have *if* you'd *been* there," she snapped and continued with a challenge. "Who the hell are you anyway? The third person in this charade, I'll bet. Did Karen and Curt leave in the boat without you on purpose?"

Cooper lifted his chin off his hands, and his cold smile in response was an expression more predatory than sympathetic and held no more humor than the answer he snapped at her across the table.

"Nice try. But I *was* there—my boat is *still* there and was seen to be by others. Clearly, if you didn't see it, or hear it, you *weren't* where you say you were. Care to explain that?"

Giving him a look of disdain, Whitney turned to Alex.

"Who *is* this guy?" she asked. "Do you know that he's been stalking Karen Emerson practically forever—that he beat her, frightened her half out of her wits, enough to drive her out of Ketchikan? Why don't you arrest him? Do you know him?"

Alex stared at her in silence for a few seconds, waiting to see if she would say anything else.

"Yes," he said finally. "I know him. And you will too, very shortly, if what I think is true. Where's the cocaine, Whitney? You might as well give it up. Did they leave you here because you've made some bad mistakes?"

"Wha—" she started to say, rising from her chair.

"I don't think so," Aaron said clearly, stepping from the doorway, where he had been nonchalantly leaning to listen and watch.

His interruption from the other end of the room drew surprised attention from all of them, as he moved to stand directly behind Jessie and, taking a handgun from the pocket of the light jacket he was wearing, pressed the barrel against the back of her head. Mouths fell open in shock and Jim started to stand up.

"Sit down," Aaron snapped.

Jim sat. "Now," Aaron told them, "you will all keep your seats, right—and your hands on the table? No questions, no talking."

With a glance at Alex, who had inched forward in his chair, "Don't even think about it, trooper. Very carefully, hand me your gun."

With clear but watchful resentment, Alex drew it carefully from its holster and handed it over.

Aaron smiled and nodded in satisfaction as he stuffed it into a jacket pocket.

"Smart boy. I assume you value this woman, so don't do anything stupid. Get up slowly, Jessie—very slowly. Come on around the table, Whitney. No one's going to move an inch now, are you, folks?"

No one did, as Whitney moved past them to join Aaron and Jessie, who had stood up slowly, as instructed. Tank rose to his feet and moved to her side, looking up questioningly at her, then at Aaron behind her. He knew what a gun was— didn't like the noise they made, but his mistress carried one when they did training runs or ran races, because of the danger of aggressive moose.

When Aaron glanced down at him he growled.

"Take care of that," Alex was told, and he reached one hand to take firm hold of Tank's collar, restraining him.

Moving the gun barrel down between her shoulders, with

a firm hold on Jessie's arm, Aaron drew her backward into the kitchen doorway, where they stopped in full view of everyone at the table.

Whitney followed, but slipped past him and disappeared into the hallway as soon as space allowed. When she reappeared she stepped close to Aaron and put an arm around his waist, so it was clear they were a couple. She was carrying the small duffel in which she had brought her clothing and personal stuff to the island. It looked heavier now—just about cocaine heavy, Jessie thought, glancing at it as Whitney stopped beside her. So if Karen and—whoever—had gone in the boat, they hadn't taken . . .

"How do you think you're going to get away from here?" Joe Cooper interrupted her thoughts from the other side of the table.

"I said, no questions," Aaron reminded him. "But thanks to you and your boat, that won't be a problem, will it?"

"It's a long walk from here to there, over a lot of hard stones—difficult enough on your own. With a hostage?"

Whitney's grin was full of sly satisfaction. "Now that I know where your boat is, I can bring it around to the cove to pick them up, can't I?"

"Get going then, Whit," Aaron told her. "Leave that. Jessie will carry it down for us. I'll watch them while you go."

She dropped the duffel close to his feet, spun to the door, and was gone.

The room was absolutely still.

Jessie could feel the barrel of the gun pressed hard against her spine and was tempted to simply drop to the floor beneath it. But that would leave the possibility of the gun being discharged by accident, or intent, at those gathered around the table, including Alex, who was in front of her.

She looked down at him and he, reading her mind, gave her a tiny shake of the head saying *Don't try it.*

Aaron caught the signal between them and shoved the barrel harder against her back. "I wouldn't try anything dumb, Jessie."

Tank growled again.

"I won't," she sighed, letting him think she had given it up.

In the silence they soon heard the sound of a boat approaching the cove below the platform.

Cooper tried reasoning again, shifting one hand on the table and speaking loudly to take Aaron's attention away from the sound—and Jessie. "There's law enforcement on the way, you know. They're flying in and can easily follow your boat."

"Just shut up," Aaron told him. "You seem to think we're making this up as we go along."

"And you're not? I could pick a lot of holes in your thinking." Cooper grinned wolfishly. "You won't get far," he said confidently.

Jessie could feel the gun move as Aaron shifted behind her and remembered his nervous pacing in the tank.

"Aaron," she asked suddenly, without moving, except to glance down at the floor to her right, directing Alex's attention. "You were in the tank with us on purpose, weren't you—so we wouldn't suspect you had anything to do with this, just like Whitney was pretending to have been hiding for the same reason? Neither of you expected to be caught out and identified with this whole drug thing, did you? But for that last couple of hours, when they didn't come back, you were afraid they meant to leave you down there with the rest of us to die. You thought Whitney would go off with them and lea—"

"Shut—up!" he almost shouted, shoving her with the handgun so hard she was forced to take a step forward and to the right.

"And she would have left you there," Jessie continued, still moving forward slightly, looking straight at Alex, who, quick to sense her intent, was ready and waiting, knowing he couldn't stop her. "You *know* she would have, if we hadn't been found before she could. So she had to try something else, didn't—"

"I said *shut*—aah . . ."

As Aaron moved to follow her with the gun against her back, he stumbled over the duffel Whitney had dropped at his feet and was momentarily thrown off balance. The hand with the gun came up as he sought to clutch at Jessie, and he almost lost the weapon as he grabbed at her shoulder with the other.

Alex, already in motion, pushed Jessie out of the way and reached one long arm to snatch the gun from Aaron's hand before he could regain his grip on it. Swinging him around, the trooper yanked his arm up between his shoulder blades and ran him against the wall.

"Get hold of Tank," he instructed Jessie, who looked down to see that the husky Alex had released was now savaging one of Aaron's pant legs in an attempt to get at the leg itself.

"Quiet," Cooper said, waving Jim and Don back into their chairs as he passed Alex and Aaron on his way to the kitchen door, where he flattened himself against the wall to one side of it.

Seeing what Cooper had in mind, Alex slapped a hand over Aaron's mouth to keep him still, and in the moment of silence that followed they could all hear Whitney's steps as she trotted up the stairs toward the kitchen door. As she stepped through it, surprise and confusion widening her eyes, Cooper grabbed her from behind.

She struggled angrily, hitting at him and twisting in an attempt to break free. "Let go of me, you bastard."

Jim went to help, and between them the two men managed to move her, still kicking and thrashing, into a chair that Jessie shoved from the table to an open space. Tying her hands together behind the back of the chair with a wet kitchen towel they finally subdued her, though she sat glaring at everyone, including Aaron, in a fury.

"Incompetent idiot!" she snarled at him. "I should have known better—taken the stuff and the boat and gone by myself and left you here."

CHAPTER THIRTY-ONE

"YOU TOOK A BIG CHANCE," COOPER TOLD JESSIE, WHEN the pair of Alaska State Troopers from Ketchikan had showed up in another floatplane not long afterward to take Aaron, Whitney, and the cocaine in the duffel into custody. They had brought with them a forensics team of two to examine the south end of the island, where Tim Christiansen lay under the blue tarp, and to take his body home for examination and eventual burial.

"Not such a big one," she said, smiling. "Alex and I know each other well enough so that he knew I was about to try something."

"He wasn't too happy about your taking that risk."

"Never is. But he wasn't in that tank, so he couldn't have known, as I did, just how much Aaron believed they would have left him there."

"Would they?"

"Yes, I think they really would. I know Karen wouldn't have hesitated for a second and, as you saw, Whitney's pretty much out for herself. The other guy, the one Karen left with in the boat, I never saw. None of us did."

"I did," Cooper told her. "But I already knew who it was."

"Who *who* was?" asked Alex, folding himself down to a seat on the helipad on the other side of Jessie and laying a hand on her shoulder.

She looked up and smiled at him before turning back to Cooper.

"Yes, who was it?"

"A rather large drug-smuggling fish I've been angling for in the last couple of years," he told her.

"Why you? I thought you were after Karen."

"Joe's an undercover agent who's been working for our side and now will be part of the cooperative effort to coordinate with the new RCMP Border Enforcement Team that Del and I met with in Whitehorse," Alex explained to her before Cooper answered. "These arrests will make a good dent in part of the smuggling traffic between here and British Columbia. But that's information you can't pass on, okay? He'd like to keep his cover for a while longer."

"Sure. But I thought . . ."

"You swallowed what Karen Emerson fed you," Cooper said with a grim smile. "You couldn't have known it was all lies. She's very, very good at that. And I *was* after her. She was my link to the real kingpin—that guy she left with in the boat."

Jessie thought about that for a minute before saying, "But they could have gone anywhere. How will you catch them?"

"They're already in custody in Petersburg. I called on the radio from Tim's boat and got both a plane in the air to track them and a Coast Guard boat to apprehend them in the lower end of the sound."

"Why did they leave the cocaine here?"

"They didn't think they had, but they were in such a hurry to leave that they didn't check till later, so they didn't know that Whitney had pulled a switch on them. They had turned around and were headed back when the Coast Guard caught up with them. Whitney is probably lucky they didn't make it. You saw how they dealt with Curt—and he'd been helping them use the lighthouse as a stash on the run north from Seattle, or Canada."

"So," Jessie said thoughtfully, "Laurie was right about someone being here when they weren't. She wanted to talk to you about it, Alex."

"She has, and I reassured her it wouldn't be happening again. Jim was pretty angry about it."

She turned back to Cooper with another question.

"Karen was never your girlfriend, was she, and you never beat her as she claimed?"

"Never." His tone turned bitter. "My taste runs more to human beings. I don't hit women—even her kind."

"She seemed truly terrified of you."

"She had reason to be. She's been running and I've been following and watching her run for—long enough. She knew I knew everything about her. But I waited, hoping she would lead me to the rest of the group. Unfortunately, I waited too long and Tim paid for it."

"You think she killed Tim? She said he was her friend."

"He was—once—a long time ago in Ketchikan, before I told him what she was into. Then he wouldn't have anything to do with her. She really cared about him, so that's what made her hate me. Yes, I know she killed him. Who else would have? She must have thought she was killing me because he was wearing my jacket after I took his by mistake that night. She tried once before, so it makes sense that she would again, the moment she had an even chance. She thought she had one—that it *was* me, not Tim."

Alex's eyes narrowed and he nodded slightly to himself. It was one important question he believed Cooper had answered correctly.

"A woman scorned," he commented, and Cooper nodded.

"Would you have killed her?" Jessie asked hesitantly.

He stared out across the waters of Frederick Sound to the mountains on the islands in the distance, but Alex thought he was seeing little of the view.

"She's not worth killing," he said finally in a level and controlled tone that displayed his abhorrence more coldly than if he had raised his voice. "I hope she'll get what she deserves in a court of law. But if she's true to form she'll probably give up the rest for some kind of consideration. She has no loyalty whatsoever to anyone but herself."

Later that evening, when everyone was gone, including Joe Cooper, Jessie and Alex, after an enjoyable and relaxing dinner with Jim, Laurie, Sandra and Don, slipped out to spend a few minutes by themselves, settling side by side on the steps of the helipad. Tank padded along behind, refusing to be separated from Jessie, and lay down at her feet.

Alex took out the pipe he had brought along and was soon puffing clouds of his favorite and familiar tobacco into the still air.

"You really had me spooked with that move you made in front of that pistol," he told her. "Wish you wouldn't do that kind of thing, Jess."

"Sorry," she said. "I felt I had to do something. It was the only thing I could think of—and it worked."

"Just barely—and because I was ready for it, and quick."

Jessie was quiet for a short time, looking up at the stars that were faintly beginning to appear in the darkening sky over their heads.

"You know," she said, "I'm sorry for Aaron. He's really a nice kid and I don't understand how he allowed himself to get sucked into the whole thing."

Alex shook his head and shrugged. "I believe he was less *sucked* into it than *suckered*. Whitney knew he was Coast Guard—saw that he was interested in her. She played him and took advantage of an opportunity for good cover. She and that Karen are two of a kind—takers."

"Karen," Jessie said flatly, "is worse. She's a piranha. She grabs whatever she can get, blames everything that goes against her on someone else, and thinks the world owes her."

"She certainly has getting what she wants down to a science—most of the time, at least. Makes you wonder what background made her the way she is, doesn't it?"

Jessie reached down to scratch Tank's ears and croon endearments to him for a minute or two. Then she leaned back on her elbows and watched the clouds rolling slowly in over the eastern hills for a minute or two.

"I think," she said finally, "that actually she was afraid of just about everything."

"Hmm-m—that could be true, I guess."

"I think she couldn't stand what she thought of herself, so she blamed other people for it."

He nodded and puffed a small amount of smoke into a ring that drifted off into the night.

"I've been afraid of things I should have let go of a long time ago too," she said presently.

"Oh, you aren't afraid of much. I think you proved that again today."

"Not much maybe, but of some things that shouldn't matter anymore."

"Like?"

As it grew dark enough, the light in the tower suddenly came on automatically and began to revolve, casting the circle of its warning light out over Frederick Sound.

"Like that." Jessie lifted a hand toward it. "Its constant purpose is preventing disaster, whether there's anyone at risk or not. It's the only way for a lighthouse to function, of course. There's no way for it to detect whether or not there is anyone in need of warning, so it's built to operate whenever it's dark, just in case.

"I've been like that. Concerned with preventing possible disaster, whether there's a real risk or not—just in case. I've been like that with our relationship, haven't I, Alex."

"So you think we might be headed for disaster?" he teased, chuckling at the comparison.

She aimed a fist at his shoulder. "No, you idiot! I mean that I don't think we *are,* and it's time to stop circling with warnings and waiting to see if we might be."

He caught the fist before it landed and used it to pull her into the shelter of his arms, where she leaned against his shoulder and settled contentedly to listen as he answered.

"If you're circling, then it's not up to me to convince you it's unnecessary. You'll figure that out when you're ready. I'm just here now, to stay—and not in any danger, that I know, of running onto the rocks."

He puffed on the pipe, then spoke again softly.

"And you do make a *lovely* light."

Turn the page for an
intriguing excerpt from

THE TOOTH OF TIME

Sue Henry's exciting new mystery
starring Maxie McNabb and Stretch
Coming in hardcover in April 2006
from New American Library

On an otherwise empty westward-tending dirt road, the small cloud of dust raised by a slow-moving thirty-foot Winnebago motor home was gently carried aside by the whisper of a breeze that wandered from a broad meadow between the road and a long high ridge to the north; an arm of the Cimarron Range of the New Mexican Sangre de Cristo Mountains. In mid-May, the meadow grass was a soft, yellow-green in contrast to the dark bluish hues of pinion pine and juniper that began at the foot of the mountains. High overhead a hawk that had nested in the rocky cliffs of the ridge was drawing slow circles against the bright blue of the sky, watching for some small mammal, a squirrel or perhaps a jackrabbit incautious enough to reveal itself.

At a spot wide enough to allow a turnaround, the driver of the motor home pulled over and stopped beside the road. After a brief pause, the door to the coach swung open, steps extended, and a woman stepped out with a camera in one hand, the end of a leash in the other. Encouraging a russet-colored mini-dachshund to follow her, she closed the door, turned, and stood facing the hills, recognizing what she had come out of her way to find and until then seen only in pictures— a pale arrowhead-shaped peak that rose commandingly midway along the ridge.

Without taking her eyes from the peak, she reached to lay her camera on the doorstep, deciding there would be time for pictures later, when the sun was low enough in the west to add definitive shadows to the ridge. Leaning back against the side of the Winnebago, she slipped the leash around her wrist and pushed both hands into the pockets of her denim skirt, concentrating on the scene before her.

Medium-slim of build and of average height, she was an attractive woman, though pretty was not a word that would apply. Handsome suited her better—and, perhaps, interesting—for there was a sharp intelligence in her hazel eyes and a thoughtful alertness about her that would offer the observant the impression that she would probably notice more than the obvious of whatever, or whoever, she encountered. The lines of her face hinted at an approach to life that was more positive than negative, leavened with a well-established sense of humor.

Reaching up, she removed a clip that held her silvering dark hair into a twist, allowing it to fall to shoulder length, and ran a hand through its crown to push it away from her face, still gazing upward at the sharp peak.

"The Tooth of Time," she said softly as if to name it aloud made it more real, thinking that it was different than she had imagined it. But in an odd way it seemed to sum up a lot of what she had experienced in the preceding weeks. "I hadn't expected that."

At the sound of her low voice, more cello than violin in tone, the dog at her feet cocked his head to give her an inquisitive look.

"Yes, lovie," she turned her attention to him. "Your walk comes now. Then, since we have the rest of the afternoon, I think I'll do a little journal keeping. Maybe I can make more sense of it all on paper than in my head."

Half an hour later the two were back inside the motor home with the screened door and windows open to the soft breeze. The woman was seated at the dinette table with a glass of iced tea, her journal, and a favorite pen in front of her, the dog napping on a rug nearby. For a few minutes, as she clipped her hair back into its usual twist, she stared out the window at the peak on the ridge, eyes narrowed in thought, then opened the journal and began to write.

Saturday, May 22

> *Time and age both have teeth—or at least one tooth, if the name of the peak is any indication. Whoever labeled it the Tooth of Time was no spring chicken. It must have been someone on the downhill side of life, someone who knew what they were talking about and—to totally jumble metaphors—named it with a rueful sense of the shrinking size of their singular piece of the pie . . .*

Through the long afternoon she continued to write, periodically getting up to refresh her glass of tea—once to make a small lunch, which she ate, sandwich in one hand, pen in the other, brushing a few crumbs from the page as she continued to record her thoughts in the journal.

> *Things that affect you strongly often creep up almost without your realizing, very like the way time passes. The older you get the faster years go by, and then—quite suddenly—you realize that there is less than half of them left. That recognition has an unexpected bite.*
>
> *I wonder why many people are so desperately afraid of growing old. Some give up and become immediately what they fear most. Others pretend to be younger, generally deceiving no one but themselves, or, just as foolishly, refuse to admit it makes a difference.*
>
> *I'm glad that, as a senior citizen, I made up my mind to take what comes along as practically as possible, somewhere in between. One of the best things I've ever done was get myself a Minnie Winnie and go off to see parts of the world I had never had a chance to visit, especially doing it on my own, with Stretch for*

company. But how many people said, "Oh, you can't do that alone, can you?" as if I were too old, or that being a woman made it something unimaginable and frightening. Most depressing was that most of the ones who questioned my intentions were women. I have found that I love to be on the road to someplace new, seeing things and meeting all kinds of people as I come to them. If nothing else it keeps me feeling, if not young, then definitely not yet old.

There are women who, left alone by death or divorce, are terrified to live without a man to take care of them. Being a self-sufficient sort, with or without a partner, I have never felt a need to be similarly dependent. I was very lucky, twice, and will always miss the companionship I shared with both my husbands; that infinitely valuable physical and emotional warmth that was a dependable part of our lives. But it does not fill me with any more anxiety to be by myself in my later years than it did half a century ago, before I married either of them.

What happened in Taos was totally unnecessary—and sad. Somehow I still feel I should have seen it coming, though I didn't know the woman and her particular circumstances before it was too late.

To even try to get it in perspective I must think back to where it all started—that, and what happened after I decided to go back to Taos, New Mexico, from the Great Sand Dunes National Monument—after I had spent the better part of two days traveling and trying to convince myself that I had left for good. I'll start again—first to those two days and making up my mind to go back that stormy day at the dunes, then from the start—the day I first arrived in Taos, and what came during and after . . .

SUE HENRY

THE SERPENTS TRAIL

At sixty-three, Maxie McNabb is cruising down the Alaska Highway in her brand-new Winnebago. With her mini-dachshund at her side and the open road ahead, she's never been happier. But before her exploration of the Lower Forty-eight gets underway, Maxie needs to figure out who burgled her friend's Colorado home—and why. And the closer Maxie gets to solving the puzzle, the more it becomes chillingly clear that her friend's life isn't the only one on the line.

"Another winner."
—*BOOKLIST*

"[Her] grasp of tense storytelling and strong characterization matches her with Sue Grafton."
—*COLORADO SPRINGS GAZETTE*

Martha Grimes

The Richard Jury Novels

Available wherever books are sold or at
penguin.com

Penguin Group (USA) Online

What will you be reading tomorrow?

Tom Clancy, Patricia Cornwell, W.E.B. Griffin,
Nora Roberts, William Gibson, Robin Cook,
Brian Jacques, Catherine Coulter, Stephen King,
Dean Koontz, Ken Follett, Clive Cussler,
Eric Jerome Dickey, John Sandford,
Terry McMillan, Sue Monk Kidd, Amy Tan,
John Berendt...

You'll find them all at
penguin.com

*Read excerpts and newsletters,
find tour schedules and reading group guides,
and enter contests.*

Subscribe to Penguin Group (USA) newsletters
and get an exclusive inside look
at exciting new titles and the authors you love
long before everyone else does.

PENGUIN GROUP (USA)
us.penguingroup.com